BUTTERFLY EFFECT

the sanguine crown series

BOOK 2

BY: SUSAN HARRIS

BUTTERFLY EFFECT
Copyright ©2020 Susan Harris
All rights reserved.
Printed in the United States of America
First Edition: December 2020

CLEAN TEEN PUBLISHING
WWW.CLEANTEENPUBLISHING.COM

Summary: Vengeance has a name, and it's Ryan Callan. Drowning in a wave of grief and guilt, Ryan pushes herself to the limit to track down the man responsible. Willing to do anything to capture her prey, Ryan finds herself caught up in not one, but two games of cat and mouse. This sequel to Chaos Theory by Susan Harris proves that vampires are back, and they're more enticing than ever.

ISBN: 978-1-63422-394-2 (paperback)
ISBN: 978-1-63422-395-9 (e-book)
Cover Design by: Marya Heidel
Typography by: Courtney Spencer
Editing by: Chelsea Brimmer

Young Adult Fiction / Vampires
Young Adult Fiction / Paranormal / Romance
Young Adult Fiction / Paranormal, Occult & Supernatural
Young Adult Fiction / Royalty

For more information about our content disclosure, please utilize the QR code above with your smart phone or visit us at www.CleanTeenPublishing.com

For Emily,
The girl who would be Ryan
And
Who is just as much of a badass as Ryan is.

Prologue

WE WERE TOO LATE... AGAIN. SHE HAD SLIPPED OUT OF MY grasp like a shadow escaping the sun's rays. I wanted to bloody scream and beat my fists against the brick wall as the scent of her lingered in the alleyway; I wanted to let loose the rage that had been coiled in the pit of my stomach for weeks.

Then again, I should have known, should have guessed that this would be the outcome. Ryan was not the type to let things lie; she went at problems like a wrecking ball until the outcome relented to her will. She was a weapon that could not be beaten.

"The sun is almost here. We will try again tomorrow."

I had heard that so many times, but just when we seemed to get closer to finding her, she vanished into thin air. Too many times I had come so close, but alas, I had failed every single time.

Vengeance had a name, and it was Ryan Skye Callan.

Jack clapped me on the shoulder, the Royal Guard all looking to him for instruction. "We will find her, Nickolai. We must."

All I could do was nod my head and motion for the guard to move out. A prickling sensation on the back of my neck had me snapping my head around. Somewhere out there, Ryan watched me from a distance, out of sight. She wished for me to leave her alone. But I had done that once before and almost lost the only person who truly knew me.

"I despise you. Are you hearing me, my liege?"

Oh, I had heard her so clearly and loudly I thought my ears would burst. Her words dripped with contempt. The guilt I felt about Krista, I would carry that for the rest of my days, but it paled in comparison to the pain I would feel if I lost Ryan to her search for justice.

My name sounded at the end of the alley. I glanced around once more, making a silent promise to the girl who held my heart.

I will not stop looking. I will find you even if it kills me in the process. I'm coming for you, Ryan Callan, whether you like it or not.

Chapter 1

I was beginning to wonder whether I was the cat or the mouse in this game.

Or games, considering I was playing two games now with vastly different roles. In one of those, I was a reaper, working my way through rogue vampires and killing anyone associated with Maxim Smyrnoi. In the space of four weeks, I had managed to rid the world of nearly twenty low-level rogues in Maxim's little cult.

Maxim would die painfully, afforded the same courtesy he had shown Krista, my human friend, the only one I'd let inside my walls in over ten years. She was dead because of me, because of what I am.

Anita Blake was right when she said *'loving the monster never ends well for the human'*. Krista didn't deserve to die the way she did. She deserved to grow old with her future husband, have kids and grandkids, and die of old age, not vampire politics.

Maxim, feeling slighted that his one true love had chosen his brother over him, had turned his hatred for the crown toward the human world, murdering college students at the night school the crown prince and I had been attending in Cork. I, being my usual charming self, bated Maxim until he'd become obsessed with me, then started sending presents to impress me. Once I had his attention, he'd become determined to make me his.

The wind slapped me hard in the face, whipping stray strands of my hair into my eyes as I glanced at the other player in the game in which I was the mouse. Every night as I hunted Krista's killer, I was also pursued by the Royal Guard and a prince who couldn't leave well enough alone. I remained downwind so he wouldn't know I was still hanging around, but his head snapped around and I caught a glimpse of his face.

His cerulean-blue eyes appeared heavy and sad, his lips cast in a permanent scowl that was almost hidden by the week-old stubble on his face. Part of me wanted to call out to him, the loneliness in my chest harder to bear than it had been before now that I'd had a taste of life surrounded by others.

My feet edged closer to the ledge as Jack, my father's best friend and the closest thing to family I had left, ushered Nickolai away before the sun could rise. I wanted to scream at him, tell him that I was glad he suffered as I did. Instead, I waited a few more seconds and then took off, jumping from roof to roof as the sun's rays followed me to the open window I needed. I ducked inside just in time.

The small, compact attic had become a sort of home to me since an ally to vampires had stumbled upon me injured one night, huddled in a dumpster, hiding from supposed friends and foes alike. I refused to come down from the attic in case it caused Rose any harm, but that didn't mean she wasn't dogged in her pursuit to make conversation.

"Come downstairs, Ryan, and have breakfast with an

old woman. Don't make me climb all those stairs with my dodgy knee."

I let loose a snort, shaking my head as the smell of a cooked breakfast lured me from thoughts of sleep, and I grudgingly descended the ladder. Striding into Rose's shop, the woman gave me a broad grin as she pushed a plate toward me. I started eating before I'd even sat down, my eyes on my food as Rose sipped her coffee.

I first met Rose when Krista had taken me dress shopping for a party I hadn't wanted to attend. Krista hadn't known that Rose was a Child of Eve, a small group of humans who knew that vampires existed and gave their lifeblood freely so we could live. Rose had also known my mother, but I still hadn't pried that story from her lips.

When I finished wolfing down my food, I took my plate to the small kitchen off the shop floor, rinsed it, and left it to drain. Smiling my thanks to Rose, I turned toward the attic ladder to sleep the day away before I went out hunting again.

"Ryan, come sit down for a minute."

"I'm tired, Rose. I can't deal with a lecture right now."

"If you don't sit your ass down right now, I'll answer one of the billion calls I've ignored from Jack O'Reilly and tell him you've been sleeping here. Or you could sit down, and I could tell you where to find two of Maxim's top-tier vampires tonight."

Now *that* caught my attention.

I didn't sit down, but I paused, arms folded across my chest, and raised a brow, trying to be as intimidating as possible.

Rose simply chuckled. "Imogen had that same look. Never did work on me."

My heart clenched, a knife piercing it as yet another

person saw echoes of my deceased parents in me. When Imogen and Tristan Callan had been murdered defending the king and queen, my life became a whirlwind of loss and grief, and I became The Daughter of Imogen and Tristan.

Just like your mother, or *You got that from your father*, became common responses to everything I did. I loved my parents and missed them every goddamn day—I didn't need daily reminders that they were gone, that I was the last piece of them on this earth.

Rose, having sensed the change in me, sighed, setting her mug down on the counter in front of her. "You know people only wish to compliment you when they say such things. You don't always need to be so defensive."

I clamped my lips firmly shut, and Rose's phone began to vibrate on the table next to her. She glanced down at her phone, and then her eyes wandered to mine as she picked it up and pressed the answer button. I stopped breathing.

"Rose."

Jack sounded tired, older than I'd ever heard him before, and I took a step back from Rose for fear he would hear me breathing.

"Jack, I'm sorry I haven't answered your calls. I've been a little under the weather."

"Cut the crap, Rose. Is my niece okay?"

Rose sighed. "What makes you think Ryan would come to me of all people?" she said. "She doesn't even know who I am."

That prickled my attention.

"Are you telling me that you didn't tell her about who you used to donate blood to?" Jack asked.

"I'm telling you that on the brief occasions I have

14

spoken to Ryan, we did not speak of my past, only that I knew of her mother. My secrets are mine to keep, Jack, and you would do well to think before you speak to me again about secrets in such a manner."

I listened as Jack sighed and offered an apology, then silence filled the room until Jack cleared his throat.

"We all just want her home safe. We all just want to make sure she's okay. We want her to know that we love her."

I let my eyes close to keep tears from welling up and slipping free of their own accord. I wanted to tell Jack I knew all of that but still had a job to do. I wasn't even sure I could go back afterward. So, I wasn't going to lie and say I would. "And if I said she knows all that? If I told you I knew she was safe even if she's not okay?"

"I would say thank you and ask for her to call me, just call me. I want to hear her voice. I'm trusting you, Rose, as Imogen once did." Jack paused before saying, "If you are standing there listening to me, kiddo, I love you. He won't stop looking for you. Not until he sees you."

With that, Jack said goodbye to Rose and hung up. I opened my eyes and met Rose's gaze as she calmly sipped her coffee.

"How did you know my mother, Rose?" I demanded, a hint of fang slipping from my gums.

"If I told you, then how would I get you to come back here every morning? You are as curious as a cat, Ryan, and until you know, I can be sure you are safe—at least by day. Once you have your vengeance, you and I can sit down and reminisce about the past."

I rolled my eyes, though I couldn't fault her reasoning. I came back every morning for the very reason she said—I wanted to know how she knew my mother and how she knew me. But it seemed I'd get no more of that information from Rose anytime soon.

Instead, I asked about the rogues high up in Maxim's resistance. Rose told me that a bartender from a recently purchased and renamed human nightclub informed her it was being run by men who looked constantly drugged to their eyeballs. This human was also a Child of Eve and knew a rogue vampire when he saw one.

My stomach sank as I licked my lips. "Has he seen Maxim?"

Rose shook her head. "Kallum said the owner hasn't shown up yet but he has been speaking to the rogues managing the club. People have been disappearing into the private areas never to be seen again. Rumor has it the boss will make an appearance soon once he recovers from a mystery ailment."

Mystery ailment my ass. At our last meeting, I'd almost stabbed Maxim in the heart with one of my sai, and even a vampire as powerful as him would need time to heal from that. A smile crept over my lips at the thought of how long it had taken him to recover from my strike.

Next time, death would come calling for him.

"Ryan, the bar has been renamed *Babochka.*"

Butterfly. Maxim had used the Russian word for butterfly, his nickname for me and the note he'd left on Krista's body—Krista, who'd had a butterfly tattoo—to taunt me. He'd opened a bar in my city, named it after me to enrage me, and it was working.

A growl rumbled in my throat and I snarled, wanting to hurt someone or something.

"Ryan, there is no way you can walk into that club. Every rogue in Ireland is looking for the ice-blonde reaper."

"Then I'll find a way in without them ever knowing who I am," I said, motioning at Rose's store with my

16

hands. "Now, I need to get some sleep if I plan to murder some rogues tonight."

Spinning on my heels, I stormed off and jumped up to the attic without bothering to use the stairs. I shut the door behind me and blew out a frustrated breath as I lay myself down on the sleeping bag Rose had given me and stared up at the ceiling, wide awake.

For weeks I'd searched for Maxim, and now he was in my grasp. I'd imagined over and over how sweet it would feel to ram my sai into Maxim's throat and finish the job his idiot brother hadn't.

Boris attempted to end his brother's life nearly fifty years ago but had failed miserably. Because of his negligence—not ensuring his brother was dead—the rogues had rebuilt in secret and stormed the royal compound in order to seize the Sanguine Crown, and I had lost my parents. Boris and I would hash that out eventually; but first, I'd finish off his brother.

And then there was Nickolai. My chest hurt every time I thought about him. I missed him more than I cared to admit, even to myself. My mind replayed all the moments we'd shared—the teasing, the laughter, the almost-press of his lips against mine.

When his mother had sent me to watch his back, the future king embarking on a mission to save all vampires from extinction, I'd never imagined we'd end up further apart than before I'd been forced into the real world by the queen.

But what was broken could not be fixed. There could be no future for him and I.

When we'd gone on our fake date to lure Maxim out of the shadows and make him jealous, Nickolai had spoken of his intentions toward me. Now, his words seemed to be on constant replay in my mind.

"I want so badly to kiss you. To claim you like I've wanted to do since you stormed back into my life. But when I do kiss you, when I claim you, it will be on our terms, not some rogue who has a hard-on for you."

I could still feel the ghost of his hands on my skin, the promise in his words. I hated that I still wanted him; I despised that even though I blamed him for Krista, I wanted to sit on the couch with him, resting my head on his shoulder.

I knew Jack was right, that Nickolai wouldn't stop hunting me. After a week on my trail, I'd had to ditch my phone because I had a hundred calls from Nickolai alone. The queen rang me as well, and I had to fight the urge to answer all of her calls. Suspecting they were also using my phone to track me, I smashed it with the heel of my boot and left it for Nickolai to find. I watched as he picked up the shattered device and threw it against a wall, roaring at Jack, asking how in the hell would they find me now.

Jack had replied that the trail of bodies would lead the way, and maybe he was right.

Once, in a heart-stopping moment, Nickolai had almost caught up with me. The memory of it ensnared me as I closed my eyes.

Rain poured down from the sky as I slashed my sai across the rogue's throat, his hands grasping at the wound in the hope it would stem the flow of blood enough for him to somehow survive, but it was futile. A heartbeat later, the rogue dropped dead.

At least he had been able to tell me, before I slit his throat, that Maxim was still in Cork and wasn't looking to move anytime soon. I wiped the blood from my one sai on my jeans and suddenly felt a presence behind. I whirled, snarling, ready to defend myself.

My eyes clashed with Nickolai's. He stood only a few feet away from me, and all the anger came roaring back as I growled and sheathed my sai.

"Don't run," he said. "Please don't run. I'm sorry."

He sounded so remorseful, so genuinely sad that I wanted to reach out to him.

"Sorry doesn't fix everything," I snarled.

With one last look, I took off running, scrambling up the wall and onto the ledge, the sound of Nickolai's footsteps booming behind me. I kept running, running away from him and my own guilt until I no longer heard his boots on the concrete and then I ran some more just to be sure he could not catch me.

My eyes sprang open as I sucked in a breath, sitting upright as I tried to remember to breathe. That moment had been the closest Nickolai had come to catching me. He'd never gotten that close again. I would follow Maxim to Russia if I had to in order to get vengeance for my slain friend, and there was nothing on this earth that could stop me.

"How many times have I told you that vengeance and anger make a toxic combination?"

I looked anywhere but in the direction of the voice as I tried to calm my mind.

"Ignoring me won't make me go away, Ryan. If it did, I'd be long gone by now. But nope, poof, here I am."

"Go away. I'm trying to sleep here."

"Nope... you're brooding and feeling sorry for yourself and isolating yourself again. That's not going to happen on my watch."

I sighed and glared at the thorn in my side. "You have no influence over what I do."

"Well, that's not true now is it?"

"Go away!" I shouted, kicking at the source of the

voice, but I ended up kicking the cupboard, my foot splintering wood as pain laced my ankle.

"Now, that was stupid, wasn't it? You've tried that for weeks now and I'm still here, wrecking your head."

I heard Rose's footsteps below as she hesitated, calling up and asking if I was okay. I grunted and she left, leaving me alone with my conscience.

A smug smile played over her lips as she shrugged her shoulders.

"You know," I said, glaring at her, "you don't have to enjoy my pain as much as you are."

"I'm not enjoying your pain, Ryan. I'm just trying to help."

"You can help me by fucking right off!"

With a roll of her eyes, my tormenter perched herself on the cupboard I'd just kicked. "I'm here because you want me here. Your guilt keeps me here. But since I *am* here, I'm going to be as annoying as Spike was in *Angel* after he died in *Buffy*."

Hands on my hips, I hissed at the smiling girl. "Of *course* I feel guilty, but I *don't* want you here. I want you frolicking in clouds like your god promises. I want you at peace and not stuck here with me. By Eve, you're not even real—I'm arguing with myself."

The girl simply shrugged her shoulders at me again, which only angered me more. "Stop using me as an excuse to run from your problems."

"Shut the fuck up, Krista," I said, pointing my finger at the ghost that was haunting me. "You don't know what's going on in my head."

"Of course I do. You're angry and standing in someone else's attic, arguing with a ghost."

Did I mention I had lost my goddamn mind?

Chapter 2

Ghosts weren't real.

Yes, I know that's ironic coming from a vampire, but our belief is that when a vampire dies, they return to the Garden of Eden to be reunited with Eve and walk in the sun once more. Vampires didn't become ghosts. They just didn't.

But as my ghostly tormenter kept reminding me, she'd been human until she died, and I was the reason she was back to haunt my ass.

Born in a small Icelandic village, my vampire mother used to sit around campfires with the rest of the village, telling stories of ghosts and trolls and *huldufólk*. She told me once, a long time ago, that we should never grieve too much for those who died, for those who mourn the loss too powerfully can sometimes trap a spirit to this world with such intense feelings. My father had scolded my mother, telling her not to frighten me with such nonsense that there were scarier things to be haunted by in life.

He was right.

So, I chose not to believe my mother because when

would I ever be around humans who died? Now, I was being haunted by know-it-all ghost.

"It's trauma," I said to myself. "It's all the goddamn trauma in my life."

"Keep telling yourself that, Ryan. Still doesn't let you sleep during the day, does it?"

See... know-it-all bloody ghost.

"You saw him again last night, didn't you?" she said.

I lay back down on the sleeping bag and propped my hands behind my head. "I have absolutely no idea what you're talking about."

"Deny it all you want, but you always get this constipated look on your face when you are thinking of Nickolai."

"No, I don't," I exclaimed, remembering to lower my voice so Rose wouldn't think I'd gone batshit crazy talking to myself.

"Oh, yes you do. I really can't understand why you're still so mad at him, Ryan. I mean, it's not like Nickolai's the one who killed me."

Propping myself up on my elbows, I glared at the ghost of my friend. Her hair still had that California sunshine look about it, her smile still as bright as it had been when her heart beat. Her skin was paler than before, but despite that, Krista didn't look like she had after she'd been brutally murdered, her blood staining her torso and bite marks all over her body.

"You're not even a proper ghost. I mean, ghosts always show up wearing what they died in. You aren't naked."

Krista rolled her eyes. "I was dead minutes after I told you to kick his ass for me. Everything after... well, I guess Maxim did that to paint a scene for you. He put a lot of effort into it to be fair. But I was fully clothed when

22

I died."

Krista glanced down at her *Sons of Anarchy* tee. She'd been wearing that when I first met her, too. "I'm lucky I like this T-shirt. Imagine if I'd been stuck wearing a pink Van Halen T-shirt for all my afterlife. The horror!"

I smacked a hand to my forehead and groaned. Was this my penance for causing her death? Having imaginary Krista give me attitude until I died? If Maxim had his way, that would be sooner rather than later, so I guess that was a plus.

Closing my eyes, I dropped my head down and tried to relax and let myself sleep. It must have worked because I jerked awake at the sound of a door being kicked in somewhere below me. I was instantly on my feet, sai in one hand and the other ready to yank open the attic door, when I heard his voice.

"I know she's here, Rose. I know you've been hiding her from me."

I couldn't breathe and daren't move for fear that Nickolai would find me, throw me over his shoulder, and drag me kicking and screaming back to court before I got the chance to kill Maxim.

"I know you consider yourself important, child, but how dare you force your way inside my home?"

I leaned closer to the hatch, despite being able to hear clear as night what was being said.

"I'll fix the door, Rose," Jack's voice said softly. "I apologize for the Prince."

"I don't need anyone to apologize for me, Jack. If she is harboring Ryan, then I will have her tell me."

Harboring? Like I was a goddamn fugitive? Harrison Ford would be jealous.

"And what would you have me do, Prince? Cast her away? Leave her to spend her days hiding in dumpsters,

23

wasting away because she doesn't eat or sleep? Because that is how I found her. She won't feed. She drinks bottled blood, but she cannot sustain herself that way for much longer. Do you want that for her when you claim to care so much? Would you not rather I harbor her and keep her safe than have her roaming the streets alone?"

Silence filled the room downstairs, and I heard Nickolai's soft footfalls as he walked across the wooden floor. I braced myself to flee, wondering if I could grab my stuff before Nickolai made it into the attic.

"I want her safe," he said finally. "I want her to know that none of us could have envisioned what happened. I want her to know how remorseful I am, and that I understand her need to blame me for what happened. I can live with that, but I just want to see her for myself. I need to see with my own eyes that she is okay."

I wasn't okay though, was I? I was hiding from my childhood best friend and having conversations with a dead girl who had vanished while I slept.

"Nickolai, let us go and search the night for her. We need to be ready when the first body hits the ground."

A small smile tugged at my lips at Jack's words. He was right; in the end, the bodies would lead the way to me. I would go to Babochka and get some answers as to Maxim's whereabouts. I dared to lift the hatch just a tad, spying Jack lead Nickolai out the door, muttering his apologies at Rose as he stopped to make sure the door was still intact.

And then they were gone.

Several heartbeats later, Rose called up to the attic that they were gone and it was safe to come down. I grabbed my weapons, opened the hatch, and dropped down to the ground, my boots clattering against the wooden planking.

I was just about to argue with Rose and tell her that I was fine when little black dots crept into my field of vision and I swayed. Rose, Eve bless her, reached out to help me, but I shrank back.

"I'm fine," I snapped at her, regretting it the moment I did.

"Sure, ya are." Rose chuckled as she went to her little fridge and brought me out a bottle of blood. I drained it without taking a breath.

"First you need to shower and change before you even contemplate heading out to the club tonight. If I can smell you then so can the rogues. Take this and put it into your hair. It will wash out in a few days, but it will do the trick for now."

Rose handed me a box of temporary hair dye, a shade of brown far from my own, very distinctive blonde. I gave Rose a small smile as she handed me a bag of clothes and then went off to the bathroom to alter my appearance.

An hour later, I emerged from the bathroom with mousey-colored brown hair that I left loose. Dressed in a pair of leggings and a long tunic top with a plunging V neckline, I smiled at Rose's thoughtfulness when choosing an outfit for me. I'd still been able to wear my sai holster without any trouble. I slipped on a leather jacket, missing the feel of my dad's jacket wrapped around me.

Rose smiled as she roamed her eyes over me. "I wouldn't even recognize you. Now, the last piece of deception." Rose handed me a little box. Nestled inside was a pair of brown contacts.

"Where do you get all this stuff?" I asked.

"A girl has to have some secrets."

The contacts burned as I placed them on my eyes, the alien feeling making me want to scrub my eyes and get them out. When I strode to the full-length mirror to examine myself, the reflection staring back at me scared me.

I looked like death. My skin was pale and my eyes looked hollow. I swallowed hard and told myself it was just the makeover. But I was in absolute denial.

"Kallum is working tonight and told me he'll keep an eye out for you. If you can't get inside by yourself, then knock three times on the side door and Kallum will let you in."

"Thank you."

Rose shook her head. "Don't thank me, Ryan. Just don't get yourself killed."

"I'll try not to."

I bade Rose farewell and slipped out the door, having already gotten directions to this new club. I walked the streets of Cork, passing for human. It was early Saturday night and the streets were already filled with people. With only a few weeks to Christmas, shops were opened late and everyone was enjoying the festive spirit—even if it was still November.

Walking past a phone shop, I hesitated outside for a second before ducking inside to purchase a run-of-the-mill phone preloaded with minutes. Before I could change my mind, I slipped into a quiet spot and dialled a number.

The phone rang twice before I lost my nerve and made to end the call. Just before I disconnected, I heard Nickolai say hello.

I couldn't speak, the words were lodged in my throat. Swallowing hard, I tried to make myself speak. But I didn't have to speak for Nickolai to know who was on the other end.

"Ryan."

The way he said my voice heated my bones. I leaned

26

my head against the wall and sighed. "You need to let me go."

"Never," he said without skipping a beat.

"Stop wasting your time on me, my liege. Find Maxim before I do, and then we can talk."

"We can find Maxim together, Ryan. Come home. Come back to the apartment so we can talk."

Snorting, I switched the phone to my other ear. "There's nothing to talk about. Maxim killed Krista, and I'm going to kill him. Nothing can stop that from happening."

"I'm worried about you, Ryan. We all are."

"Please don't do that, please don't pretend you care."

"You're my friend, Ryan. Of course I fucking care."

My laughter was bitter as it bubbled from my lips. "We aren't friends, my liege, not anymore. Rid yourself of any foolish notions. I no longer bow to the crown. I should have left long ago. I should have put myself first rather than duty and loyalty."

"Ryan."

"No, Nickolai. Just... no. If I had stopped trying to be my parents, I wouldn't have been subjected to being mocked and ridiculed. Maybe I'd have spared myself all of this fucking heartache if I'd just left long ago."

Again, I shifted the phone, realizing my mistake. "I shouldn't have called you. I won't make the same mistake twice. Let me go, Nickolai. You were a fool to ever think there could be an us. I was just a poor, stupid little girl, still waiting for a happily ever after, but people like me don't get to be happy. Goodbye, Nickolai."

I contemplated crushing the phone in my hand, but I had one more call to make.

"Yeah?"

Jack's gruff voice make me smile. "Hello to you, too."

"Kiddo? Is that really you?"

I couldn't stand the kindness in his voice, so I switched gears. "Make him stop looking for me, Jack. Make him stop, and I'll keep in touch with you. If he keeps looking for me and Maxim decides to leave the country, then my ass is on a plane and you won't lay eyes on me ever again."

"Wait a sec, kiddo. Wait a goddamn *second*!"

Jack knew I was going to hang up, and I issued my instructions one more time. "I mean it, Jack. If Nickolai doesn't stop hunting me then I'm a ghost. You'll never find me. But if he stops, if he leaves me alone, I'll call you once a week to let you know I'm alive. He keeps coming for me, and this is the last time you'll ever hear my voice. Tell Atticus he trained me well. I do love you, Uncle Jack. I hope to speak to you soon."

I crushed the phone with my bare hands and tossed it into a bin as I slipped back into the steady stream of people on the sidewalk, losing myself in the crowd as I walked toward a seedier part of town. I didn't need directions to find this place of Maxim's; the illuminated lights and signage guided my way. Even as early as it was, a steady queue of people stood shivering in the cold, waiting to be admitted.

A group of girls made their way into the queue and I pretended to be with them until we got to the top of the queue and the bouncer, a rogue, could smell that I wasn't human. Either that or he could smell the lack of alcohol on me.

"Now, hold on a second there, missy."

His accent was Russian, which sent anticipation surging through my veins.

"*YA zdes', chtoby tantsevat' i pit*"—*I'm here to dance and have a drink*—I told the bouncer in a heavy Russian

28

accent as I smiled and flashed my fangs at him. He leered and motioned for me to go in without even checking me for weapons.

Slipping through the curtains, I made my way down a corridor, music thrumming under my feet. I nodded as a human opened the door for me, and then I stepped into the club.

The bar ran in a semicircle all around the vast space, with mirrors from ceiling to floor. Seating areas filled with awfully patterned couches looked out over the dancefloor, where girls danced on platforms dangling from the ceiling. Each girl was wearing butterfly wings on her back, while lingerie that left little to the imagination adorned the rest of their bodies.

Across the room, curtained areas hid some of the patrons from view, while others enjoyed the fact that people were watching them. Bile pooled in my stomach as I let my eyes fall to a door that was marked private. I saw a woman lead a man in his late fifties into the private rooms after he flashed a wad of cash at her.

Trying to remain unnoticed by all the men striding around with guns, I leaned against the bar and surveyed the sights of this vomit-inducing club. Human women tried to dance drunkenly around poles, their friends hunched over and laughing at their failed attempts, stupidly unaware that monsters lurked in the shadows.

"I thought you could do with a drink."

I glanced over my shoulder to see an attractive young man, maybe a few years older than me, smiling softly as he pushed a tall shot glass in front of me. About five-five with reddish-brown hair, his face was littered with freckles, but that did nothing to diminish his handsomeness. He could easily take the fancy of any customer who might like a stereotypical Irishman.

I assumed this was Kallum, the bartender who'd been giving Rose information, and as I spied the apple tattoo at the nape of his neck, I knew I was right. My gums ached at the thought of sinking my fangs into his neck; I could almost taste his blood on my tongue.

Kallum's smile deepened, flashing dimples that seemed to go on for miles, and he gave me a knowing look. "I can offer something else to drink as well if you need it. All you have to do is ask."

The monster in me snarled. I wanted to indulge my need to feed—this self-imposed starvation was starting to affect my reaction time and fray my nerves, which made me a liability.

I flashed Kallum a smile. "If I say yes, will it get me behind that door?" I asked, inclining my head toward the door marked *Private*. Hopefully, anyone watching was thinking Kallum was simply trying to charm the pants off a customer.

"No," he said, keeping his rakish grin in place, "but I can get you close enough that you could get inside yourself. Follow my lead."

Kallum strode across the bar and spoke to a rogue, who leered in my direction. I glanced away, twirling my hair in my fingers as I downed the shot of vodka and almost coughed at the sheer strength of it.

The rogue pushed Kallum toward me, and Kallum sauntered back, slid his hand up my neck, leaned in, and brushed his lips against my ear. "I told him you were a court vampire who snuck out and wanted a taste of outside life. He gave us the curtain nearest the door you're looking to get into."

I laughed and wrapped my arms around his waist, letting Kallum lead the way as I kept an eye out for Maxim or anyone else I might recognize.

30

Once we were in the room, Kallum stripped off his top, and I held up a hand to stop him.

"Hey, keep your clothes on, buddy."

Kallum pushed me down onto a chair in the room and whispered, "We are going to have company in about five minutes, and it needs to look like you want a feed-and-fuck. If we get caught, you might survive but I'll be dead."

I lurched forward and swapped our positions, climbing into Kallum's lap and shoving his head to the side. My fangs elongated as I ran a hand over the pulse at his neck, just over the apple tattoo, and he shivered. For a moment, I resisted, reveling in the painful burn of desire in my veins as I denied myself what I wanted.

As footsteps approached, I sank my fangs into Kallum's flesh, and we both groaned as his hands caressed my ass and I drank deeply. The curtain opened behind us, and I dragged my fangs from Kallum's neck long enough to growl menacingly at the guard who asked if he could stay and watch.

The curtain closed, and I sank my fangs into his neck again, drinking down the sweet-tasting blood. It tasted so damn good I didn't want to stop. It had been so long since I'd fed from a vein, and now, as the hunger dulled just a tad, I fought against my desire to drink this man dry and forced myself to stop.

Retracting my fangs, I licked the curve of his neck, rejoicing in the newfound strength coursing through my veins. My senses were sharper, my body felt alive.

Kallum grinned at me through the haze of post-feeding afterglow. "You know, if you wanted to continue with the second part, I'd be happy to."

I stumbled off his lap, unsure what he meant for a second, but then he shifted the bulge in his pants and my cheeks flamed with heat.

Kallum looked surprised at my reaction and chuckled. "You are the rogue reaper, and you blush a shade of crimson when offered sex? I like you, Ryan."

"I would happily take you up on your offer, but I still have a very pissed-off royal prince with designs on me in tow, and I like you enough not to want to see him tear your head off."

Kallum chuckled and let out a contented sigh as I wiped my lips and peeled back the curtain to see if the coast was clear. With one last glance at Kallum, I used the cover of the curtain to reach out and grasp the door handle. I gave it a quick twist, slipped inside, and shut it quietly behind me as I entered the lion's den.

Chapter 3

THE MOMENT THE DOOR CLOSED BEHIND ME, I GAVE MYSELF a second to adjust to the red lighting, pressing my back against the textured wall. Groans and moans sounded from various rooms lining the large corridor ahead. I grimaced at the tell-tale crack of a whip and the undeniable sounds of pleasure as I began to edge my way along the corridor.

I had made it maybe fifteen steps when a rogue rounded the corner. His eyes widened when he saw me, and I pretended to stumble, acting like a drunk patron who had gotten lost. He grinned. Calling out something in Russian I couldn't quite pick up, another rogue appeared from around the corner, and the two smiled as they came toward me.

Stumbling forward, I placed one hand on the floor, the other releasing the dagger hiding in my boot. Retching loudly, I heard the rogue's chortle as they stood over me. The adrenaline of the impending fight, mixed with the strength I had gained from drinking Kallum's blood, pounded in my ears.

"Poor little drunk vampire. We have some fun, *da*?"

Hilt of the dagger firmly grasped in my hand, I slowly rose to my feet, flashed my fangs, and grinned. "Oh yeah, I'm gonna have some fun, boys. You, not so much. Let's get ready to rumble."

They stared at me blankly, and I rolled my eyes. "See, that's the problem with you old vampires. You guys don't appreciate the finer things in life. I mean, how can you live your lives without the classic that is PJ & Duncan's "Let's Get Ready to Rhumble"? Did you sleep through the nineties or what?"

The two rogues glanced at each other, and I pounced, plunging the blade into the skull of the nearest one. He dropped to the ground the moment I yanked back my blade. The remaining rogue stared at his dead comrade for at least two heartbeats before he yelled for help and dove for me.

I dodged his blow, flattening against the wall and spinning to face him, the sound of approaching footsteps sending another rush of adrenaline through my veins as the rogue pulled a machete with a serrated blade form nearly thin air, the long blade already stained with blood.

I grinned. The rogue didn't look after his weapons, which meant they were already weakened. It also showed me how little he was trained. The doofus had probably been told to pick a weapon and had gone straight for the one he thought would make him look toughest.

Idiot.

He came at me, and I blocked his blow, kicking out with my foot and catching his knee. He went down with a grunt, stabbing forward with his machete. I blocked his blow again and drove my knee into his chin as he fell; and then he was out, dropping the blade with a clatter.

The sound of footsteps halted as I bent down and sank my blade into the side of his neck, severing the

34

rogue's carotid. Some of his blood splashed onto to my face, and as I rose, I wiped it off with the back of my hand. Standing before me were six more rogues who'd come to aid their friends. I relaxed my stance, bending at the knees, my dagger ready to strike as I reached out my free hand and beckoned them forward.

Not a single rogue moved for what felt like forever, each one glancing to see if any of the others would be brave enough to have a go. I could smell their fear and it excited me. They were afraid of me, and I liked it.

As the rogue reaper, I had begun to carve out a legacy for myself that was free of the shadow of my parents, one that defied the crown and all I had been taught to serve. I was finally finding myself, a path that was my own.

It was exhilarating.

One foolish soul lurched forward, pushed by one of his cowardly mates, but he still came at me, committing to the forward motion. With the flick of my foot, I kicked up the dead rogue's machete and let the incoming rogue's momentum to drive the blade into his stomach.

His eyes wide, he clutched at the machete, yanked it out, and then tried to stem the bleeding. I reached out to grab his hair and slammed his head against the wall. With a sickening crack, another rogue was gone from the world.

Two of the rogues turned and ran away, leaving two still looking at me. The scent of their fear washed over me like the sweetest perfume.

"If you don't want to end up like your buddies, then just tell me where Maxim is and I'll be on my way. Better I take my temper out on Maxim than you guys, right?"

Neither rogue replied, they simply snarled and growled like that would intimate me. I took a step in their direction and quickly flung my dagger. It hit its mark, lodging in the eye of the rogue on the left, who screamed in pain. His friend took one look at his buddy and bolted out of view.

Unsheathing my sai, I darted after the rogue, following the scent-trail of fear in the air. A satisfied customer stumbled out of one of the rooms, and I shoved him back inside. His bedfellow took one look at me and slammed the door shut.

Seconds later, a fire alarm wailed from inside the club, and soon enough, humans poured into the hallway from every room. I gritted my teeth, dropping my gaze and hoped the lighting would help to shield my face so the humans would not see the blood streaked across my skin. I slipped my hands inside my jacket to hide my weapons and slowed my pursuit. As the crowd began to thin, I pressed forward once again.

To my right, a door sprang open and I came face to face with one of the last people I expected. With hair the color of caramel and skin to match, Farrah Nasir paled in the red-light glow of the hallway, her own fear so strong it crinkled my nose. She was half dressed, the buttons of her blouse done up wrong as she clasped a hand over her mouth at the sight of me.

Farrah, though not the worst of the bunch, was part of the self-proclaimed Heathers, Natalya Smyrnoi's band of bitches who had made my childhood even worse by bullying and harassing me. Farrah was also the daughter of Idris Nasir, the leader of the Royal Guard and a man who considered me a thorn in his side.

"Oh, by Eve, Ryan! What are you doing here?"

I heard a female call Farrah's name, and I arched my brow. "I think the more interesting question is what is Idris Nasir's little princess doing slumming it in a strip club and brothel?"

For a moment, I felt ashamed at myself for needling her because I knew very well why she was here. But Farrah had ridiculed me for being different my whole life, and all the while she was harboring a secret of her own—one that her father would disown her for.

"Please, Ryan. You owe me absolutely nothing. I'm begging you not to tell anyone you saw me here."

I shrugged my shoulders. "Who would I tell, Farrah? In case you hadn't noticed, I have my own shit to deal with. Take my advice, through; secrets have a way of coming to light when you least expect it. Just be ready for it."

Leaving the stunned vampire to her thoughts, I continued following the trail of the rogue I'd been chasing. A bloody handprint along the staircase at the end of the hall guided me up to another dark hallway on the floor above.

The hall was eerily quiet, and my senses pricked as I came to the door at the end of the hall. I placed my hand on the handle, noting it was warm and slightly sweaty from being recently used. Ear against the door, I heard not a whisper of sound.

A smart person would walk away. After all, an ambush could be waiting for me beyond the door, and as highly as I rated my skills, I was no match for a hundred rogue vampires lying in wait. I would either die quickly or be dragged to Maxim to die slowly and painfully. But I'd never claimed to be smart.

"Ryan, don't go in there."

"Go away, Krista. I can't bloody deal with you right now."

"Nothing good will come of you walking through that door. Maxim isn't there. You do not need to go in there. Please, Ryan. Just go home."

"You're not even real," I muttered to myself. Ignoring the ghost's warning, I took a step back, recoiled my foot, and kicked the damn door in.

The room was utterly dark, the only illumination coming from spotlights that wandered around the obviously huge room. This was clearly a ballroom. A large dancefloor filled the center space, with a bar running along one side. The periphery of the room was filled with circular tables draped with dusty sheets, chairs sitting upside down atop them.

I caught the scent of blood that had soaked into the floorboards. I could smell it off the thick curtains masking the moon from the room, too. This was where the rogues partied and humans died.

An army of rogues was waiting, just as I'd suspected, the spotlights flickering over their faces, illuminating the hunger in their eyes. The fear that had previously laced their scents was now gone; they knew even the rogue reaper was no match for a hundred male vampires.

But what I wasn't expecting was the slideshow that flashed against the massive screen on the back wall. Images flashed onto the screen that were already burned into my mind—images of Krista's death—and I covered my mouth to stifle the scream of anguish threatening to burst from my throat.

"Oh, my butterfly, it does pain me to see you hurt so much."

Anger overwhelmed my pain as I whirled round, trying to pinpoint where the voice had come from, where Maxim taunted me from, and how many rogues I would have to get through before I could make him bleed.

However, as Maxim's voice began to speak again, I snarled at the realization that the asshole wasn't here;

he'd never been here.

"You look so beautiful, Ryan, a warrior through and through. Even with colored hair and eyes, not a vampire alive does not know about you, my butterfly."

"Don't fucking call me that!" I screamed, eliciting a croaky chuckle from Maxim.

"Lay down your weapons, Ryan, and my associates will bring you to me. We can talk."

Sheathing both my sai, I stretched my arms out in front of me. "Come on, Max. Come get me yourself... or are you afraid of a little ol' girl? No wonder Mia left you hanging."

A snarl rang out through the speakers, and Maxim swore in Russian. I smiled, glad to have hit a nerve, and then answered him in his native tongue, asking if he liked having his lackies do all his dirty work for him.

"Beautiful and smart," Maxim said, the surprise evident in his tone. "I can see why the prince searches for you as madly as you search for me. Does that mean that you care more for me than you do the prince, my butterfly?"

I snorted. "Puh-lease," I drawled. "There's no contest. Nickolai is a prince."

"But that matters little to someone like you, Ryan Callan."

"If you hadn't been going around murdering people and killing my friend to get to me, you wouldn't even be on my radar, Max. When I kill you—and I will—you'll be long forgotten as I get on with my life. The history books won't even mention your name outside a brief reference to a rogue who tried to steal the crown and died a failure."

"Would you come with me, Ryan, if I promised to tell you who killed your parents? Would you promise to let me live if I told you who had betrayed them? Whose vengeance is more important to you—your parents, or a human girl who was part of your life for a millisecond in vampire time?"

For a second, I had no answer to that because I couldn't trade either; each was equally important to me. What Maxim lacked in his understanding was that vengeance was vengeance, and I would not trade either to keep him alive.

"You know what, Max? You talk too much for someone who doesn't have shit to say. I'm not stupid. You know what I worked out from our little chats? You may have played a hand in the coup, but you did not kill my parents. Someone inside the court did. Someone used the rogues to try and take the crown but failed. Was it Boris?"

Maxim's sardonic laugh greeted my suggestion, oblivious that I'd already guessed Boris wasn't vampire enough to attempt something like that.

"My brother never had the stomach for bloodshed. He couldn't even kill me. No, I will not share this revelation with you just yet, my little butterfly. I want to feel the race of your pulse when I whisper the truth in your ear. I wish to feel the sharp intake of your breath on my skin as you realize what a tapestry of lies has been woven. See you soon."

Maxim's voice cut off as my heart hammered in my chest. The rogues began to draw closer, the lights flickering over their features. Maxim might not want me dead yet, but he wanted to see me broken, willing to bend to his will.

"Ryan, the window!"

Krista's voice broke through the building wave of panic in my chest. I glanced at my ghostly friend, tears

40

streaming down her face as she stared at the images for a moment before she cried at me to watch out.

I ducked a punch to the side of my face, glancing as I moved at the window to which Krista was frantically pointing. As the army of rogues descended upon me, I took off at a sprinter's pace, using my vampire speed to duck and weave around them. I was certain Maxim had ordered them not to hurt me too badly. Winded as I was, I ignored the elbows to the ribs and punch to the face I received as I fought with every defensive move I had to make it to the window.

The curtain fluttered ahead of me, offering a glimmer of moonlight, and then suddenly one of the speakers fell over... and then another. I paused, frozen in disbelief as I watched Krista, anger written all over her features, destroying the movie equipment. Almost as shocked as I was, the rogues were distracted by Krista's actions long enough for me to make a beeline for the window. I said a silent prayer to Eve and then smashed straight through the glass, the shards piercing my skin as I went into freefall.

I tried twisting my body to make a graceful landing, but seconds later, I smacked into the pavement below, letting loose a scream as I heard a bone in my right wrist snap. Somehow, I'd managed not to crack my skull open on the concrete, and the alleyway had blocked my fall from human eyes.

Before I could assess myself further, the door at the side of the building opened and I really thought I was about to die. My body was still in shock from the fall, and there was no way I could get my stupid ass off the ground. Pain raged throughout my body, but I could not tell where it began and where it ended.

Even a vampire hurt like hell if she fell two stories

41

out a window.

"Jesus Christ, Ryan. Let me call Rose."

I groaned in relief at the sound of Kallum's voice and heard myself ask him for a phone. He handed it to me, and I dialed a number, knowing there was no way Kallum could haul my ass out of this alley before sunrise.

When a male voice answered, I managed to grind out a few words, telling the man who answered that I needed help and to come alone.

I tried to hand the phone back to Kallum, but I was starting to fade. I heard Kallum tell Atticus where we were, and then Kallum pressed the phone to my ear as Atticus spoke to me.

"I'm on my way, Ryan. I'm minutes away. How bad?"

I couldn't speak. Dizziness washed over me as I tried to wipe the blood from my face, forgetting about the broken wrist. As fire sparked in my bones, I let out another scream of agony.

The phone was whipped away from my ear as Kallum tried to get me to talk.

I must have passed out, because the next moment I was being lifted carefully by strong arms as my body jolted and a fresh wave of pain wracked my body. I felt tears fall from my eyes but I was too broken to care.

A car door opened, and I cracked my not-so-bruised eye to see the last person I expected to see jump out of the car. The queen looked visibly ill at the sight of me, ordering Atticus to lay me down on the backseat of the car.

Darkness engulfed me again briefly, and when I came to next my hair was being smoothed by the queen as she ordered Atticus to take us to Nickolai's apartment. I began to rise, my body still in the throes of shock as I begged Atticus not to take me to Nickolai's.

I heard the queen sigh as she told Atticus to take me to Rose's, easing me back down again.

"Oh, Imogen, dear friend," I heard her say. "What am I do with your daughter?"

And then my body and mind could take no more.

Chapter 4

I CAME BACK TO CONSCIOUSNESS WITH A JERK AND TRIED TO sit upright, but a tsunami of pain stopped me in my tracks. I groaned, lying back in a bed that was not my own and inhaled a breath, the air burning in my lungs as I clenched and unclenched my fists. I didn't even try to open my eyes just yet; even I wasn't that much of a masochist.

The broken bones were healed, even if they were a little tender, and I was glad for it, because as soon as I was on my feet again, I'd be back on the hunt. I tried to sit up again, and a wave of nausea and dizziness washed over me. I rolled to my side as I went to get out of the bed.

"As fun as it is to watch you struggle so, I would ask that you try not to injure yourself any further than necessary."

At the sound of the regal voice, I hung my head as every single moment of what had happened came rushing back. Cracking open my eyes, one still slightly blurry and obviously swollen, I glanced up to see Queen Katerina sitting in an armchair at the foot of the bed. She balanced a dainty cup of tea on her knee as she regarded me. Her hair was pulled back in a ponytail, her clothing far from the elaborate dresses she wore at court, a simple black legs and training top zipped up the front. On her feet were pink tennis shoes that for some reason made her seem more human.

"I would bow, my liege, but I'm sure I'd tip over if I did."

"Must you make jokes, even now?"

I shrugged my shoulders, hissing at the stab of pain. "If I didn't joke about my pitiful life, my liege, then I would drown in my tears."

Katerina didn't respond as Atticus entered the room, simply lifted the teacup to her lips and took a sip.

I made to sit up, and Atticus rushed to my side to help me into an upright position. When Atticus was certain I wasn't about to leap from the bed to escape, he perched himself at the side of the bed and handed me a bottle of blood.

"You've been force-fed blood since you went unconscious, but you still need more to heal. Drink this while your new fanboy recovers enough to feed you again."

I bristled at his tone, tilting my head to scowl at him. "Are you mad at me for getting hurt, or mad at Kallum for helping me?"

Atticus frowned, shaking his head as he gave me a smile that didn't quote reach his eyes. "Both. I'm mad that you went off on a suicide mission by yourself. I'm mad that you took a swan dive out a window with a couple dozen rogues baying for your blood. And I'm mad as hell that you're making me lie to both Nickolai and Jack right now."

The relief on my face must have been visible because Atticus tipped the bottle so I was forced to drink, then took the empty bottle from my hands. He got to his feet and bowed to the queen, pausing at the door. Turning back to face me, his lips pressed into a scowl as he asked, "Why call me and not Jack? Why me of all people?"

I sensed the queen watching our exchange with mild curiosity. I didn't wish to crack myself open in front of Katerina, expose the secrets of my heart and mind, but I had little choice. I owed Atticus my honesty.

I wrapped my arms around myself protectively. "Do you remember your graduation to the Royal Guard?" I asked.

"Like it was yesterday," he replied with a faint smile, pride in his tone.

"Do you remember what you did afterwards?"

He blinked in surprise and nodded, his eyes darting to the queen.

"I was so pissed off," she said. "They announced the new round of trainee guards right after, and I wasn't on the list. What was the point of everything I'd gone through if I wasn't going to be exactly what my parents wanted me to be?"

"Ryan... you don't have to explain."

"I do." I sighed, dropping my chin. "I had a run-in with Nattie. She said her father had told her that the queen had forbidden them to let me into the class. I was eleven years old, and I went to the roof that night to wait for the sun."

Ignoring a gasp from the queen, I continued. "You found me, and you sat with me until the sun began to rise. You asked me to give you a day—to stay alive just one more day and give you a chance to fix things. You sounded like you meant it, so I agreed.

"I was never sure how you did it, how you managed to change her mind. But you beat down my door at sun-

46

down that day, dragged me to class, and never told anyone about that morning. That's why I called you—because you helped me when you had no obligation to do so."

"Ryan," Atticus' voice was thick with emotion as he gave me a warm smile. "I would have done that for anyone. But you... I saw myself in you—alone, isolated, full of self-loathing for being different. I sat on that roof long before you did, but I couldn't go through with it. I believe Eve wouldn't allow me to end my life then because I was meant to sit beside you that morning."

Without another word, Atticus excused himself, leaving me alone with the queen. We remained in an uncomfortable silence for an age, Katerina setting her teacup down before she folded her hands in her lap.

"Had I known my attempts to keep you safe had impacted you so, I would have made different choices."

"Coulda, shoulda, woulda. Doesn't matter now."

Glancing toward the door at my words, Katerina smiled. "I always wondered why he chose to use up his one favor on you. Now, I know."

"I'm not sure I understand," I said, confused.

Turning her attention back to me, Katerina looked almost fragile as she explained. "It is a long secret tradition that anyone who ascends to the Royal Guard is granted a favor from the queen. Some ask for gold; some ask for other materialistic gains. Atticus used his favor to bring you into the trainee class. I always wondered why he'd ask this of me for a girl he hardly knew. And now I know."

My heart tightened in my chest. I knew I'd never be able to repay Atticus for what he'd done for me. He had gotten me in the door and had helped me all the way. I would be eternally grateful to him.

47

"You will soon get to ask your own favor of Nickolai, once you see sense and allow yourself to use the tools of the guard to find Maxim."

"What did my parents ask for?"

Rose had been right when she'd said I was curious as a cat; I just had to know what my parents had asked of the queen, to know them more, to learn of them outside of what I remembered.

"Your parents asked for the same thing—the right to love one another and still be members of the guard. Tristan asked it of me first, and I would not deny him. When Imogen asked me the same question, I told her she could choose another as I had already given my blessing."

Katerina rose, and for a moment, I thought she would not tell me what my mother had asked for. Then, to my relief, Katerina began to speak once more. "I have tried every single day to live up to Imogen's request, but I have failed. She asked that if she and Tristan were blessed with a child and ever fell in battle, that I would raise the child as my own."

"My liege... I... I have not made that promise possible. For that I am very sorry."

Katerina dismissed me with the wave of her hand. "I was the adult, Ryan. I had an image in my head of how I would raise a daughter, and nobody expected the rebellious spirit that you would grow to be. Apart from your parents."

Turning to leave, Katerina paused and tilted her head back to me. I watched her mull over thoughts before she spoke again. "I offered my son the same favor, and he knew what he wanted without skipping a heartbeat. Nickolai asked for me to give my blessing to the woman he chose as his queen."

My mind spun back to what Nickolai had said after

I told him his father wanted me married off and how he could hardly send me back when he had done the same. My heart raced even as my head told me that it would never be me.

"It doesn't mean he would choose me," I murmured. "I wasn't born to be a queen."

"When my son was seven years old, he watched you as you played with Tristan. You called him over, and my son looked to me and said in that determined tone of his that one day he would marry you." Katerina paused. "Only time will tell."

"Why would you tell me this? Surely you want someone better for him, someone more suited to queendom?"

Katerina raised a brow. "You mean like Natalya? That girl will never find herself married to either of my children. Nickolai went out with her to appease his father. I know what love looks like, Ryan, and my Nico looks at you like Tristan looked at Imogen."

For a moment I found myself wondering why she didn't refer to herself and Anatoly as being in love. But then all the other information started racing through my already-pounding head, and my brain started spinning as it struggled to process everything.

"Just before I go, Ryan—Nickolai is beside himself over the girl's death."

"Krista. Her name was Krista," I growled, unsure why the queen's words had sparked my anger.

"Of course... Krista. Nickolai blames himself as much as you do for her death. Had we not sent you both to that college campus... well, we cannot change the past. The crown has paid for her body to be repatriated back to her country. I asked for them to collect her body from the morgue at around ten this evening. Say goodbye, Ryan, and then come home."

The queen was gone before I could say anything else, and I dropped my face in my hands and cried my goddamn eyes out. I wasn't sure how long I cried, but it must have been for a while.

As I wiped the snot from my face, I heard the queen leave with Atticus, asking Rose to let her know if she needed anymore assistance.

"Dude, you look like a hot mess."

Lifting my face from my hands, I stuck out my tongue at Krista, who laughed and plonked down on the chair vacated by the queen. She curled her legs up under her body and ran her eyes over me.

"I mean, you slept for three days. One would think you'd look a little less dead than you did in that alley."

"Says the actually dead ghost?"

Krista grinned. "Touché." Her grin faltered as I threw back the cover and slowly swung my legs out until my feet landed on the carpet. "What are you doing?" she asked in alarm.

"I'm going to see you," I grunted, trying to ignore the pain of sore limbs and stiff muscles as I stood on shaky legs.

"I hate to break it to you, Ryan, but I'm right here."

"Not *you*—dead you," I explained as if it made sense.

"Um hello, like that's any clearer? You need to lie back down. Maybe you have a concussion. Did you hit your head when you flew out the window and smashed into the concrete?"

"No, you idiot. Your body is being flown back to the states this evening, and I need to... hell, I dunno... Someone should be there."

I was in no state to be standing, much less making my way across the city to the morgue, but even as it took me an age to dress, each movement a kiss of agony burn-

50

ing inside me, I was soon dressed, my hair pulled roughly off my face, the blonde starting to blaze through once again.

Ghost Krista sighed and winked out of sight as I opened the door and stepped into the main area of Rose's shop. The Child of Eve shook her head, ushering out her customer as I rested against the wall and took a breath to steady myself.

"Katerina told me you might be about to do something stupid," Rose said as she turned back to me, "but I explained that was a lot of things you do."

"Leave the jokes to me, Rose. They need a dash of bitterness to hit the mark, and you... you have no bitterness in ya."

The statement would have hit its mark if I hadn't tried to walk at that moment and nearly faceplanted. Reaching out to catch myself, I grabbed a shelving unit and winced at the pain in my wrist, my eyes watering.

Rose came forward and handed me a fifty euro note. I protested that I had money in the attic, but she wouldn't hear of it. "Neither of us are in any condition to climb those stairs, my girl. And besides, your twisted sense of morality will ensure you at least attempt to come back in order to pay me back." She smiled. "There's a cab outside to take you to the morgue. No arguments, just go."

Rose went behind the counter and retrieved my sai, then helped me slip them on even as my face flamed with embarrassment. It took a few attempts to get out the door and into the cab, but soon I was getting out of the cab and standing outside the morgue.

I had meant to slip inside unnoticed and say goodbye before they came to take Krista away, but it was already five to ten and I knew my body wasn't up to stealing inside in time. I heard the sound of a van reversing and glanced at the black van parked at the side of the morgue.

Tears welled in my eyes as I moved to the building next to the morgue, a medical training center. A fire escape led up the side of the building and I climbed every single step with a tuck in my heart and my lungs burning. I deserved every single flicker of pain.

By the time I reached the roof, I had barely enough time to perch on the ledge and watch as they wheeled solid oak hardwood coffin out into the chill of the night. Krista was being sent home in the finest of coffins, the queen having spared no expense. I wished I could see her one last time; I wished I could wake up from this nightmare and walk onto campus and have Krista sidle up next to me, link her arm in mine, and everything would be right in the world.

I stayed as they hoisted her body into the van, closed the doors, and locked her inside. The mortician slapped the doors, and the van drove off slowly—painstakingly so—until it turned out of view.

Now that she was gone, I didn't know what to do with myself. I was so tired I couldn't face the thought of going back down the goddamn stairs anytime soon. Glancing toward the sky, I offered up a prayer to Eve, hoping that Krista, who had been a friend to vampires, might be looked after by our deity.

"Please Eve, watch over my friend as she takes her final journey home. Give her peace and guide her toward her final resting place. I ask it of you for the blood I have sacrificed for your children."

"Hey, kiddo."

I started at the sound of Jack's voice, almost losing my balance and taking another fall to the ground. I managed to scramble to my feet at the last second, bracing myself for a fight, my fangs bared and my sai in my shaky hands.

Jack's expression flickered from concern to hurt and then back to concern again as he took in my current state. Holding out his weaponless hands, he cautiously inched closer even as I took a step back.

Jack was standing between me and the escape ladder. I glanced over the side of the building, darting my eyes all around as I tried to figure out how many of the Royal Guard were circling me. I was a fool to have believed that the queen wouldn't rat me out to the guard.

"Hey kiddo, it's a long way down, especially after the fall you took the other night. How 'bout you and me go somewhere and talk? Just you and me."

A shadowy movement in the corner of my eye caught my attention, and I snarled. "Fuck you, Jack. Don't stand there and lie right to my face."

"I ain't lying, Ryan. Everyone, stand down. That's an order."

I growled low in my throat as the shadows retreated, and Jack gave me his attempt at a bright smile.

"See? Just me and you. Everyone just wants to make sure you're okay."

"Cut the crap, Jack. I could count on one hand the number of people who care about my well-being. I'm too tired to deal with this shit tonight, so either move aside or come for me."

"Aw, come on, kiddo. It doesn't have to go down this way. I don't want to hurt you."

Bracing my feet, I bent at the knees and held out my sai, one hand in front of the other as I blocked out the pain. In a sudden burst of movement, I lunged forward, but my reactions were slow and Jack was in full strength. I managed to slice my sai down his forearm as he made to block my move, but Jack grabbed the collar of my top at the same time and tossed me to the floor of the roof.

Pain bit at my side as I rolled out of the landing into a standing position, ignoring the wobble of my knees as I squared my shoulders. Taking in Jack's horrified expression, I know that I have already won the fight—Jack doesn't want to hurt me anymore than I already am. But I have no issue in hurting him in order to get off this roof.

I sucked in a breath and charged forward, my sai poised to strike.

Chapter 5

I held my own for maybe five minutes before my body started to rebel against me. To be fair, it was Jack's lack of force that let me keep going for so long, the vampire blocking my strikes with his forearms and sidestepping the tips of my sai with embarrassing ease.

I was pretty sure a toddler could've walked onto this roof and handed me my ass right now, but I would not stop fighting to leave. I would not stop hunting Maxim until I could watch the life drain from his eyes as I finished the job Boris should have done all those years ago.

And then my mind wandered back to what Maxim had said to me in the ballroom. *"I want to feel the race of your pulse when I whisper the truth in your ear. I wish to feel the sharp intake of your breath on my skin as you realize what a tapestry of lies has been woven."*

Maxim might be a sadistic killer, but he'd never lied to me. Had he skirted around the truth? Hell yeah. But why was it that I trusted him to keep his word even if he killed me after he honored it?

Now, as Jack shoved me hard and I landed on my ass, I growled, the sound pitiful as I painstakingly hauled myself up and spat blood from my mouth. I was fighting a fight I could not win. I knew it, but I was stubborn as hell and wouldn't concede.

"Never ever think you can win every fight. Pick your battles. There is no shame in living to fight another day."

My father's words bounced around in my mind as I felt a wave of dizziness wash over me. My knee buckled as I came within striking distance of Jack, and I dropped the sai in my right hand. Jack surged forward to stop my fall, but I snarled, low and vicious, and stabbed weakly with the sai in my left hand.

It totally missed the mark, and I panted as I tried to rise, awareness of another prickling at my senses. Strong arms hoisted me up from behind, and I coiled my left arm back and dug my sai into the leg of whoever was trying to hold me captive.

I spun away from Jack, who was still shouting for everyone to stand down. The scent of copper hit my nose, comforting as the smell of warm cookies on a lazy Sunday afternoon as I shoved Zayn away from me. An animalistic growl ripped from his throat as he lunged at me again, but I somehow managed to avoid his grasp.

Pain bloomed in my side as I rolled and grabbed my discarded sai, my eyes darting to the morgue roof behind Jack. If I was feeling a hundred percent, I could absofuckinglutely make the jump. However, I was sure I currently had some internal bleeding after reinjuring myself, and as my hands trembled, I wondered if I could catch the ledge.

"Come on, Ryan. I just want to talk to you. No one is here to hurt you."

"Really? And that's why the Neanderthal put his hands on me, is it? No wonder I have trust issues."

Jack flinched, and I liked that I'd hurt him, even if he

was one of the only vampires I trusted. Decision made, foolish as it was, I slipped my sai into their sheaths. Jack's face relaxed, as did his stance. I flexed my feet, trying to work out how fast I could run before either Zayn or Jack could catch me. I was standing smack in the middle of the roof.

"Now, this may be one of the stupidest plans I've seen in my undead life."

Glancing to my right, I saw Krista rolling her eyes at me and grinning. Now I was caught between a dead girl and a group of highly trained vampires.

"Are you thinking again? It looks like it hurts."

"Shut up, Krista! Can't you see I'm trying to figure out an escape here?"

"It doesn't look much like an escape, Ryan. Looks like suicide."

"That's rich coming from the dead girl," I bit back, earning a snort from Krista.

"I'm just saying, it's a long way down."

"Shut up, Krista. Please, shut the hell up!"

The roof was suddenly quiet, the vampires studying me as I snarled at an invisible person. I huffed, realizing that everyone now knew I'd finally lost all my marbles. I glanced at Jack, who was watching me with an expression I knew only too well—pity. A growl rumbled in my chest as I sucked in a burning gulp of air.

"Last chance, Jack. Move or I do. I asked you both to stop hunting me, so you will either have to take me by force or let me go. I should've never trusted the queen."

Surprise flashed in Jack's eyes as I feigned to the left. The two vampires on the roof with me fell for it. As soon as they followed my misdirection, I whirled and bolted toward the other end of the roof. Pumping my arms hard, I drew on any remaining strength I had to move myself forward.

Jack called my name as my booted foot hit the ledge of the roof, and then I was in the air. I knew the moment I left the roof that my stride had not been long enough to make the jump, my pace all too slow. And now, as injured as I was, I knew there could be no recovery.

I didn't even try and fight it as I missed the ledge of the opposite building by a mile. For a split second I hovered in mid-air, and then I was freefalling, the air rushing up to meet me, my hair whipping across my face as I closed my eyes to avoid seeing the ground coming up to meet me. With my eyes closed and the air against my skin, I didn't feel a single thing—no pain, no grief, no loss. I wondered if this was what it felt like to be free. I waited for the blissful flare of agony as my already broken body reached the ground, but it never came.

Familiar arms caught me around the waist as a familiar scent washed over me before we crashed right on through a window. I felt the pinprick of shards on my skin, the sound of breaking glass ringing in my ears as my fall was broken by a hard, male body whose arms were tightly wound around me.

My eyes sprang open and all the air was stolen from my lungs. Cerulean eyes stared back at me, a mixture of relief and anger flashing through them as I tried to wriggle free. But Nickolai would not give me an inch.

The prince looked far from his normally composed self—stubble dusted his face, his hair was unruly, and his eyes looked tired as they ran over my body. Even disheveled, Nickolai looked good enough to bite, and I was suddenly overwhelmed with this *need* to touch him.

My fingers grazed the side of his cheek, and Nickolai let loose a shuddering breath. I scratched the stubble on his jaw for a moment, yearning to lean in and press my lips to his, to feel the stubble against my lips as I moved them along his jawline.

Horrified at how easily I was swayed from my mission, I snatched my hand back as if touching Nickolai had burned me. And maybe, somewhere deep in my soul, it had.

"Hey, Ryan, you're gonna have company in about two minutes," Krista said from somewhere behind me. "If you don't want it to look like you and the prince are about to get naked, then I'd haul your ass off him."

I shoved at Nickolai's chest, and he let me go. Scrambling to my feet, I turned to my ghostly companion and muttered, "You could have warned me sooner!"

"I didn't want to ruin the moment," she said with a grin. "Plus, I'm not opposed to seeing your prince naked, either!"

"*Krista*," I hissed through clenched teeth.

The ghost chuckled as Nickolai got to his feet, studying me with a tilt of his head as I looked at the broken glass window and tried to plot out my escape.

"Ryan."

I shivered at the tone, unable to ignore the instinct to obey my future king. Just then, the door to the room crashed open, and the entire trainee group flooded in on Jack's heels. Part of me wanted to smirk at the limp in Zayn's gait, but mostly I wanted to curl into a ball and cry as pain coursed through my entire being.

"Ryan."

Closing my eyes was the last act of defiance I could muster. With closed eyes I could ignore the face of my liege and try to remember that I had a choice. I didn't, really; and resistance was futile.

"Ryan, open your eyes."

Unable to defy Nickolai in my weakened state, I

complied, letting all the hate and anger I could seep into my eyes as I glared at him. I didn't hate him, not really, but I hated that he would use such a tone with me and take away my free will; it was the only thing I had left. A wave of grief cracked open my heart, and I slumped my shoulders in defeat. Everything suddenly felt meaningless. I had no fight left in me. They had taken everything from me. I was utterly alone.

Swallowing hard as the trainees surrounded us like students observing some lab or something, I could read their expressions in my periphery and felt the mocking tone of their sneers as if I were being struck by bullets. Their eyes taunted me. Their body language was relaxed as if the mission were over and the petulant girl had been safely rounded up by the men.

"If the bitch was mine, I'd knock some sense into her," Zayn ground out.

Nickolai's head snapped around, breaking the spell he had me under. Before he could respond to Zayn's comment, however, Jack punched Zayn square in the jaw. The vampire would have been knocked into next week if Edison hadn't blocked his fall. Nickolai, having realized his mistake, whirled back to me, but I had already regained some control.

My eyes darted to the window, and I was pretty sure I could land on my feet if I jumped down the one floor. I took a step toward the opening, my boots crunching on broken glass.

"Don't you *fucking* dare!" Nickolai ordered, his tone feral, his fangs peeking out.

"I told you to stop following me," I said. "I asked you to let me be, but you don't listen! I'm so goddamn close to getting my hands on Maxim."

"You look ready to keel over, Ryan. You are no match

60

for a male rogue vampire in your current state."

Nickolai was calling me weak. Shame and embarrassment flushed my skin. I *felt* weak, incapable; but it killed me that the one person I wanted to see me as strong saw me for the pathetic mess I was.

"Be reasonable, Ryan. You don't always have to go it alone."

His tone, angry with a sprinkling of condescension, raked against my composure. I took another step back, negating Nickolai's advancement. "I do," I snarled. "I always do."

I pointed to the gathered group. "Do you know the half of what they did to me? Do you know the hell I went through while you watched from your royal perch? I can't trust them to have my back in battle. They'd throw me under the bus, stroll back to the crown, and tell them I fell in battle because I was female."

I should have stopped then; I should have taken my words and locked them into the place in my mind where I put all the awful things in my head. But I was so fucking tired of pretending. So, I let my words be my weapons, striking out with my voice against those who'd hurt me because I didn't have to strength to strike with my fists.

"Did they tell you about the low blows? The whispered threats? The pranks? The threatening letters under my door to try and make me quit? The sick note that said I should've had my blood spilled just like my parents? I walked into *every* fight knowing my teammates didn't have my six even if I saved their asses—even if I was ten times the fucking soldier they were."

I couldn't stop the verbal shitstorm flowing from my lips. My skin was on fire and sweat dripped from my forehead. The entire room was utterly silent as I stabbed my finger to my chest. "I told you once why you and I could never be, and the real reason is because I don't trust them to have your back. I could never be queen because I don't trust them to have mine."

Nickolai sucked in a breath, and I knew that my words had hit their mark, a sniper shot to the chest. But I also knew Nickolai; I knew he'd heard what I hadn't said. I'd never said I didn't want him, and that would be all that mattered to him.

My blood pounded in my ears and my vision blurred as I took another step toward the window. When no one moved to stop me, I leapt for the opening in the glass. I didn't make it far, as Nickolai grabbed my wrist and yanked me back.

Without thinking, I whipped a concealed blade from out of nowhere and plunged it into Nickolai's shoulder. I ignored the roar from Jack, from the trainees, and from the internal voice in my head that told me to run. My eyes were glued to the knife embedded in Nickolai's shoulder.

The crown prince didn't so much as flinch, ripping the blade out with his free hand and dropping it to the ground. The scent of his blood roused the monster in me, and I licked my lips without thinking.

Our eyes clashed, and my body was on fire as the sound of Kingsley Day's voice dragged me back to clarity.

"She has committed treason, Jack. She has committed *treason!*"

And by Eve, I had. I had, without any provocation, drawn blood from my future king. I had bloodied a member of the royal family, and that was a crime punishable by death. Nickolai would have to take my head and burn my body. It would kill him, but he would do it.

Stumbling back, I felt eerily calm. Lifting my gaze to Nickolai's once again, I noted that whatever he saw in my eyes terrified him. Chewing on my bottom lip, I made to clasp my hands behind my head in surrender when my body finally decided it'd had enough.

Powerless to stop myself, my body crumbled to the ground and I saw stars as my head hit the tiled floor. Rolling over in the broken glass, my eyes stared up at the ceiling. Then Krista was crouched down next to me.

"Oh, Ryan. My death is not worth causing you all this pain."

But it was. It really was.

I lifted my fingers, imagining I could feel the icy coldness of Krista's skin against the raging fire of my own as tears slipped from my eyes. "I'm sorry, Krista. I'm so, so sorry I failed you."

Then Nickolai was hauling me up off the ground, blocking Krista from view as he smoothed the hair from my face. I struggled a little in his grasp, trying to get away from him even as my body protested, but I was so damn tired. My head lolled to the side, and Jack's face came into view. I heard him ask Nickolai if he could carry me, and then I must have blacked out because the next thing I knew, I was cradled in Jack's arms, my head against his chest, the hum of an engine surrounding me.

"I need to go, Jack. I need to find Maxim."

"We will, kiddo, we will. Just rest up for now; we're almost there."

"Am I going to die?" I asked.

A hiss left his lips at the coldness of my tone, no fear at what may come. "They'll have to go through me to getcha, kiddo. They'll have to take me before they can take you."

And then Jack started to hum an old Irish ballad, one that had been a favorite of my dad's, one that he used to sing with pride, even though the daft man didn't have a note in his head even if he could rattle the keys of a piano so hauntingly. Jack swept his hand over my hair as he hummed, and when I closed my eyes I could imagine that I was back at Murphy's, sitting in my mother's lap as my dad sang "A Song for Ireland," the entire pub still as they listened to him.

Jack continued to hum as I wrapped my arms around myself, keeping my eyes closed, trying to fall into my memories and imagine I was still whole and not irrevocably broken. But that was all it was, a memory and a foolish dream. I knew that when I opened my eyes, all I'd be left with was the nightmare I'd been living for the last ten years.

But I supposed that's what grief did to a person, whether they're human or vampire. People tended to fixate on memories and fantasies of things that could never be. Maybe the grief stricken couldn't let go of their memories of lost loved ones because those thoughts were constant, heart-breaking reminders of a great story they never expected to end so suddenly.

Chapter 6

My father clapped Anatoly on the back, his signature grin illuminating his eyes as he tried to mollify the king's trepidations.

"It will be grand, Toly. The boy has to learn how to take a blow, and no other vampire would dare try and hurt him."

As if on cue, Nickolai yanked the ends of my hair and I whirled around with a scowl, punching the prince in his shoulder. He grimaced and stuck out his tongue. Though two years older than me, the prince had the maturity of a toddler.

"Tristan, it's unfair to expect Nickolai to fight back against a girl. It would not be a fair fight."

My father let loose a whoop of laughter. "Don't let my Imogen hear ya say that. She'd bleed ya just to prove a point. I'm offering my daughter up for this, Toly. However, if you can find another poor soul who has no problem wounding the crown prince, then we can surely leave."

Nickolai and I stood next to each other, both watching our parents intently. At six years old, I already knew fighting was a way of life for us vampires and that we protected the crown at all costs. I knew that was what I'd do when I was grown—protect Nickolai with my life just like my parents *had vowed to do.*

When Anatoly gave a brisk nod, my father steered me away from the king and prince, crouching down low so his deep hazel eyes were in line with my own lavender ones.

"Baby girl, you got this. No need to show up the prince too badly—we want Nico to have some confidence in his swordsmanship."

"It's okay, Daddy. I won't hurt him too much. He's my best friend. And I know I need to let him win."

Wrinkles creased my father's brow. "Who told you that you needed to let Nico win?" he asked with a frown.

Pursing my lips together, I ducked my eyes, staring at the floor until my chin was lifted and I had no choice but to look back at my father. "I was playing hide-and-seek and I heard Momma and Auntie Kat talking, and Auntie Kat said that perhaps I should let Nico win so as not to hurt his con-fid— confide—"

"Confidence?"

I nodded my head and swallowed, waiting for a lecture or for my father to tell me Auntie Kat had been right and I needed to let Nico win for he would one day be king, no matter if the thought of letting anyone beat me when it was not fairly achieved sat uneasily with me.

Instead, my father let a growl rumble in his chest. "You do not have to let Nico win, Ryan. Never dilute who you are because others don't understand you. I bet if you had spoken to Momma, she would have told you the same. If Nico beats you fair and square, then so be it. But if you are to grow to protect him, you must be better than he is. You do you, baby girl, and never be afraid to just be you."

Getting to his feet, my father handed me my sword, a small replica of his own katana. The familiar weight of it in my hand was as comforting as any blanket. Resting his hand on my shoulder, my father steered me back to where Nickolai and Anatoly stood.

Nickolai grinned at me and winked, and I returned his smile. The entire training room was empty, the usual spectators having been banned from the room to let the prince find his footing without all eyes on him.

"The first to draw blood is the winner. A nick or a scratch is sufficient. No cheap shots."

I listened intently as Anatoly continued with a long list of rules that were no doubt meant for me. I rolled my eyes at Nickolai, letting loose a quiet snort, and Nickolai barked out a laugh.

When the king stopped speaking, our fathers sent us off to the practice mat to square off against each other. My father stayed close by but gave me enough space to concentrate. I bowed my head to Nickolai, and he did the same before we began.

Sparing was nothing new to Nickolai and me, but this was the first time we would spar with weapons that could inflict serious harm on one another. I had sparred like this with my mother and father, but never with Nickolai.

While I was lost in my thoughts, Nickolai charged me. I sidestepped the attack and used an elbow to his kidney to wind him. Turning, he faced me again, the laughter gone from his face. This time, he waited, circling me like a predator, and I followed him as he did, moving so that my back was never to him.

Nickolai struck out suddenly, his eyes darting to where his father stood, and I knew that his heart was not in this fight. As the tip of his sword came at my face, I dropped to my knees, ignoring their sting of protest. Nickolai stumbled in surprise, and I used his distraction to my benefit. Shifting my own sword upward, I aimed to prick the prince's skin, just under his cheek. But Nickolai moved at the last second, and my blade slashed along his cheek, blood welling and dripping *down his face.*

The prince didn't cry out, only protested when I was yanked upward by my shoulders into an upright position. My sword fell from my hand as I was spun around, and my eyes widened as the king lifted his palm to hit me.

The blow never came.

My father grabbed the king's wrist, his face a mask of calm. "My liege, you will not lay a hand on my daughter. She has done naught wrong. If you strike her, then you and I will be having more than words."

The king looked at me with such hatred that I couldn't understand, even as Nickolai pulled me away from the two men. Yanking on the sleeve of my shirt, I lifted it to Nickolai's cheek and wiped away the blood, apologizing.

Nickolai shook off my apology, leaning in close to my ear. "Next time we spar, show me how to do that."

I grinned up at my best friend, oblivious to the tension in the room at that moment, but I remembered that my father and Anatoly had never been the same since that day.

Blinking my eyes open, I stretched without thinking, but my body didn't argue with me as it should have. I was toasty warm and comfortable, not holed up in a cell as I'd expected. Glancing around, I found myself tucked up in Nickolai's bed in his apartment on campus, a sliver of light peeking through the closed curtains.

The light led my gaze across the room to where Nickolai sat in a chair by the door. He had headphones on, and I could hear the hum of a hip-hop track. His arms were folded in his lap, his eyes closed as if he were asleep. But I knew better than that.

Sitting up in the bed, I took the duvet with me so it was tucked up under my cheek. Nickolai still hadn't opened his eyes, and I was grateful for the reprieve as I reached for a nearby glass of water and sipped it cautiously.

I could hear the sound of heartbeats outside and wondered if this was just a luxury prison instead of a cold cell. Setting the glass down, I twirled the ends of my returned-blonde hair between my fingers.

"Are you going to pretend to be asleep for much longer? I'm just so excited to find out when I get my orange jumpsuit," I drawled, trying to keep my tone neutral but unable to stop bitterness from seeping into my words.

Slowly, the crown prince opened his eyes, and for a second, I forgot to breathe. Those eyes, deep like the vastness of space, clashed with mine and stole my breath. He slowly removed his headphones, rising from his chair to come sit on the end of the bed.

"You're awake."

I rolled my eyes so hard I was surprised they didn't fall out of my head. "No shit, Sherlock. Now, am I a prisoner, or can I be on my way?"

Nickolai glared at me for a second. Memories of what I'd blurted out washed over me, and I ducked my head, biting down so hard on my lower lip I drew blood.

"You spiked a fever. Your wound was infected. You were delirious and rambling."

I wondered what Nickolai would say if I told him that I had been deliriously taking to a ghost long before I spiked a fever.

"How long was I out?"

"Five days. We gave you something to help you sleep so you could fight the infection—"

Panic flared in my chest. Nickolai had drugged me? I shuddered, a chill sweeping over me as I tried to catch my breath. Memories of Braydon and the awful night my drink had been spiked came on so suddenly that I couldn't hear or feel anything but Braydon's breath in my ear and his hands on my skin.

"Ryan, look at me." Hands on the side of my face, Nickolai growled and used his alpha tone, forcing me to look at him. "You are safe here. Jack gave you a sedative so you would sleep. I stood by and watched as he gave it to you. If I haven't been here, then Jack has been. No one else has stepped into this room without Jack or me present. I would never hurt you."

I swatted away his hands. I wanted to chase away the panic in my chest. feel something else. Blinking away tears, I reached out and grazed my fingers against the stubble on Nickolai's chin. Sitting up a little straighter, I leaned into him, knowing that if he closed the distance, I could rid myself of the weight in my chest if only for a few minutes.

Fingers around my wrist, Nickolai pulled my hand gently away, swallowing hard. I could taste his rejection all the way down to the pit of my stomach. My teeth clenched, and I snatched my hand back, embarrassed.

With that I was out of bed, my legs a little unsteady as I searched for clothes to put on. When I found none, I made for the bedroom door, but Nickolai barred my way.

"Ryan..."

"Don't 'Ryan' me, Nickolai. Get out of my way. I need to get back to hunting Maxim."

"No."

There was an order in that tone, and I balked at it. Again, here was another reason why we would not work. He didn't respect me enough not to play top vampire with me. He would order me about and expect me to follow him. I could do that if he was just my king, but... fuck it.

I stepped around him, and Nickolai grabbed my arm as I yanked open the bedroom door.

"Let go of my arm, my liege, or I will break it."

A shocked gasp erupted from those in the next room. Nickolai dropped his hand, and I strode out into a gathering of male vampires. Eyes bulging, they ran their eyes over me; I realized I was nearly naked except for a vest and my panties.

Rolling my eyes, I pointed to Atticus, who came forward as I motioned for him to unbutton his shirt. "Gimmie."

Atticus glanced over my shoulder at Nickolai, his fingers stopping dead as Nickolai growled for them all to leave. They hesitated, even Atticus, but none seemed foolish enough to voice their concerns.

"Forgive me, my liege, but the bitch is not stable. You should not be left alone with her."

I stood corrected.

"Get out of my sight, Nasir. Your comments have frayed my nerves enough."

Nickolai handed me a tee as the vampires all piled into the lift. I gave Atticus a small smile and flipped off Zayn Nasir as he shot me a look of pure contempt. The doors closed with a clank, and I pulled Nickolai's tee on over my head as I walked to the fridge. I ignored the heat of Nickolai's gaze as I pulled out a bar of chocolate and tore into it.

"You should really eat something with more sustenance."

I ignored Nickolai, brushing past him to sit on the couch, tucking my legs underneath me.

Blowing out a breath, Nickolai set himself down on the table in front of the couch, facing me, resting his chin in his hands, elbows on his thighs. "How long are you going to stay mad at me, Ryan?"

Nickolai's tone was low, barely a whisper, but I still

heard the tiredness in his tone. I wanted so much to give him assurances, to tell him that I was no longer mad at him but at myself, for it was my own foolish fault for not holding my ground. I shouldn't have let Krista befriend me. I shouldn't have let Nickolai chip away at my walls. I was angry at myself far more than I was angry at him.

"How long are you going to keep me here for?" I countered.

"Until you agree to fight by my side and hunt Maxim together."

I shook my head. "I can't do that, Nickolai," I said softly. "Hunting with you means hunting with the trainees, and I can't do that."

"And if I promised it would just be me and you? Would you let me help you then?"

I wanted to, by Eve I did. Yet, the soldier in me could not put him in danger even more than I already had. I'd already stabbed him without thinking twice about it.

Changing tactics, I cleared my throat. "I'm sorry I stabbed you."

Flashing me a lopsided grin that made my heart skip a beat, Nickolai shrugged. "It's okay. It wasn't the first time, and it probably won't be the last."

I snorted, allowing a small smile to ghost my lips as I got to my feet. "I need to go, Nickolai. I need to catch up to Maxim."

"He knows where you are, Ryan. He's always known. He sends me little postcards, sometimes with pictures of you hunting. Sometimes, the things he says..."

I could imagine what Maxim was saying to Nickolai, taunting him, teasing him to anger. I could see Nickolai tense as I let go of a sigh. "They're only words, Nicky. Whatever he says, it's only to provoke a reaction. What better prize for a rogue like Maxim than to see the future king wound into knots for a girl who isn't worth it."

Nickolai's head snapped in my direction, his jaw clenched as if he were considering saying something that would slice us both open and never heal. Instead, I turned away, moving to stand by the window and gaze out at the city.

I could feel Nickolai come to stand beside me, felt the slight brush of his fingers against mine. We stood, watching the city for a few minutes as the doors to the elevator hummed to life and I saw Jack stride out of the open doors reflected in the glass.

His face was serious as I turned to face him, surprised at the angry tears in his eyes. "Don't you *dare* do that to me again," he shouted. "Don't you dare force me to hurt you even if it's for your own good. Don't you dare break my heart again like you did on that roof."

I made to apologize when the vampire engulfed me in a hug so tight, I thought my bones would crack. I let him hold me but didn't return his hug, even though I wanted to. When Jack stepped back, I glanced away, ashamed of my actions but trying to remain detached.

Jack frowned, turning his attention to Nickolai instead of me. "My liege, the Sanguine Council has agreed to your meeting and the location. They will gather downstairs within the hour. I have the trainees rearranging the room, and the bar staff have been dismissed for the night."

The council was coming here? Then that was my cue to leave.

"Well, I'm gonna make like a banana and split," I said lightly. "Adios."

"You're not going anywhere, Ryan. Much as I hate to admit it, you know Maxim the best. You can get inside his head. We need you to find him."

73

"But I don't need *you* to find him. I can do this by myself."

Nickolai had been relatively calm up until now, so I couldn't stop myself from jumping when he punched his fist through the wall. "By Eve, Ryan, can't you stop trying to lone-wolf it for one fucking minute? Stop with the cold, ice-queen act and... and... just bloody *stop*."

I flinched at the use of the nickname given to me by Nattie and her group of dimwits. Jack began to chastise Nickolai, but I held up my hand to stop him.

"It's okay, Jack. I can take it. I never expected to hear it from him, but it proves what I've been trying to tell him for, like, forever. We're too different, opposite ends of a society that would rather mock me than celebrate me. Better I know now."

Nickolai paled as I went back into the bedroom to find some clothes even as ice crept over my heart and latched on.

"That wasn't what I meant, Ryan. I'm not like them."

My hands on the door, I gave Nickolai a small smile. "That's the problem, my liege; you are, and you don't even realize it. One day, I hope that changes. But for now, all cards on the table, I can never go back to being someone I'm not. If that makes me an ice queen, then so be it."

Then I closed the door right in his face, shutting down any chance that we could find a way through this.

Chapter 7

IT TOOK ME SOME TIME, BUT I MANAGED TO FIND SOME OF my clothes left over from when I'd stayed here. I quickly dressed in leggings, a pair of sneakers, and, even though I didn't want to give Nickolai any false hope, I tied a knot in the front of his T-shirt so it fit me a little better. Grabbing a hoodie and tying it around my waist, I pulled my hair back off my face and then braved heading back outside the bedroom.

Two things waited for me when I stepped outside. My sai lay on the table, cleaned and gleaming, and next to them sat the queen. Twice now, Katerina had shown up after I'd been injured, her beautiful features marred with concern. I wasn't worthy of it considering how badly I'd treated her, and it irked me to think her concern was simply due to an obligation made to her best friend.

"Had I known that you would stride off and cause such a commotion, perhaps I would not have told you about the human girl's remains being sent home."

"If you were that worried about me, you wouldn't have told Nickolai and instigated the commotion."

Katerina stared at me for an age as I gathered up my

sai, slipped on the straps, and instantly felt more comfortable. I was about to head to the door when Katerina said my name. Out of respect for her, I paused, turning back to face her.

"There are another six months, Ryan, before I am obligated to release you from my charge. Until then, I am well within the rights afforded me by both your parents to force you to stay."

As my legal guardian, Katerina was right.

"You may choose how you spend the next six months. You may work alongside Nickolai to hunt down the rogue responsible for your friend's death, or you may spend the next six months confined to your room in the compound, with one hour a day to train, until you turn eighteen. Even then, I can decide to not grant you emancipation until your twenty-first birthday."

Anger boiled in my veins. "You can't do that," I hissed. "I raised myself. You don't get to pull the guardian card now just because you want to keep your son happy."

Katerina rose and brushed imaginary dust off her lap. "Foolish girl, I do this to keep you alive. By Eve, Imogen would scream at me for letting you hurt yourself like you do, filled with self-loathing and an attitude that somehow you deserve all of this pain."

I made to retort, but Katerina held up a finger to hush me. "The choice is yours, Ryan. Some have said that my affection for Imogen has blinded me to your faults, and certainly letting you do as you please has not endeared you to the council. But Maxim is fixated on you and will not stop until he has you. That makes you a weapon of the crown, and I will wield you as needed. Choose wisely, Ryan. Next time you run; I will not give you a choice."

I stood in silence, mouth open in shock, as she

walked past me to leave. Though unable to respond, I caught a glimpse of her hard-faced expression wavering before she slipped into the elevator and was gone, leaving me to mull over her words and the not-so-easy decision I had to make.

On one hand, I wanted to balk at her offer, dare her to try and lock me into my rooms until, Eve forbid, I turned twenty-one. On the other hand, I could not stand by and let them hunt Maxim down without me. His death would come by my hand, not by anyone else's. But if Katerina thought I would obey without the standard Ryan flair, then the queen was mistaken.

I let the mask of indifference that Nickolai hated so much fall over my features as I called for the elevator and made my way downstairs. Striding across the lobby, I nodded my head to Carter Reeser as he manned the door, preventing anyone from entering or exiting the room. He held open the door for me, and I stepped inside the viper's nest.

The little bar that sat inside the lobby of Nickolai's apartment complex had been transformed. Gone were the comfy chairs and low tables. Instead, a large rectangular table was in the middle of the room, three chairs on either side of the length. One highbacked chair was placed at the head of the table for the queen, and Nickolai was just pushing in his mother's chair as I entered the room.

The room hushed the moment I entered, the trainees of the Royal Guard watching me with eager eyes as if they wanted me to kick off. I ignored them all as I ignored the current members of the Royal Guard and hoisted myself up onto the bar counter.

A murmur of voices began to sound, then quietened when the queen lifted her hand to silence them. When all was still, Katerina sat back in her chair and motioned for Nickolai to speak.

"Maxim Smyrnoi has issued a challenge to the crown," Nickolai began. "He has said that one day soon, he will come for the crown. However, he's conditionally offered to end his war with us, take his rogues and leave Ireland to take his chances in Europe. Additionally, he's offered to provide us information that we've sought for over a decade."

Boris leaned forward to look up at Nickolai. "And what does my brother want in return? I will not give up Mia to him."

Nickolai stalked around the table, pausing to clasp Boris on the shoulder. "Fear not, Boris. He was quite clear he didn't want his brother's sloppy seconds."

Boris snarled but was quickly halted by a glare from Jack. "Then what does he want?" he hissed.

"Me," I said flatly. "He wants me."

The room was still for a moment, and then it burst into commotion. I blocked out the voices and comments, finally understanding what my purpose in all this was. Maxim wanted me just as much as I wanted to kill him. If the crown handed me over, then I would find a way to kill him eventually.

"If any one of you thinks I would trade *any* vampire to lessen the chance of war," Nickolai growled, silencing the room, "then I would not be the king you want me to be."

Nickolai couldn't even look at me, and I knew I needed to make this choice for him. He would never make it for us—not while he was conflicted over the small feelings he had for me.

"It's smart," I began, reaching behind me, snagging a bottle of Jack Daniels, and ignoring the click of Boris's tongue as I took a gulp from the bottle. "If we work this right, like a Trojan horse, I can kill him. I can get into his head—I'm already there—and I can convince him he's won. And when Maxim thinks he has me under control, I'll gut the fucker like a pig."

Jack strode up to me, took the bottle from my hands, and gulped down a mouthful before winking. "If Maxim is as smart as he's indicated," he said, "he'd never believe you would go to him docile, kiddo. If you play like you're agreeable, he'll suss that you're not on the level."

Folding my arms across my chest, I tilted my head. "Maxim is so blinded by his infatuation with me he'll *want* to believe me. He's hinted that my parents died by an inside job. If handing me over to Maxim sniffs out the traitor in our midst, then I'll go."

"No," Nickolai ground out, a growl rumbling in his chest. "I will not let one of my subjects offer themselves up to a madman."

"Technically, my liege"—my heart pounded as I smirked at Nickolai, wanting to anger him— "I'm not your subject yet; I'm hers. And as she so bluntly told me before this little soiree, until I'm eighteen or twenty-one—or I suppose until that little tiara is on your head—she owns me. If my queen tells me to set myself on fire and burn that bastard alive, then I am legally *and* honor bound to obey. What say you, my queen?"

Jack whistled through his teeth as Nickolai's face turned a vicious shade of red, his eyes darting from his mother to me. I snatched the bottle from Jack and tipped it at Nickolai before drinking deeply, relishing the burn at the back of my throat.

"My lieges," Idris interjected, "it is obvious that the girl is not mentally stable. I mean, she has been overheard speaking to the dead."

It was my turn to blush, heat warming my cheeks as Nickolai whirled on Idris and the son standing over his father's right shoulder.

Giving the pair a wolfish grin, he bowed his head to his mother. "Should I tell them the news, or would you like to?"

Idris's jaw ticked as Katerina sighed. "The decision was made," she said, "to start giving my son more responsibility as he nears his ascension to the throne. The first step was to hand over the Royal Guard. Nickolai has been using these past few weeks to assess and determine the future of the guard."

I snorted, drawing a smug smile on Nickolai's lips, though he did not shift focus. The crown prince held Idris's steely gaze until the other vampire finally looked away, realizing the boy who would be king was finally setting his own pace.

Watching Nickolai stride over to stand before Idris and Zayn, I felt a wave of pride wash over me, even as sadness punched my gut. He'd always had the air of something special about him, and there was not a sinner alive who could deny that Nickolai had been born to be king.

"Idris Nasir, the Crown would like to thank you for your service, but it feels fresh blood is needed to ensure the survival of our species. The Royal Guard needs a leader who walks into battle with his troops, not one who sits back and lets other fight his battles. As of now, you are relieved of your duties and Jack O'Reilly is promoted to Commander of the Royal Guard."

I smiled at the shocked expression on Jack's face as Nickolai came to stand before him. Jack dropped to one knee, fisting his hand over his heart. "My blood and my sword are yours, my liege; may I be worthy of the position you have bestowed upon me."

I'd never heard Jack sound so formal before. Standing, he and Nickolai clasped forearms and solemnly nodded their heads to one another.

Turning back to the table, Nickolai continued. "The Crown is also promoting Atticus St. Clair to Second; and as his new position precludes him from performing his official duties as court liaison, Zayn Nasir will take his place as our representative to the United States."

Zayn exploded in rage as I burst out laughing. "You can't do this to me," he cried. "I am the best damn guard in that class!"

Nickolai was in front of Zayn a second later and had the cadet lifted off his feet and shoved against the wall in a flash. "Wrong," he growled menacingly. "The best damn guard in that training class is sitting on the bar necking a bottle of JD, and that is why *she* will be my personal guard. *You* were ordered to keep the rooftop events to yourself, and you immediately ran to Daddy to tell tales."

Zayn paled.

"Loyalty to the Crown comes first," Nicholai continued, "family second. If I had my way, you would not graduate to become a guard; however, we are short on soldiers."

Dropping Zayn, Nickolai peered down at the shocked vampire as Zayn spluttered, stopping only when his father kicked him.

"Pack your bags, Nasir. You leave for America tomorrow."

"My liege," Idris pleaded, his voice pathetic as he addressed the queen. "Have a word with the prince. He cannot send my only son away from his family. This is ludicrous."

"Careful, Idris. You overstep," the queen said in a low warning tone.

The entire room was now weighted with tension as I continued to drink from the bottle, listening intently as Nickolai continued.

"Now that you all know the Royal Guard answers to me first, Jack second, and Atticus third, decisions will be made about the rest of the class in the coming days. We will be watching, so it is up to you to prove you deserve to be part of the group."

Katerina took over from Nickolai, who moved to stand between Jack and me. The implication of his words, that I was to be his personal guard, cast an anchor around my heart and weighed it down to my toes. I would not argue with him here, but should the time arise for him to take a queen, I would use my favor to ask for him to release me, if I stayed after the queen gave me my independence.

"Nickolai has also spent time with some of the female members of the court, and a few have expressed an interest in taking some self-defense lessons. They do not wish to be unable to defend themselves should they need to. I have granted this, and they will start as soon as we have a minute to arrange some tutorials."

The men in the room bristled, their eyes wandering over to me. I grinned, wondering which sap would be forced to watch as the Heathers pissed and moaned about breaking nails. The queen took that moment to glance over her shoulder and flashed me a smirk of her own.

"I'm sure Ryan will make time to arrange this once she settles into her new duties as a fully-fledged member of the Royal Guard."

I choked on the gulp of JD I'd just taken, staring daggers at Jack as he smirked. I'd rather pull off my finger-nails than train my tormentors.

Katerina rose, and the rest of the stunned council rose with her. "We will leave Nickolai and his new guard to speak and work out where they will go from here." She paused as she passed by her son, motioning for him to come closer. The moment he lowered his head, she pressed her lips to his cheek.

Jealously prickled inside me, which took me by surprise since I didn't remember the feel of my mother's kiss on my cheek.

Lifting her eyes, the queen locked her gaze with mine. "Be safe, Guard Callan."

I bowed my head. "My liege."

The moment the room emptied, leaving me, Nicko-lai, and Jack to ourselves, Nickolai took the bottle from my grasp and drained the remainder.

"Jaysus, Nico," Jack exclaimed. "What the hell have you done?"

"Your face was worth keeping it a secret. The guard is yours, Jack, and should have been yours after Tristan passed. If it had gone to you like it was supposed to, then perhaps the bullying and boys' club wouldn't have happened."

I leaned over and gently punched Jack in the shoulder. "My dad would be very proud of you right now, Jack."

"As he would of you, kiddo."

I chased down the emotions threatening to send me adrift, relying on my usual sarcasm to deflect from what I was feeling. "So, when am I being handed over to Maxim? Cause seriously, I'd rather take my chances with Maxim than spend a minute trying to wrangle the Barbie brigade."

Nickolai rolled his eyes as Jack chuckled. "We are

83

not handing you over to Maxim. We will not bend to his will."

"Nickolai, with all due respect—"

"And by that she means 'what the hell are you planning?'"

Scrunching up my face, I nodded. Nickolai scrubbed a hand down his face, pulled a nearby chair over, spun it around, and threw his leg over the seat so he faced us, his arms crossed over the back of the chair.

"Right now, we're playing Maxim's game. He wants Ryan, and it's boosting his ego having her estranged from the court and running herself ragged chasing after him. It gives him all the power, watching from afar."

"Hey," I exclaimed, only slightly offended. "While I can't technically argue with your statement, I feel obliged to do so anyway."

Nickolai grinned. "I wouldn't expect anything less."

Jack leaned against the bar, folding his arms across his chest. "While all this flirting is cute, kids, what do we do about Maxim?"

"Aw," I said, patting Jack lightly on the arm, "if you think this is flirting, then I suppose it was Eve's blessing that Atty kissed you first."

Nickolai chortled as Jack nudged my jaw with his knuckles. Then the crown prince got suddenly serious.

"Think of Maxim like a fire burning his way through us. The fuel to his fire is Ryan. If we remove the fuel, we'll starve him, and then Maxim will grow frustrated and seek her out. He'll have to play by our rules, giving us the upper hand."

"I'm not sure I follow you, Nico."

But I did. I knew exactly where Nickolai was headed, and the only ingredient he needed to put his plan into motion was me. I wasn't sure how he planned to keep me away from Maxim. And I was desperate not to admit that my direct approach had not worked out.

"You want me to stop chasing after him." I stated rather than asked. "You want me to stand down."

Nickolai shook his head. "I want us to play the long game. Maxim is obsessed with you, and he thinks you're obsessed with him. If you back off, just for now, it will irritate him. He'll seek you out. His rogues will report back that you're getting on with your life and he matters little to you. It will unnerve him, pulling at his own insecurities until he makes a mistake."

"And then his blood will paint my sai as I slice into his jugular."

"And then his blood will paint your sai as you cut the bastard's throat."

I grinned, wondering how long I could play the long game before my impatient nature got the better of me and I went off book. For now, I would go along with Nickolai's plan, and when Maxim was dead and our species saved, I'd decide if I could stand beside Nickolai as his personal guard.

If not, I would use Katerina's favor to ask Nickolai for the one thing he would never agree to without being oath-bound to do so. I'd ask for him to let me go.

Chapter 8

THREE DAYS.

Three goddamn days.

That was how long I lasted before being stuck indoors drove me insane. The first day, I'd lounged on the sofa, eating my weight in junk food and watching Hallmark movies. The second day, I'd been distracted by Nickolai asking me to help evaluate the trainees, despite my protests that maybe I wasn't the best person to help him because the only qualities I knew they possessed were being douches, and that didn't seem an appropriate answer.

Jack came by as we were waist-deep in paperwork, giving his and Atticus's assessments. We discussed the candidates as well as the female vampires who wanted to learn self-defense. Nickolai asked me who would make the best fighting candidates should the need arise. I snorted, stating that I couldn't really say until I saw them in action. With a grin, Nickolai inclined his head and said he would arrange that.

We went through files and reports until the early hours of the morning, and I fell asleep right there on the floor using some file folders as a pillow. I woke snuggled up in Nickolai's bed, still in yesterday's clothes, with no sign of the prince.

Getting out of bed, I made my way to the living area to find Nickolai right where I'd left him, neck-deep in paperwork. To be fair, it was the most relaxed I'd seen him in ages, as if he finally was settling into the role he was born to fill.

Part of me was wracked with guilt for blaming him for Krista's death, for running away, for hurting him. However, I knew the blame lay with me and me alone. It was just easier to blame Nickolai than to carry the weight of grief with me. But hey, what was one more dead body to add to the baggage I already carried with me?

"Have you told him that my death wasn't his fault yet?"

I ignored my ghostly friend, just liked I'd managed to do for the last three days, catching myself before I responded and earning more than one curious glance from Nickolai. Right now, Nickolai was hunched over the vast array of paperwork on the table. He too was wearing yesterday's clothes.

"Did you sleep at all?" I asked him.

Nickolai lifted his head to lock his gaze with mine. "How could I sleep with you snoring up a storm in there?"

"I don't snore. I purr."

"I bet you do."

The undertone in his words hit me hard and I blushed, earning a chuckle from Nickolai as he went back to examining papers, answering phone calls, and sending emails. I made coffee, showered, and cleaned the apartment. Then I spent a good few hours lost in my thoughts and pacing the apartment.

"You can't keep ignoring me, Ryan," Krista said.

"Wanna bet?" I muttered under my breath.

Nickolai peered over at me, and I ground my teeth together.

"I've got no one else to talk to."

The sadness in her tone hit me like a sledgehammer to the gut and I staggered, hissing, until a hand settled on my shoulder and I whirled round as if I'd been burned.

"Hey, hey—it's just me. You okay?"

Nickolai's face had concern written all over it. I wanted to step into him, wanted the touch of his fingers grazing my skin, but instead I stepped back, leaning my back against the cold pane of glass behind me.

"I know we agreed to keep me out of Maxim's line of sight, Nickolai, but if I have to spend another day locked up in here, I'm going to lose what's left of my mind."

Nickolai reached out and tucked a strand of hair behind my ear.

I sucked in a breath, suddenly hyperaware of his closeness, of his scent, of everything about him. Swallowing hard, I dared to lift my gaze.

Mischief sparked in those goddamn gorgeous eyes of his as he smiled, all boyish and charming. "Then it's a good thing we've been summoned to the compound."

I rolled my eyes and sidestepped him, wrinkling my nose. "If you've gotta go in front of your mother, then you need to shower, my liege. You stink."

"You could wash my back for me."

"Hard pass."

Nickolai grinned even wider. "Don't tell me you haven't thought of getting me naked and wet."

I hadn't, but I damn well was now.

"I've thought about drowning you, though, if that helps."

His smile lit up his eyes, the tension in the room

bursting like fireworks as Nickolai pulled his shirt over his head. I turned my back, blowing out a breath. The cocky git was still laughing as he ducked into his bedroom. Minutes later the shower was running, and I tried to banish all rebel thoughts from my mind.

The elevator doors chimed, and I turned my attention to the smiling face of a Child of Eve as he strode into the room, my duffel bag slung over his shoulder. Kallum flashed me a sexy, dimpled grin, and I rolled my eyes, which only sent him into a burst of laughter.

"I like this version of you better, Ryan Callan. That mouse-brown hair and plain eyes were far too unextraordinary for you." Dropping the duffel, Kallum came forward and ran a finger down my hair. "It doesn't even seem real."

I opened my mouth to retort when a growl sounded from the behind me.

"Don't you touch her."

With a sigh, I winked at Kallum and turned to Nickolai. "Okay, relax. Kallum helped me out of a jam when I was on my own. He's a friend of Rose's. Tone down the possessive crap. You might be my liege, but you do not own me."

Turning back to Kallum, a small smile tugged at my lips even as Nickolai came to stand behind me, his hand clasping the nape of my neck. "Forgive the crown prince, Kallum. He's used to people being in awe of him."

Kallum's eyes widened and he bent low at the waist, his freckled face paling as he spluttered. "So, *he's* why you declined my fang-and-bang offer? I can see why."

The hand on my neck tightened, Nickolai's aggression kicking up another notch. I elbowed him hard in the gut and, as the prince grunted in pain, slipped out of his grasp and dragged Kallum to the elevator.

89

"Better not mention that in front of the rabid animal, Kallum. Male vampires can be a little possessive, even when absolutely nothing will ever happen between us. Is that," I pointed to the duffle, "my stuff from Rose's?"

He nodded. "She said to pop by when you can. She misses your company."

With a snort, I patted Kallum on the cheek. "Tell her I said that's a bloody lie, but I'll come by as soon as I can without causing danger. Be safe, Kallum—don't go back to the strip club."

Reaching down to squeeze my hand, Kallum gave me a weary smile. "I'm good, Ryan. Rose arranged for me to go to a more upmarket club. Stop by sometime."

With one final bow in Nickolai's direction, Kallum was gone and I was left to face a very pissed-off Nickolai.

"Fang and bang?"

Keeping a comfortable distance between us, I hoisted myself onto the kitchen counter and folded my arms across my chest. "That's what they called it at Maxim's club when vampires wanted a little more to go with their blood. Not that it's any of your business, but I drank from Kallum at the club, and if I hadn't, I'd probably not have survived the fall. I have no interest in Kallum, so you can tone down the aggressive BS, Nickolai. It's fucking irritating."

Nickolai growled at my tone, taking a step toward me, and my heart skipped a beat. My mind imaged him closing the distance between us, tilting my head so I looked up at him, and then crushing his lips to mine... and there would be no going back.

I felt my fangs itching to pierce through my gums, my body humming in anticipation. Nickolai inhaled through his nose and his eyes flashed red. He took another step.

And then his phone rang.

The spell was broken.

Shaking my head, I slid off the counter and turned my back to Nickolai as he snarled into his phone.

"*What?*"

I drained a bottle of blood and rinsed out the plastic to give myself something to do. I heard Nickolai mutter "five minutes" into the phone, then a beep, and then it was just him and me and a massive elephant in the room. Nickolai said nothing as I strapped on my sai, pulling my dad's jacket on over to conceal my weapons.

Clearing my throat, I said, "I take it our lift's here?"

A curt nod was all I got, and I sighed, annoyed that the rollercoaster I was currently on showed no signs of stopping to let me off. While I waited for Nickolai to collect himself, I began to riffle through my duffel and take out my clothes.

"Don't unpack. This place is compromised. When we come back from the compound, we'll be moving to a new suite of rooms across campus."

"Has Maxim made himself known?"

Nickolai said nothing, which confirmed everything.

"You can't keep secrets from me, Nicky—especially not where Maxim is concerned. Tell me."

A muscle in the prince's jaw ticked as anger seeped into his expression. "He sent rogues to case the building. He wrote you letters. He sent a rogue to walk into this building and kill all those in here until you broke and left with him. He threatened to come for you and take you far, far away from me and said I'd never see you again."

"I'd rather die than let him have me."

"Don't you think I know that?" Nickolai yelled, his shout rebounding inside the suddenly very compact apartment. "You react before you think! You put yourself in grave danger without a thought to your own safety. You are reckless and impulsive and have no sense of your own mortality."

"Keep on listing all my best qualities; it's very endearing," I drawled, ready for this conversation to be over. "Can we just leave now?"

"I can't lose you again, Ryan. I can never go back to the last decade."

"You know what, Nickolai? Why the hell did you make me your personal guard if you don't think I'm up to the task? You do realize your personal guard's the one who takes the bullet for you, right? So that's me now—the girl who will take a bullet so you don't have to. If you can't stomach that, then why claim I'm the best and make me your guard?"

A flash of guilt crossed his features as I studied him, and I wondered what about my question had made him feel so guilty. Suddenly, it dawned on me that maybe he didn't think I was the best person for the job; he just wanted me close to keep his eye on me.

"No," I said, my eyes widening in disbelief. "That's not it, right? You didn't give me the job just to make sure you and Jack could keep an eye on me, did you? I deserve the truth, my liege. Am I the best person to guard you, or did you just want to protect me?"

"Both."

I stumbled back as if he'd hit me, the blow of that single word more painful that any punch or slap I'd ever taken. In one single word, Nickolai had taken away any pride I'd in the position I'd been given. In one single word, everything I'd worked so hard to achieve had been set alight and was burning inside my chest.

"I'll see you downstairs."

"Ryan, wait... I didn't mean it like that... please give

me a chance to explain."

"That is quite alright, my liege," I said icily, facing away from Nickolai as I pressed the button to close the doors behind me. "You've said enough."

I was seething with anger as the lift descended quickly to the lobby. As I stepped out of the elevator, I could feel the rage on my skin. Spotting Jack, I made my way over, the other vampire taking one look at me and realizing that something was wrong.

"You okay, kiddo?"

"Make him pick someone else, Jack."

"What?"

"Make him pick another personal guard. One who doesn't cloud his judgement and cause him to make choices based on his heart and his damn possessiveness."

"I'm not sure what you mean, kiddo."

Anger now a viper coiled in my chest, I spun to face Jack. "Nickolai chose me because he wants to keep me safe, not because I'm the best damn warrior in that class. He has this notion that he wants me for his queen. I am not and will never be queen. Make him choose someone more suitable so he can stop fucking with my head."

Strong hands landed on my shoulders. "Kiddo, when Nickolai suggested making you his sole personal guard, both Atticus and me questioned his motives. While we agreed it was the right choice, we wanted to make sure he was picking you for the skills you possess, not because of his feelings for you."

I whistled between my teeth as Jack continued moving with him as he walked outside, wondering if every single vampire was watching the soap opera that was Ryan and Nickolai.

"He told us he didn't just need someone who was skilled with a weapon, but also someone smart who

93

could help him make big decisions—someone who could be his guard *and* his confidant. He wanted someone who understood court politics but who was not afraid to challenge him, someone who would call him out and argue with him."

The hairs on the back of my neck rose, and it took all my self-control not to whirl around in the direction of what was most likely a rogue. Instead, I let a silly grin curve my lips and embraced Jack.

"Rogue," I whispered as Jack released me.

Jack opened the car door for me to slip inside, but I waved him off as Nickolai emerged from the elevator. He took one look at my face and forced away whatever was banging around in his head, giving me a silly smile of his own.

Instead of coming to me, he clasped Jack on the arm and leaned in. Jack chuckled and ruffled Nickolai's hair. I stood waiting as Nickolai made a big deal of coming to stand in front of me. While I wanted to scream at him, wanted to rebel against what my heart was beginning to feel, I reached out and zipped up his jacket.

In response, Nickolai brushed my hair from my forehead and pressed his lips to my skin. My toes curled, and I let a contented sigh slip from my lips as Nickolai held out his hand. I took it, wondering how much of this was an act for the rogue and how much was just me.

I let Nickolai help me into the car, sliding to the far side as Nickolai got in and Jack followed suit. Nickolai stayed on the seat next to me, while Jack moved to sit across from us. Nickolai reached for me, and I was instantly sitting on the same seat as Jack, my gaze firmly fixed on the world outside.

"Don't be like that, kiddo."

I said nothing, merely angled my body away from

94

them, listening as they spoke about the plan of action for what was apparently a two-day trip. Nickolai had dinner with his family this evening before sunrise and in between, he had a meeting with the trainees and a conference call with the American president of vampires to see about adding some resources to our guard.

"Do you need me at your meeting, my liege?" I was still looking out the window, so I couldn't see his face as he replied to me.

"Not for all of it," he said. "Jack will be with me, but I'd like for you to watch with me as Jack runs some drills and we assess the trainees—possibly spar with them for me. Is that okay with you?"

"Perfectly, my liege. I would appreciate some time to myself, if that is okay."

"You spend enough time on your own. Why would you need more alone time?" Nickolai bit out.

"I'd like to be left alone while I visit the lake where I scattered my parents' ashes. I'd prefer no one watch me should I cry. If that is quite alright with you, my liege."

Silence suffocated the car, further intensified when we arrived at our destination. The vehicle ground to a halt and Jack opened the door, muttering about how he was too old for teenage drama. Slamming it behind him, he left me in the car with Nickolai.

"Can we talk, Ryan? Just you and me?"

"I don't think we have much else to say, my liege."

"Cut the 'my liege' crap, Ryan, you know it wrecks my head."

The order in his tone was natural; I doubted Nickolai even knew he had used it, but that was the problem wasn't it.

I let loose an exhausted breath. "I can't do that, Nickolai, because that is who you are, and I am who I am. You will always give me orders, and I will be hon-or-bound to obey."

"What if I promised that when it's just us, we're just Ryan and Nickolai. Do you remember when we were kids and we pinkie-swore to leave titles at the door and just play? We made a blood oath once to never stop just being Ryan and Nickolai to one another. Can we at least try?"

Hand on the door handle, I pushed open the door. "That was the foolish thinking of children, Nickolai—children who did not know life can't always go their way. If we were normal vampires without the weight of the crown or legacy looming over us, then perhaps. But we are not normal vampires."

I scrambled out of the car, shut the door, and turned to find Nickolai standing in my way.

"What do you want, Ryan? What do you want from me?"

Chapter 9

Standing in the shadows of the carpark, I wondered what, exactly, I did want from him. Maybe having feelings for Nickolai was easier because deep down, I knew it was safer knowing we could never be together. Nickolai may want me as much as I wanted him, but we could never be more than friends.

"I want," I started, then shook my head, feeling foolish for even attempting to explain exactly what I wanted. "I don't want anything from you, Nickolai. One day, I want to be just known as Ryan Callan. Not tragically followed by 'Imogen and Tristan's orphaned child.' I want someone to see me for me, not my past. If I'm lucky enough to find someone, I want them to not be ashamed to kiss my forehead in public or hold my hand. Not just to do it to piss off a sadistic rogue.

"I doubt that will happen for me, Nickolai. I doubt it very much. But, on days when I can't drown my demons, I can imagine that maybe one day, when I wake up, I can wake with a smile rather than a sense of doom in my heart."

I brushed past Nickolai, who was staring at me like

I'd been speaking a foreign language he didn't understand. Taking the stairs two at a time, I flung open the door into the main hallway, nearly smacking Kristoph in the face.

"Aw shite, Kris, I'm sorry."

Kristoph grinned at me as he held open the door and stepped back. "Always with such a fine entrance, Ryan."

The sound of footsteps echoed behind me, and I winked at Kristoph, stepping into the foyer and bowing to the queen and king as they waited for their son to come into view. Some of the council had gathered, along with their children. Nattie glared at me like she hoped I would spontaneously combust.

I made my leave, heading for the winding staircase that would lead to my sanctuary, my safe place. I could feel the weight of people's eyes on me as I started up the stairs.

"Ryan."

I paused as Nickolai said my name, turning slightly as Nickolai bypassed his parents and the rest of the court. His face was filled with determination, as if he was resolved to do something. He seemed contented with himself.

Since I was standing two steps from the bottom, we stood at the same height. My heart raced and I tried to lower my eyes, but something primal inside me screamed at me not to. Nickolai tucked a rebellious strand of hair behind my ear, something he had done many a time before.

He grinned at me then, a slow, sly smile that flipped my stomach. I didn't get a chance to react as he leaned in and pressed his lips to my forehead. The entire lobby inhaled a breath when I did, each one of us shocked as the prince staked his claim in front of the court, giving me what I had said I wanted, dangling a happily ever after in front of my face.

His grin deepened as he took in my shocked expression. "You and I will finish our conversation later. I'm really interested in hearing more about the things you want."

My cheeks flamed as the son of a bitch winked and sauntered off, leaving me standing there, a furious shade of red, as Kristoph clasped his brother on the shoulder and the queen followed her sons. The king threw me a murderous glare, and as the council began to focus solely on me, I bolted up the stairs.

Once in the confines of my rooms, I slammed the door shut and leaned against the doorframe. I'd tried everything in my arsenal to convince him we couldn't be. Now, the damn fool had basically told the entire court of his intentions, and no other vampire would look in my direction. Not that I wanted them to, but still; not a single vampire in the compound would go against their future king.

And what if he did that just to have whoever's helping Maxim report back to him that the prince is kissing you in public? It could all be a ploy.

"There you go, trying to look on the downside once again. You can be a right Debbie Downer when you want to be."

Dropping my chin to my chest, I sighed deeply. Once I'd calmed my racing heart, I lifted my gaze to meet Krista's. Looking the same as always, my friend sat on the weapons trunk at the end of my bed.

"I see that doubt creeping in, Ryan Callan. You have nothing to hide in here from. You need to remind them exactly who you are."

A spray can rolled in my direction as Krista winked

out of view, and I bent down to pick it up. Turning the can over in my hands, I headed for the bathroom. Stripping off my jacket and my sai, I shook out my hair and popped open the spray can.

I continued to work my magic until the ends of my hair were now a shade of purple, highlighting the lavender of my eyes. I gave myself two braids, left off my jacket and sai, and stripped, redressing in loose workout pants and a vest. I slipped on my trainers, just for the walk down, and made my way downstairs.

The sound of my name stopped me in the hall, and I bristled slightly until I saw who it was that'd called me. Scarlett Hamilton walked slowly toward me, a small bundle in her arms. She must have had the baby while I was out hunting Maxim. Her cheeks were hollow and she looked thinner than usual, but Scarlett gave me a warm, welcoming smile as she stopped next to me.

"I swear she only settles when we pace the floor with her."

I didn't know what to say to her and stood there awkwardly until Scarlett spoke once again.

"I never got the chance to thank you for looking after me that night when I wasn't well."

"I did nothing special, Mrs. Everett," I replied, shrugging my shoulders.

"Would you like to hold her? Her name is Ava."

"By Eve, *no*," I exclaimed, wincing as the child stirred and her mother hushed her. "I mean... thank you, but I'd be terrified I'd hurt her. I've never held one before."

The next thing I knew, Scarlett had offloaded the tiny vampire into my arms and I was suddenly so afraid I couldn't even breathe. Glancing down, I saw such peace in her tiny features, so very like her mother's, that I felt jealous. Hopefully she would have a future free of the pain I carried.

Carefully, I handed the infant back to her mother and stepped away, hoping to escape this uncomfortable moment before Scarlett spoke.

"Your mother used to pace the floor with you, Ryan. You only settled when you were on the move, too. None of the other girls were like you as babies. Maybe my little one will follow after you."

And then I was gone, almost leaping down the remaining steps because my head was beginning to throb and I couldn't take any more. I didn't stop moving until I was in the training room, the door slamming shut behind me, echoing in the silence as I kicked off my shoes and walked to the center of the mats.

I stretched out my limbs, warming up my muscles in the silence, letting the routine of it all seep into my marrow until I was at peace once again, the swirl of anxiety quieted for now.

Once I was suitably relaxed, I walked over to the sword rack and took a katana off its perch. I preferred to work with my sai, but as most vampires stereotypically went for swords, I made sure I could wield one as well. I reached for the remote and turned on the speakers, music filling the room as I skipped a couple of tracks until I found a Yungblud track I liked.

Going to stand in the middle of the room, I held the sword in the palms of my outstretched hands. Closing my eyes, I inhaled a breath, flipping the katana up and catching it with one hand. I let my body go, and it fell into a rhythm that came from years and years of practice, twisting my wrists so the blade moved like and extension of my person.

As the song ended, I tossed the sword upward, still with my eyes firmly shut, and listened. Even with the pulsing beat of the track filling the air, I knew the moment the sword began its decent, its blade pointed downward. As a whisper of air ruffled my hair, I clapped my hands together and felt the hiss of metal against my flesh.

A coppery scent hit my nostrils, and I could hear my mother's voice in my ear. *"Never be afraid to bleed, Ryan, for the moment you are afraid to bleed is the moment you are lost in battle and in life."*

Ignoring the sting of the cut on my palms, I tossed the blade again and caught it by the hilt.

"Oh by Eve, that was quite something to watch."

My head snapped toward the voice, and I glared at Farrah Nazir as she gave me a small smile. I walked over to the sword stand, wiping the blade clean of my blood before setting it back in its rightful place, and then turned the music down to a more appropriate level.

A throat cleared behind me, and I glanced over my shoulder to see Farrah holding out a bottle of water. I arched my brow, turning to take the bottle from her out-stretched hand, and uttered a thanks before I realized Farrah was not going away anytime soon.

"What can I do for you, Farrah?"

"I know Prince Nickolai said we could learn self-defense, but some of us were hoping you would be the one to teach us."

I look at the girl as if she were out of her mind. "So, the group who bullied and shamed me for trying to be as good as the boys now wants my help? Kinda messed up, right?"

Farrah kicked at the mat. "You can be quite intimidating, Ryan, and most of us... most of us didn't want to go against Nattie. But none of us want to die, either."

"How am I intimidating?" I barked, surprised when

Farrah flinched as if I'd struck her.

"You are beautiful, smart, can kick a grown man's ass, and you don't care what people think about you. For you, it doesn't matter about power or prestige—you just want to be the best. I admire that."

I studied Farrah for a moment, then smiled. "If you're trying to flatter me so I'll keep your secret, you don't have to. I won't tell anyone."

Farrah gave me a tired, sad smile. "I told my liege I was gay when he had a private meeting with each of us. He came with me when I told my parents. My father hasn't spoken to me in days, and now with Zayn gone, my dad feels as if his family is disgraced."

"Don't take this the wrong way, Farrah, but your dad is kind of an asshole."

Farrah barked out a laugh, then sobered. "I won't argue with you," she replied. "I'm tired of being someone I am not, and I need you to help me."

She clumsily tried to lift a sword that was far too heavy for her—or even me—to wield effectively.

"Put that back before you hurt yourself," I said. "You need to learn to defend yourself so you can run away as fast as you can before you learn to wield a sword. Then again, maybe you should use a dagger or throwing stars."

Farrah grinned. "So, you'll help me?"

"If Maxim doesn't kill me, then sure, I'll help you. Doesn't make us friends, though."

"Of course not."

When Farrah didn't immediately walk away, my heart sank as I realized that she intended to start learning right now. I wondered where to start with someone like Farrah, someone who'd attended ballet classes and etiquette lessons. Then again, ballet training would mean she was agile enough for the basics...

At that exact moment, Edison St. Clair strode into the training room, inclined his head to us and strode over to the treadmills. I thought of my friendship with Atticus; this was his brother. Maybe, maybe we could find a way to be civil to one another.

"Hey, St. Clair, can you help us out?"

Edison looked as startled as Farrah did when I called out, but the trainee came over and asked what we needed.

"You heard that our liege would like all interested female vampires to learn self- defense?"

"Yeah, Atticus mentioned it to me."

I nudged Farrah with my shoulder. "Well, Farrah's the first to volunteer. You want to help me give her a little demonstration?" I asked. "I want her to see how she can use her natural skills. That it's not all about swordplay."

Edison glanced at Farrah, who nodded. "Sure," he said, "what do you need me to do?"

"Pretend to be a rogue and try to take me down."

"No weapons?" my fellow classmate asked.

"Nope, just you and me. Don't tell me you're not dying to punch me."

Edison shook his head, but he was grinning ear-to-ear as I turned to Farrah.

"You used to dance," I began, "so moving quickly and with precision will be your greatest asset. You can also focus on what's going on around you even as your body moves in complex ways; that means you can see what's coming at you, anticipate it, and decide how best to respond. No one is saying you have to physically fight someone—you just need enough space to run away as fast as you can. Got it?"

"Yes."

Stepping up to face Edison, I craned my neck and motioned with my hand for him to come get me. Edison charged, and I sidestepped him by simply moving. Edison spun quickly, his clenched fist coming for my face. I ducked backward, kicking up my leg and twisting my body so that my foot gave Edison a little nudge.

Edison chuckled as we circled one another, and it hit me then that I was sparring with a teammate who *wanted* to spar with me. Edison could have played dirty, showing me up in front of Farrah, but he didn't.

The next time Edison came at me, I weaved from side to side so none of his blows could catch me. When he reached out to grab my shoulders I leapt up and kicked him with the bottom of my feet, and Edison went down, letting out a groan as his back hit the mat.

Farrah watched with such awe I was a little embarrassed. Walking over to Edison, I held out my hand, and as the vampire looked at it my stomach dropped as I recalled many a time when I'd done the same and it was slapped away.

I began to pull my hand away when Edison grasped hold of it, and I helped him to his feet. Nodding to Edison, I called Farrah over.

"You see how I let Edison use up most of his energy by letting him attack me?"

Farrah nodded.

"That's what you need to do."

An uneasy silence fell over us as the door to the training room opened and Nickolai, Jack, and Atticus strode in.

"Edison," I said, "you fancy helping Farrah out while I'm not here? I mean, just show her some basics and keep her away from the knives, yeah?"

"I can do that."

"Thank you."

Atticus called me over, and I went easily into his embrace.

"When you gonna greet me like that?" Nickolai muttered.

I snorted. "Around the 12th of never."

I dragged Atticus over to where Farrah and Edison stood. Atticus play-punched his brother who, in turn, tackled Atticus, taking him to the ground. I laughed, watching as Nickolai went to stand beside Farrah and leaned in to whisper in her ear.

She smiled at Nickolai, who squeezed her shoulder before he kicked off his shoes, slipped off his jacket, and rolled up his sleeves.

"Let's give Farrah a proper show."

"Hell no," I said. "I'm not sparring with you."

"Do it, kiddo. I love seeing our liege get his ass handed to him," Jack taunted with a grin.

I flipped him off. "It's a real shame that nobody asked for your opinion," I said, barely getting the words out before I was shoved forward. I had just enough wit in me to roll with it into a low crouch, turning with a snarl.

Nickolai was grinning at me like an idiot as he stalked forward, a hint of fang showing as he reached out to grab me. I rolled sideways and swept my leg out, catching him mid-stride and causing him to stumble.

I looked up at Farrah. "The bigger they are," I called to her, "the harder they fall."

Nickolai growled as I popped up from the floor and began to side-kick me, aiming his feet into my ribs. I blocked each strike with my forearms, biding my time until I counted exactly three seconds between Nickolai's strikes.

I counted in my head, and then as he lifted his leg to

kick me again, I dropped down to my knees so his kick was off balance. When he tried to regain his footing, I caught his ankles and yanked his feet from under him.

Nickolai fell face-first into the mat and rolled over to his back. He was breathing hard, but there was a lopsided grin on his face. Ignoring the heat in his gaze, I turned to Farrah.

"One lesson the boys won't tell you is, as a girl, never be afraid to play dirty. They never expect it, and—"

My legs were suddenly swept out from underneath me, and I hit the mat hard, letting out an *oomph* as I laughed, realizing that Nickolai had used my own move against me. Pinning my arms over my head, Nickolai leaned in, his breath as hot as his voice was rough in my ear.

"What you just did? Making nice with Farrah and Edison? That does nothing to prove you can't be my queen. In fact, it proves how right you are to be my queen."

I sucked in a breath and tried to free myself from his grasp, even as Nickolai leaned his nose against my neck and pressed his lips to the pulse of my throat, his fangs a tease on my skin.

Chapter 10

"Now I get it. Frosty was never going to be interested in any of us mere vampires," Edison said with a chuckle. "It takes a prince—no, a future *king*—to melt all that ice."

Heat flamed my cheeks as Nickolai snarled, his cerulean eyes fixed on mine and whatever expression had crossed over my face. My heart raced, beating so hard I thought it might explode.

"Get off me," I ground out as Nickolai continued to look at me as if he couldn't believe what Edison had just said and my reaction to it.

Letting go of my wrists, Nickolai eased off me, sitting back on his haunches as I scrambled ungracefully away from him. I quickly got to my feet, adverting my gaze from Jack and Atticus, too, as embarrassment sank into my bones. I couldn't stand to be here with everyone's eyes on me.

I spun on my heels and, cursing the tears welling in my eyes, hurried out of the gym and down the corridor. I didn't want to go back to my room, but I had little choice of where else to go.

"Ryan... wait."

Nickolai's voice carried down the hallway, and I shook my head, needing to be anywhere but here right now. A hand landed on my shoulder and I spun, shoving Nickolai so hard he took an unsteady step backward.

"Don't touch me."

"Why are you letting something petty that Edison said ruin all that good work you just put in? Why let something so insignificant bother you?"

I blew out a frustrated breath. "You wouldn't understand."

"I'm trying to, Ryan. Help me understand." Nickolai opened a door to one of the classrooms and stepped aside to let me by.

Part of me wanted to turn away and leave him standing there, reinforcing the fact that nothing could happen between us, much as I craved it. Instead, I strode inside and waited for Nickolai to close the door behind him. He pulled out a chair and sat down, resting his clasped hands in his lap. I gave him my back as I went to the window to watch droplets of rain slide down the panes.

"What did Edison say that upset you so much? Or was it what I said?"

"No matter what I do, no matter any good I may do," I said slowly, keeping my gaze on the rain outside, "there will always be those who think I got where I am because of your mother. I'm not oblivious to the fact that most of the trainees think I'm your personal guard because we're sleeping together."

"But we're not..."

I heard the unspoken word and ignored it with a little shake of my head. "That doesn't matter; they think we are. I made progress today with two people who made my childhood even more hellish than it had to be.

109

And then you went and undermined all that in one fell swoop. Edison may have been joking, but he heard what you said. I need to carve my own path, Nickolai."

"Edison is an idiot whose ego is bruised because he's envied you since we were teenagers."

Rolling my eyes, I turned to face Nickolai. "That's ridiculous, Nickolai. What could Edison be envious of me for?"

"His brother spent more time training with you than he ever did with Edison. Atticus made *you* his protégé, not Edison. He's jealous of the bond you both have."

I made to speak but I had no words. Again, I was being blamed for something that was out of my control. I was tired of all this court bullshit and mind games.

"It doesn't matter, Nickolai, I can't erase the past. I can't go back and undo my parents' deaths. I can't make Atticus spend quality time with Edison. I can't undo anything, and I'm so sick and tired of always being blamed for doing what I had to to survive."

"Let me ask you a question, then. When this is all over, when Maxim is dead and we know whether or not we can save our race, what does Ryan Callan want?"

I blinked at his question. To be completely honest, I wasn't sure what I wanted. I'd spent the vast majority of my short life trying to be the best and become a member of the Royal Guard. I'd achieved that, and it hadn't filled the gaping hole in my chest. I had gotten what I always thought I'd wanted, and I felt no different than I had before.

"Don't answer me now," Nickolai said. "One day soon, I will ask you that question again, and no matter what your answer, I will do everything in my power to make it happen."

"When did you become so fucking reasonable?" I

ground out, surprised as anger laced my tone.

Nickolai's face fell as his own anger filled his eyes. "I can't win with you, can I? I try and keep you safe, and you accuse me of ordering you about. You tell me you want someone who is not afraid to show their affection in public, and when I do, you lose your shit. And now I try and be reasonable, and you get angry at me? Do you just find excuses to get annoyed with me, Ryan?"

My lips twisted into a scowl, but I didn't answer him.

"Oh, here you go with the silent treatment. What are you so afraid of?"

"I'm not afraid of anything."

Nickolai's smirk hit me like a gut punch.

"Like *hell* you're not. You are afraid of your emotions. You're afraid of letting anyone see the real you. You are absolutely terrified of not living up to everyone else's expectations, and most of all, you're afraid of failing."

My jaw popped open in surprise as tears welled in my eyes. What gave him the right to just throw all of that at me? Who, by Eve, did he think he was?

I saw him flinch at the water in my eyes, and I folded my hands across my chest. "How dare you hurl that at me? You want me to be brutally honest, my liege? Well, buckle up. You spent your entire life trying to be the king you thought the vampires wanted instead of the king they needed. You are utterly afraid of the future and being tied to someone you don't want in order to keep the Romanov line going.

You accuse me of being afraid of failing, but look in the mirror. You'll see the face of someone who cannot stand the thought of failing. You dated the vainest of creatures in order to keep your father happy and secretly asked your mother to let you choose your own wife."

I shook my head and laughed, a cold, harsh sound.

"I don't know why I'm wasting my breath. I was better off when I was the loneliest girl in the world."

"There are different measures of loneliness, Ryan."

I snorted. "And what would you know about it, Nickolai? You had it all growing up. You were never alone. You were surrounded by a multitude of people every single day."

"You can be surrounded by a million people, Ryan, and still feel alone. I had friends who were friends because I was a prince. I had mentors who were so because I was their future king. I was always *my liege*, never *Nickolai*. People were afraid to spar with me because of a throne and a crown. I only had one real friend my entire life who didn't treat me differently, and she abandoned me."

Oh, I was really pissed off now.

"I'm sorry if grieving for my parents meant I couldn't play with you. I'm sorry that the fact that I was left orphaned meant that Your Royal Highness felt he had no real friends. I'm sorry that the steps I took to stay sane meant that you lacked someone who would punch you in the face, but that's life. And did you ever ask yourself why I pushed you away?"

A muscle ticked in Nickolai's jaw, but I wasn't done yet. "I did it because I couldn't bear to lose you, too. It was better to watch from afar and see that you were alive. Even if that meant having to stomach you with Natalya. I never stopped making sure that you were safe."

Nickolai stood suddenly, his chair scraping across the floor as he came toward me. I rooted my feet to the ground, refusing to be intimidated. Nickolai stood within striking distance of me, but I didn't so much as blink.

"Is that jealously I hear in your voice, Ryan?"

"No, I think you'll find it's disgust."

Nickolai's lips curved into a smile. "I think you're jealous. Would it help to tell you that Nattie doesn't set my blood on fire like you do? I never once craved her as much as I want you. There are moments when all I can think about is kissing you."

Swallowing hard, I rolled my eyes and pretended I was unaffected by his words. "It doesn't matter. My body may want you, but it will never happen. My body wanted Kallum when I was drinking his blood, but I still said no. How many times did you tell Nattie no, or any other girl, for that matter, who wanted to sleep with a would-be king?"

I strode past him, ready to leave him to digest my words, when I heard him mutter something under his breath, so low I couldn't hear him.

"What did you say?" I bated him.

"I never slept with Nattie."

I snorted in disbelief. "And you expect me to believe that? You guys dated for six months, and Nattie was begging for it so much she practically panted after you. So forgive me if I don't believe that you and Nattie weren't at it like rabbits."

"You can believe me if you want or don't. Doesn't stop it being the truth. You wanted me to be honest, so I'm laying it all out for you. Nattie wanted to, but I said no. She came to my room the night of your birthday to seduce me and I almost did because I was lonely, and then you appeared, and I knew I could never be with Nattie."

I glared at him hard for a second. "Are you expecting me believe that you've never had sex?"

After I said the words, I realized I didn't want to know the answer. I held up a hand to stop him from answering. "Never mind, I don't want to know. It doesn't change anything. We are who we are, and nothing is going to change that. You tell me you want me to be queen, but have you thought about what that means for me?"

"I'm not sure I understand."

A sad smile tugged at my lips. "I know. And that's what hurts so much. If we gave in to this attraction, one of two things would happen. Either we'd realize that we were better off as friends and I'd have to watch you take another as your own and maybe have my heart broken, or two—we'd fall in love and I'd agree to be your queen. I would have to step down from the guard and give up both my family name and personal identity, forever known as the king's wife."

Nickolai blew out a breath, however, I didn't give him a chance to answer. "I would be giving up who I am to be with you. It's not like you could stop being who you were born to be, Nickolai. Fate is a fickle bitch, and I'd grow tired of being someone I am not."

"And if I said I'd give up the crown for you? If I renounced my title?"

"I would never ask you to do that. I would never *let* you do that. Nickolai, you were *born* to be king. You would grow to resent me. And I would still lose you in the end."

Jack opened the door to the room, thankfully interrupting any further comments that Nickolai might have. He looked from me to Nickolai and then back to me.

"You okay, kiddo?"

"I'm fine, Jack. I'm gonna go get some fresh air and clear my head."

"Would you like some company? I want to get some advice from you."

I made to say no, that I needed this time to myself, but there was something in Jack's eyes that made me rethink my answer.

"Sure."

The smile that lit up Jack's face was blinding. "Brilliant. Just give me a few minutes with Nickolai, and I will follow you out."

I left without another word, heading straight out of the room and crossing the hallway, opening one of the doors that led outside. The rain still fell, the icy droplets cooling my skin as I walked down the grassy embankment and stood inches from the lake.

The moon was reflected in the water below, her glow so bright it was calming and beautiful at the same time. I lowered myself down onto the grass and felt the dampness seep into my clothing, but I didn't mind. Suppressing a shiver, I stared out into the lake, losing all the words I had wanted to say since my encounter with Nickolai.

"I wish you guys could tell me what to do," I said quietly. "I wish I could be sitting here beside you both, Mom giving me advice on boys and Dad scowling. I feel like I'm drowning. I really miss you both."

No answer came from Eden, the place where all vampires went upon death—not that I'd expected there to be, for my warrior parents had been recalled to their rightful place beside Eve in Eden.

"Kiddo?"

I glanced over my shoulder at Jack with a sheepish smile on my face.

Jack sank down next to me, nudging my shoulder with his arm. "When I'm trying to make an important decision, I like to have a word with your Da, as well. I imagine what Tristan would say back to me, for he never spoke a word of untruth. Didn't know how to."

Looking back toward the lake, I leaned my head

against Jack's shoulder, needing the contact. "It feels silly, talking to them like this. But I still do it."

"It's no sillier than humans who go to a grave and visit their dead. The person knows their loved one is gone wherever humans go when they die, that it's only bones that lie beneath their feet, but they still go and offer up a prayer."

I nodded my head ever so slightly. Wanting a change of subject, I asked Jack what advice he could possibly want from me.

Jack tensed, but I let him take his time. "I already spoke with Nickolai, have yet to go to the queen, but I was considering asking Atticus to be my mate."

Darting upright so I faced Jack, I gave him my biggest smile and threw my arms around him. "By Eve, Jack, that's amazing! I'm so happy for you both!"

"I'm absolutely terrified. If the queen says yes, then it means outing us both, and there are enough ripples in the court at the moment."

"So," I wiggled my brows and grinned, "you came to ask the person responsible for most of the ripples how to deal?"

Jack chuckled. "If you want to think of it like that, then yes."

"I mean, we could all be extinct in a few years. Why not spend it with the person you love?"

Jack held my gaze for a few seconds. "It really is that simple for you, isn't it?"

"Yup," I replied with a shrug of my shoulders. "We're going to war whether we want to or not. Some of us may not make it through. Why waste a second being unhappy and someone we aren't?"

Again, Jack studied me until I squirmed where I was sitting and glanced back at the water.

"Atticus is going to tell his parents and brother tomorrow about us."

"If his parents react as Farrah's did, I'd happily go and be menacing with him."

Jack laughed again and drew me in for a hug. Night began to slip away, the moon giving way as dawn approached. We could both feel it, the tiredness in our bones that meant the sun would soon rise. We got to our feet and walked silently back to the compound. While I headed for the stairs, Jack headed for the soldier's quarters, giving me one final hug before he let me go.

"Ryan, don't stab an old man, but maybe you should take your own advice. I mean, here you are denying what could make you truly happy. If we all die anyway, would you go to Eden filled with regrets?"

Jack left me then, and I loitered in the foyer. Before I could take myself out of it, I backpedaled and slipped inside the doors leading to the royal quarters. The royal section of the compound was entirely quiet, my footfalls silent as I rounded the corner.

Walking to Nickolai's door, I knocked softly twice but got no answer. A mixture of relief and regret washed over me as I chastised myself for being so stupid.

I backed away from the door, ready to retreat when I spied a mass of caramel curls and flattened myself against the wall. Nattie was having a very heated conversation with someone on her phone. I just caught the end of her side, where she told person at the other end to give her some time.

The call seemed to end there as Nattie growled in frustration, then went back inside Kristoff's room.

Intrigued as I was by my eavesdropping, I walked away, climbing the stairs to my room as exhaustion began to weigh upon my body. All I wanted was to lie down on my nice, comfy bed and sleep a dreamless sleep.

I shoved open the door to my room and froze at the sight that graced my eyes.

Chapter 11

Nickolai was sprawled out on my bed, one hand behind his head, the other hand holding open the Anita Blake book I'd been rereading. His eyes were fixed on the pages as if he were devouring each word, and Nickolai didn't spare me a glance when I strode in.

"What the hell are you doing here?" I demanded, feeling my cheeks heat as I remembered I was the one who had just left his bedroom. I also wondered exactly where he was in the book.

"Shush, I'm reading. It just got interesting. I'm not sure why Anita was so reluctant about Jean-Claude. Even I'm swooning a little."

I marched over and grabbed my book, clutching it to my chest as I glared at Nickolai, who only grinned back at me, folding his other hand behind his head.

"Get off my bed, Nickolai. I'm tired and want to go to sleep."

"Nothing stopping you. This bed is big enough for two. It's quite comfy, I must admit."

I snarled as I set the book down on my weapons trunk and walked back over to the bed. Nickolai held my gaze, and I reached out and gave his shoulder a shove.

"Move over, then. This is my side of the bed."

He blinked as if he'd expected me to throw his ass out the door, or at least put up more of a fight, and then dutifully rolled over, leaving me to pull the covers back. I grabbed my pyjamas, which consisted of shorts and a vest top, and motioned to him to turn around.

When he did, I quickly stripped and redressed, leaving my hair in the braids before I slipped under the covers. The bed was warm from the heat of Nickolai's body, and I tried not to dwell too much on that, even though Nickolai made that impossible as he kicked off his shoes, pulled his tee over his head, and tossed it on the floor. Slipping under the covers, he turned to face me with a smile.

My cheeks flamed. "You better clean up your mess this evening. I know a prince must have a maid running around after him, but us peasants clean up after ourselves."

"Maybe I'm hoping if I leave my T-shirt here that you'll wear it and think of me while you're in bed."

By Eve, my blood was burning. "Whatever helps you sleep at night," I muttered. "You ain't all that, Nickolai Romanov."

"Then why has your face gone all flushed?"

I decided it was best not to answer him; I simply turned out the lights and tried to relax my body enough to sleep. But falling asleep wouldn't be as easy as it was before.

The mattress shifted as Nickolai made himself comfortable, and I could feel the intensity of his gaze on me. I felt him tug on the ends of one of my braids, and I flopped over in the bed, not realizing he was barely a breath away from me.

We stared at each other, my heart beating wildly against my chest. I barely had time to think as Nickolai wrapped his arm around the waist and drew my body flush to his, my head against his chest, his chin resting on my head. I froze, unsure of where to put my hands.

Nickolai sighed. "Go to sleep, Ryan. Your thoughts are keeping us both awake."

The tension in his body relaxed, his breathing slowed, and I knew the bastard would soon be asleep. I shifted my body ever so slightly, trying to get comfy but hesitating to sling my hand around Nickolai.

Sensing my hesitation, he grabbed my arm and placed it around him. I closed my eyes for just a second.

Banging sounded at my bedroom door, and I darted awake, trying to untangle myself from Nickolai as the prince stretched and yawned. The door was flung open as I pulled a dagger from under my pillow and crouched on the bed.

Jack stormed into my room, Anatoly hot on his heels. Jack took one look at me, spied Nickolai lounging in my bed, and grinned broadly for a second before sobering. The king looked appalled as he barked at Nickolai to get up.

"The entire compound is in red alert looking for you, Nickolai, and you have the audacity to lay their yawning?"

"I wasn't aware that my sleeping arrangements were the concern of the court, Father. I will take that under advisement."

The hostile exchange between father and son made me feel uneasy, but Jack came forward. "There is a rogue at the main gate with a message for the crown and he'll only deliver it to the rogue reaper."

I jumped down from the bed. "Then let's go shoot the messenger." I made to stride out of the room when a thought popped into my head.

"Hey Nickolai, pick up your tee from the ground."

"I think we have more important things to worry about than picking up my laundry."

Jack snickered as I rolled my eyes.

"No, you doofus; give me the T-shirt and when I walk out there wearing your clothes, smelling of you, the rogue will report back to Maxim that I went to greet him straight from your bed."

Nickolai grinned as he tossed me his T-shirt, and I pulled it over my head. I slipped my feet into my chucks, Nickolai's tee falling just below the knees. I wanted to take my sai with me, but this wasn't a fight I was going to. This was a gathering of information.

Blowing out a breath, I braced myself for the inevitable stares as I left my bedroom, Nickolai right beside me, taking Jack's hooded top from him as we walked down the stairs. The entire court was gathered in the foyer, the scent of their fear thick in the air. Katerina was doing her best to reassure them that the rogue could not come into the compound.

Nattie positively glowed with anger at the sight of me and Nickolai, even as Kristoff winked by her side. Even bloody Katerina could not stop the smile on her lips.

I went outside, halting once the main doors closed behind us. Turing, I faced Nickolai, ignoring the heated glare of his father's eyes. "The king stays here," I said. "You can come if you follow my lead, but the king stays here."

"How dare you! You do not get to order me about like a mere minion."

"No offense, my liege, but your obvious hatred of me is palpable. We need to convince the rogue that the entire court is waiting in anticipation for a royal wedding. Maxim will never believe that you would allow your son to romance me when you hate me so deeply for some reason."

I said no more to the king as I strode forward, the Irish winter meaning that even though it was just after four in the afternoon, the day had long turned dark. I heard Nickolai have some words with his father as Jack came up beside me.

"Do I need to have the birds and bees conversation with you?"

"Not unless you want me to do the same with you. I mean, I'm betting Atticus looks damn fine naked."

Jack chuckled as our feet crunched over the gravel. I heard Nickolai's footsteps as he jogged to catch up with us and let him slip his hand into mine. We took our time reaching the main gate, dragging it into a ten-minute walk to give the impression we could care less that a rogue had shown up at our compound.

Atticus and Edison stood sentry at the gate, their faces void of emotion. The only movement they made was to fist a hand over their hearts as Nickolai approached. Atticus tried to grab my attention, but I was focused on the rogue standing just outside the gate.

The rogue was standing in front of an SUV, and I sized him up as we approached. He was about Jack's height, with mousey brown hair that hung loose to his shoulders. His face was vampire-pale, eyes reddened, teeth stained, I noted, as he snarled at me. He had scars all along the side of his throat that looked like old burns, and his top lip was also scarred. I would remember this face, and I would kill him one day.

"Reaper," he hissed at me, a look of pure contempt on his face. I wondered if I had killed any of his friends.

Hopefully.

"Rogue," I replied with a bored tone in my voice. "What's so urgent that Maxim sent you to disturb my sleep? It was a late day, so I'd like to maybe get some more sleep."

The rogue inhaled and sneered as he caught Nickolai's scent on me, his eyes darting to the crown prince, who took the opportunity to grin smugly.

"Maxim wanted to ensure that you knew he was still very much thinking of you. He asked me to tell you that the Crown may try and hide his butterfly from him, but he will not rest until he sets you free."

"You go back to Max and tell him the Crown is not hiding me away. Has he ever heard of the honeymoon phase? I mean, my liege is quite athletic—as you can see for yourself—since our return home, we've barely left the bedroom. I don't need to be set free."

I heard someone snicker behind me but ignored the sound, my focus completely on the rogue.

"Nevertheless, Maxim has sent you a gift."

The rogue opened the back of the SUV and dragged out a bound girl, her mouth gagged. Her hair had been dyed as close to my ice-white as possible. Her eyes, swollen and red from crying, were filled with terror. She wore the barest lace bra and panties, and her entire body was covered in fresh butterfly tattoos.

As I stared in horror, the rogue tilted the girl's head and sank his fangs into her neck. She screamed against her gag, and then the rogue ripped his fangs out and snapped her neck. He flung the girl at the gate, her blood still dripping from his fangs.

"Their blood always tastes so much better when they are afraid."

I didn't realize I was moving until I felt Nickolai

ensnare me with an arm around my waist. I struggled against him, wanting to kill the rogue with my bare hands.

The rogue wiped the blood from his chin with the back of his hand and then licked at his hand. I knew then that Maxim had wanted me to be disgusted, wanted me to be sickened by the rogue's actions.

I was done playing into Maxim's hands.

I stilled in Nickolai's arms, and he instantly released me. Tilting my head to the side, I let a slow, deliberate smile curve my lips.

"What's your name?" I asked.

"My name doesn't matter."

"Humor me."

"Cedric."

"Cedric." I walked closer to the gate and gripped the bars. "I want you to enjoy your time left, Cedric. Someday soon, when you least expect it, I will come for you and you will die. I won't make it quick or painless. I will savor the scent of your fear as you feel death coming for you. Death *is* coming for you, Cedric. *I'm* coming for you."

Stepping back from the gate, I dismissed him with the wave of my hand. "Now, be a good little minion and tell Maxim to stop sending idiots to taunt me because all that does is piss me off. If he wants me, he can come get me. I'm ready whenever he's got the balls to face me."

The rogue hesitated for a second, but I'd already turned and begun to walk away. Everyone else followed suit, save Atticus hanging back to make sure the rogue actually left.

When I heard the SUV drive away, I spun round and headed back to the gate. Nickolai didn't say a word as I yanked it open and dropped to my knees beside the dead girl's body.

Reaching out with the hem of Nickolai's tee, I closed

her eyes and muttered a prayer to Eve before I rose. Facing Jack, I heard myself begin giving orders. "Find out who she was. I want to know her name. If she has family, kids, make sure they are looked after. Take it from my trust fund. Fix her up so the human police can find her body. Ensure she has the burial she deserves."

"You got it."

I let my feet move, heading back toward the compound. I knew Nickolai was on my heels as I stormed inside and again felt the weight of the court's gaze settle on me. Katerina came forward and went to cup my cheek, but I flinched back. If she touched me, if she offered me any sympathy, I would crack right open and expose myself to the vultures of our court. I could not let that happen.

"What happened, Guard Callan?"

"Not now, Mom," I heard Nickolai say. "Please, just let us by."

I'd already stepped around Katerina before he finished speaking. The crowd parted before me, and I jogged up the stairs and into the sanctuary of my room.

Krista greeted me for a brief moment, but she blinked out of view as soon as Nickolai came in and closed the door behind him. Without another word, he steered me toward the bed and forced me to climb in. I kicked off my shoes as I went. I was exhausted, both emotionally and physically drained.

Nickolai pulled me into his lap, and I stiffened out of habit but let him hold me. Selfishly, I curled into his embrace and breathed in his scent.

"This isn't on you, Ry. Please don't blame yourself."

When I said nothing in reply, Nickolai jostled me. "Are you listening to me?"

"It's hard not to when you keep droning on."

"There's my girl." I heard the teasing in his tone even as my stomach fluttered at his words.

A rap of knuckles sounded on the door, and Nickolai sighed.

"The joys of being the supreme ruler, my liege." I meant to sound light-hearted and teasing, but it sounded a lot more bitter than I'd intended.

I made to apologize when Jack's voice, muffled through the door, called out, "I'm coming inside, so please be decent. Atticus is with me."

Trying to slide off Nickolai's lap, I was stopped by a firm hand on my thigh.

"Don't."

Normally, I'd growl and buck at his order, but today... today, I would humor him.

Jack and Atticus came in, and I listened as Jack reported that the girl had been brought inside from the elements and that he had tasked the trainees with doing research to find out who she was. He would supervise them to ensure they did right by her.

I thanked him, my eyes heavy as Nickolai played with the ends of my hair.

"I am sorry to intrude," Jack continued, turning to Nickolai, "but your mother would like to hear from her son what transpired outside." Jack glanced at Atticus before continuing. "You should know that Katerina and Anatoly have had words—in front of the court—and your father has questioned Katerina's decision to give you so much responsibility when your energy seems directed elsewhere."

"My father is a bitter old vampire who cannot stand that when I become king, any semblance of perceived power he has will evaporate. I will deal with him in my own time."

"It's my fault," I began, chewing on my bottom lip. "Isn't it? I'm not sure what I did to make Anatoly despise me so much, but he's your father, Nicolai. You shouldn't fall out with him over me."

Nickolai yanked one of my braids. "Contrary to what you think, the world doesn't revolve around you, Ryan Callan. My father and I have never seen eye to eye, not since I was a young boy and spent some time learning from Mom. He has his own protégé in Kristoph, which isn't a good thing."

"Not to rush you two, but Katerina is waiting in the meeting room. I'm sure Nickolai wants to get in early so as not to ruin the rest of the night."

Jack looked to Nickolai, and as the three shared a smile, I became overtly suspicious.

"Something to share, Nicky?"

Nickolai dropped me from his lap, laughing as I shrieked in surprise, my reflexes the only thing that stopped me from taking a dive off the bed. I grabbed a pillow and aimed for his head, but he dodged with a laugh.

"It's a surprise. Just be ready by ten, leave your weapons at home, and wear something pretty for me."

Ignoring his last comment, I placed my hands on my hips and gave him my fiercest glare. "I'm not going anywhere with you without my sai, Nickolai, and I'm not going *anywhere* unless you tell me where we are going."

Nickolai motioned for Jack and Atticus to leave, and they did, leaving the door open behind them. I could hear their footsteps as they retreated down the stairs. Nickolai stalked toward me with an expression that could only be described as determined.

"I'm asking you to trust me. I'm asking you for one night. I'm asking you to overlook your fears, your reservations, and the opinions of others, and just give me this one night. Please, Ryan? I'm begging you."

By Eve, I didn't want him to beg so I just mutely nodded, swallowing down all the voices in my head that screamed at me that this was a bad idea.

Nickolai tapped my nose lightly, and I growled. Walking toward the door, he glanced over his shoulder as he began to pull the door closed, then paused. "Don't forget to wear something pretty for me," he said, closing the door as fast as he could behind him.

As my shoe hit the back of my door, I could still hear Nickolai laughing as I growled my frustration.

"Oh my god, Ryan. You need to start getting ready! Have you shaved your legs? Do vampires need to shave their legs? Let me see in your closet. Do you have anything in color? Let's avoid black if you can. Do you have curling tongs? Can you use said curling tongs? We don't have enough time!"

I groaned, dropping my chin to my chest as I wondered how I could punch a ghost.

Chapter 12

AFTER SPENDING AN AGONIZINGLY LONG TIME IN THE shower to not only avoid Krista and her ramblings but also to try and talk myself out of whatever surprise Nickolai had lined up, I finally dried off and resigned myself to getting ready. If I were being wholly honest with myself, I'd admit there was a flutter of excitement in the pit of my stomach. However, in the back of my mind, I needed the night to be a disaster. If this was Nickolai's way of persuading me that we could be together, I had to be the reasonable one and show him it wouldn't work.

Krista tried to get me to wear a dress, but, after I reminded her of what happened the last time I wore a dress, Krista *hmm*'d, rolled her eyes, and tossed a pair of black jeans and a soft cashmere top at me. I pulled on the skinny black jeans but rejected the cashmere. Instead, I grabbed a tee from my chest of drawers that read "This is what a badass looks like."

I let my ice-white hair hang loose around my shoulders, adding a fresh spray of purple to the ends. Despite Krista's insistence that I wear makeup, I just put some gloss on my lips and decided that was enough.

I had just about slipped on my dad's leather jacket, the clock barely striking ten, when a short tap sounded on my door. I glanced at Krista, who winked and disappeared with the biggest smile on her face. I kicked at a pair of boots as I strode across my bedroom and opened the door.

Nickolai stood with his hands in his pockets, a boyish grin playing on his lips. Dressed in dark blue jeans and a casual knit sweater that looked strokably soft in the same cerulean blue as his eyes, his hair slicked back apart from that one rebellious strand that fell into his eyes, Nickolai looked like every girl's dream guy. He was a teen-movie heartthrob, and I felt a sudden wave of panic wash over me.

I slammed the door right in his face.

Retreating to my bed, I sat down on the edge as I heard a sigh and then my bedroom door opened and Nickolai strode in.

"Want to tell me what just happened?"

Right, no thanks. I wasn't about to tell him that I felt like the girl the hot guy goes out with in teen movies because he made a bet with his buddies. That I, Ryan Callan, was insecure and second-guessing myself.

Instead, I lifted my head. "I've just decided that this shouldn't happen. I mean, I need to make you understand that nothing is going to happen with us. Maybe your parents will find some royal vampire noble and you can forget all about me."

As if he could taste the lies in my words, Nickolai came to stand in front of me, then dropped to one knee.

I nearly lost all reason.

The next thing I knew, Nickolai was slipping my feet into my boots and lacing the things up. When he was finished, he patted my calf and told me to get over myself.

Still reeling from seeing him down on one knee, I let him take my hand and start to lead me from the bedroom. Snapping back to reality, I pulled free of his hand and went to my weapons trunk to grab something to take with me.

"Ry, come on. No weapons tonight. Just you and me. Please."

I glanced down at the dagger in my hand and peered over my shoulder at Nickolai. I shouldn't have looked because the next thing I knew, I was setting the dagger down and heading back over to where he waited for me.

Placing a hand on the small of my back, Nickolai escorted me out of the room. My eyes darted through the halls immediately, and I wondered how it was empty of anyone strolling about. As if he sensed my question, Nickolai began to speak.

"The Americans are arriving tomorrow. My mom has roped every single vampire into preparations for the president's arrival."

"Shouldn't we be doing that as well? Instead of whatever you have planned?"

"Would you rather sit down with Nattie and my mom to discuss floral arrangements?" Nickolai asked with a chuckle as I shuddered. "Thought not."

We quickly made our way across the foyer and descended to the underground garage. I expected the town car to be waiting for us, ready to drive us on Nickolai's little surprise jaunt, yet the garage was empty.

Well, not quite empty. Nestled next to the official royal town car was a sleek, black Ford Mustang, its paint gleaming as if it had just been rolled off the showroom floor. I ran my fingers over the bonnet as I made my way round to the passenger side of the car.

"Early coronation present from my mom," Nickolai

explained, unable to mask the sheepishness in his tone.

"As far as presents go, your mom gives good gifts."

Without another word, I slipped inside and leaned back in the seat, fastening my seatbelt as Nickolai got in and did the same. There were no back seats in this car, and my heart began to race as I imagined all the ways we could be attacked or blindsided and Nickolai kidnapped or killed.

"Hey, what's wrong?"

I chewed on my bottom lip and shook my head, rubbing my hands on my thighs as I tried to rein in my overactive imagination. Nickolai took my silence as permission to continue and steered the Mustang up and out of the compound.

Forever the soldier, my eyes scanned the roads for any signs of threat. This late on a Thursday evening, the roads were relatively quiet. Apart from the odd taxi or truck, it was just Nickolai and me cruising the motorway that linked the city's suburbs together.

Nickolai tapped his fingers on the steering wheel in time with the music, the happiest smile on his face as he indicated and left the motorway, driving toward a usually busy shopping mall. The parking lot was empty as Nickolai pulled his car into one of the free spaces, and after switching off the engine, he got out and walked round to open the door for me.

I swung my legs out and stood, my eyes darting around as I braced myself for attack. I could feel the fear and anger beginning to build the more we lingered out in the open.

Nickolai motioned for me to head toward the main entrance. When we neared, I heard the door being unlocked, and a very human security guard welcomed us as we stepped inside. Then he locked the doors once more.

The guard went off whistling, leaving us standing there, in an empty shopping mall as my anger continued to simmer, although I wasn't sure who I was angry at, or why.

I walked beside Nickolai, following as he ventured up the escalator. As we stepped off at the top, I saw the movie theatre in front of us and shook my head. Stepping back, I stupidly would have taken a tumble down the escalator had Nickolai not reached for me.

"Hey, you've been on edge since before we left the compound. Tell me what's going on."

"I'm not going in there," I blurted out, folding my arms across my chest. "You bring me to an empty cinema, where I haven't been able to ascertain security before the future king decides he needs some salty popcorn, where I don't have a weapon to my name. There is no one here to stop Maxim from ambushing us, and I can't relax because I keep seeing all the ways you could die!"

When Nickolai grinned at my rant, I let loose a savage growl and made to leave. He caught my arm and pulled me to him, lowering his lips to my ear, and I almost didn't hear him for the hammering of my heart.

"Take a second and look around you," he said. As I did, Nickolai continued to speak. "Jack and Atticus are using this as a training exercise. We have more Royal Guard and trainees here than at the compound. The trainees are learning how to blend in. I knew you'd be worried about safety, so I made sure that even though I wanted us to have a moment to ourselves, there's an entire army here to protect us."

I made to speak, but Nickolai continued.

"I know you, Ryan. I asked the management to close early, so we have the entire place to ourselves. Jack is a speed dial away and so is a weapon for your hands. I made sure that even though the best damn soldier is not armed to the teeth, we have enough security in place to ensure we are safe."

Stepping back from me, Nickolai held out his hand, and the ice around my heart melted just a fraction thinking of all the effort he'd gone to just to put me at ease, knowing full well that I would be concerned about his welfare. Before I could chastise myself and make a less foolish decision, I reached out and took Nickolai's hand.

We walked into the theatre, bypassing Edison working at the popcorn stand. He ignored us, his eyes dismissing us immediately, and I was pleased by that, knowing Nickolai would feed that little nugget of information back to Jack and Atticus.

Nickolai walked us down to the very back of the cinema and held the door to the Imax open for me. I gave him a small smile and headed in, trying not to shiver as his hand found its way to my back again. Halting, I glanced around the theatre to try and pick a spot that would be the best place to sit, a place where I could see all the entrances and exits.

Nickolai gave me a knowing smile and inclined his head toward the back. In the very back row, two seats were surrounded by a vast array of food and drink. As we climbed the steps and got closer, I saw that Nickolai had gotten my favorite junk food, chips, and sugar jellies. He'd even managed to find a lemon-flavored drink I knew full well the company didn't make anymore.

I sank into one of the seats as Nickolai did the same. Reaching under his seat, he handed me a fleece blanket. I arched my brows at him, and he grinned.

"I know you like to watch movies with a blanket to be cozy."

I frowned even though I was cracking open inside. Nickolai had gone to so much effort, just for me. Breaking his heart would be harder than I thought.

I fluffed out the blanket and, big as it was, covered us both with it as Nickolai poured me a drink and set it down in the holder on the seat. Leaning back in the seat, I bounced it a little as I stared at the blank screen.

"I know you've got a new car and all that, but if you think I'm sitting here through *Fast 15* or whatever number they are on now, then you're mistaken, mister."

Nickolai chuckled, a sound that I felt in my bones as the lights dimmed and the movie began. What played wasn't what I'd expected at all—it wasn't even a movie that was supposed to be in theatres. This was a movie I adored secretly and had been searching for a copy of since it was removed from streaming TV a few years ago. I tilted my head to look at Nickolai, noticing the clench of his jaw as he waited for me to react.

He didn't have to take me to expensive dinners or lavish parties. Nickolai knew enough about me that he understood I wasn't the kind of girl who was impressed by money and expensive gifts. I was the kind of girl who liked comfy blankets as much as sharp blades; who thought an empty cinema playing one of my favorite Christmas movies was a perfect date; who felt receiving sweets and a drink that wasn't being made anymore was a luxurious gift. And ensuring the night went smoothly by surrounding us with the Royal Guard, proving they'd have my back, was a brilliant touch. If all went well, I might start to think that we could do this, Nickolai and me.

The hopeless romantic in me applauded his efforts, and I wanted to show my appreciation as much as the control freak in me would allow me to. Snuggling into the seat, I rested my head against Nickolai's shoulder and tried to relax as the tension slowly released from him.

As the Crown Prince of Aldovia returned to take his throne, as he fell in love with the reporter posing as a tutor, I made a mental note to not do as Amber did in the movie, allowing myself to fall for my own crown prince. While stuffing my face, eyes glued to the screen, I reached for popcorn at the same time as Nickolai. Our fingers brushed, and the air became increasingly warm, tension crackling as the movie played out.

Hugging my knees to my chest, tears pricked my eyes as Amber saved the day and Richard was crowned king. In my head, I pictured myself standing by as Nickolai was crowned and then walking away like Amber did. I wasn't sure our ending would be nearly as happy as *A Christmas Prince*.

The lights came on, and I tried to hide my face under the blanket so Nickolai couldn't see my obviously red eyes from trying not to cry.

"The warrior with a penchant for jumping out of windows is felled by a romantic movie. Every day I am surprised by you, Ryan Callan."

"Speak a word of this to anyone, and I will kill you, Romanov."

Nickolai laughed, and I lifted my head to look at him. When our eyes met, he stopped laughing and his eyes suddenly filled with hunger. Watching my lips, he leaned in slowly. He was a breath away from kissing me when he grinned, snagged my drink, and drained it, scowling at the sour taste.

"Now I know what to get you for Christmas: me."

"Nah, just give me a DVD of what just played and I'm all good. I mean, I don't think I could find a bow big enough for your ego."

"No need for a bow; I'll just show up naked."

"Yeah, cause your mom would *love* you walking around the compound in your birthday suit," I joked.

"It's not my mom I'm trying to get to fall in love with me."

My heart clenched so tight I thought it might burst. Shifting in my seat, I folded up the blanket I was totally taking home with me and got to my feet. "I mean, it's good you watched this, Nicky. It's nearly a biography of your life—even down to the slutty ex who moved on to another royal thinking it would make her a princess or queen or whatever. Kris isn't as bad as Simon was, but Nattie is def trying to get above her station like Sophia was."

"Where are you going?" Nickolai asked, his tone husky as I looked around.

"Well, when the movie is over, people tend to leave the cinema."

"Not when I've rented it out for another couple of hours. Sit down, Ryan. Now it's time to watch one of my favorite Christmas movies."

The lights went down again before I had a chance to argue, so I sat down and turned to the screen. As the opening credits started, I barked out a laugh. Nickolai peered over at me with a grin.

"*Die Hard* is not a Christmas movie, Nicky."

"It takes place at Christmas, so it's a Christmas movie."

"If you say so, Nicky. If you say so."

I sighed as I covered us with the blanket again and allowed Nickolai to slip his fingers into mine, watching in amusement as he mouthed the words to nearly the entire movie. Nickolai seemed so at ease, like when he was at St. Patricks, among the humans. Here he was, letting his own guard down, showing me that he trusted me enough to be himself.

And as happy as I was in this moment, I couldn't help but feel ashamed of just how much joy I was feeling, especially when I had a serial killer on my ass and a friend's death to avenge.

As if sensing the tension in me, Nickolai glanced over. "You okay?"

I didn't want to spoil this night for him. I'd give him this memory of us, free of taint and taken in the spirit in which it was meant.

"All good, Nicky. We're good."

When the movie was over and I had eaten my weight in sweets, I let Nickolai lead me from the theatre, taking my blanket with me. Far too soon, we were in the car and headed back to the compound, daylight on the horizon. I almost hated the fact that we were on our way back to reality.

When Nickolai parked the car in his spot, he killed the engine and sent a quick text, explaining that he was telling Jack we had made it back in one piece.

"Sometimes, I don't know if he's more concerned for your safety or mine." Nickolai said, his tone light as he slid the phone into his pocket.

"Out of the two of us, who is more likely to end up bloody?"

"Touché."

Before I could stop myself, I removed my seat belt and leaned over to press my lips to Nickolai's cheek. "Thank you for tonight. I had a really nice time."

"Ryan..."

I ducked out of the car and headed for the stairs as Nickolai called my name again and asked if he could walk me to my door.

Shaking my head, I held out my hand to stop him from stepping closer to me. "I don't think that's a good idea. If you walk me to my door, I'll ask you to stay. Then you and me could end up doing something we can't come back from. I'm... I'm not ready for that yet."

"*Yet*? So, you're telling me there's a chance?"

"I'm not making any promises, okay?"

I knew by the massive, smug grin on Nickolai's face that he was hearing what he wanted to hear. I supposed, after he'd gone to so much effort tonight, I'd let him grin smugly as I took the steps two at a time.

"But there's a chance, right?" Nickolai called after me.

I didn't turn or break my stride, but I did allow myself to smile because maybe there was a chance.

Chapter 13

"WHAT THE HELL IS WRONG WITH YOU?"

Lifting my gaze, I paused my bite of cereal as Edison plonked down at the table opposite me. I eyed him with suspicion as I chewed, waiting for him to continue. When he declined to elaborate despite a glare from me, I set my spoon down and leaned back in my chair.

I usually waited for the trainees to finish eating before venturing into the dining room for breakfast. Today I'd been first in the door, other trainees and Royal Guard members coming in shortly after I had poured myself a blood-infused coffee. Ignoring the stares, I tried to smile in greeting, but that seemed to just get me more suspicious looks.

"Again, what the hell is wrong with you?"

"Nothing's wrong with me, St. Clair, other than I want to punch you for asking me anything with that tone."

Edison flashed me a fangy grin. "Everyone is freaked out because you're smiling. It's unnerving. Like a killer who smiles before they go all stabby."

I rolled my eyes and growled, earning a bigger grin

from Edison.

"See, that's more like it."

Pushing my half-eaten bowl away, I leaned back in my chair. "What do you want, Edison?"

Dropping the grin, Edison leaned in and his face got serious. "I wanted to say sorry about what I said the other day. I was trying to be funny in front of Nickolai and my brother. I didn't mean to hurt your feelings."

"Because I don't have any, right?" I retorted with a tilt of my head.

"Damn it, Callan. You can be so intimidating, you know that?"

I shrugged, snagging my mug and taking a sip. When I stayed silent, Edison sighed and held up his hands.

"Listen, the guys want to know if you would train with them some day. Now that Nasir is gone, we want to make amends for being so blinded by him. I mean, we all tried to be the best, and we were so busy ignoring you that you snuck in and actually *are* the best."

Running my tongue over my teeth, I stared, considering his statement.

"Don't answer me now," he said quickly. "We all heard what you said on that roof, that you didn't trust us to have your back. That hit us hard in the nuts, Callan. We always thought you ignored us cause you knew you were better than us. Give us a chance to prove we can be trusted."

"Trying to make nice with me to curry favor with Nickolai or your brother won't work, you know."

Edison got to his feet and shook his head. "Our liege doesn't need to know we've had this conversation. This is one guard to another. Think it over, Callan. And stop smiling like a serial killer; you're turning everyone off their breakfasts."

I laughed as Edison walked away, which caused more vampires to glance in my direction with curious looks. I tipped an imaginary hat to them as Nickolai strode into the room, his eyes immediately clashing with mine. The entire room seemed to stop breathing, bowing and fisting their hands over their hearts as Nickolai strode over to me.

Ruffling my hair as he sat down beside me, his knee touching mine under the table, Nickolai reached over and snagged my coffee mug, taking a sip. I snarled, taking back my coffee as Nickolai nudged me with his shoulder.

"How are you this morning?"

"I'd be fine if it wasn't for everyone staring at me. Or for Edison apologizing and asking me not to smile because it unnerves people."

Nickolai let loose a burst of laughter and asked me how I was smiling. Embarrassed, I gritted my teeth and tried to smile, which made Nickolai laugh even more. Now, every single vampire was staring at us. I pushed back my chair so hard it scraped against the tiled floor, making to leave, but Nickolai rested a hand on my arm.

"Ryan, sit down, please. I'm not mocking you."

How did he know that's what it felt like? How did he know so much about me when I hardly knew myself?

I did as he asked, and a single glare from Nickolai had everyone averting their eyes.

"Edison said I was intimidating."

"He's right. You are."

I peered over at Nickolai. "Do I intimidate you?"

"What answer do you want that won't have you mad at me?" Nickolai teased, which meant I *did* intimate him.

Blowing out a breath, I frowned, picking up my spoon and playing with my food. We sat there in silence for a few minutes before Nickolai leaned in.

"I had a really nice time last night."

I swallowed hard. "Me too."

"After the introductions to the Americans later, you want to spar a little? Just you and me?"

I smiled.

Nickolai chuckled. "I thought that would make you smile."

Jack strolled into the room then and made a beeline for Nickolai. Standing, I gave Jack a hug and went to leave when Nickolai called out to me.

"I expect my guard beside me today when we meet our American cousins."

I inclined my head. "My liege."

Heading back to my room, I showered and changed into my guard uniform, smoothing the material. My fingers grazed the yellow stripe that said *Trainee.*" I pulled off the stripe and set it down on my dresser, allowing myself to enjoy the feeling of achievement as I looked at myself in the full-length mirror.

My hair was pulled back into a plated braid, the stray strands pinned off my face. Somehow, I felt older than my seventeen years. Then again, I'd never felt young, had I?

The phone in my room rang, and I stared at it, not knowing for a second what to do. This was a landline connected to the main compound switchboard. No one ever rang my extension. No one.

I walked over to the wall and picked up the receiver. "Hello?"

There was silence for a heartbeat, but I heard a sharp intake of breath and immediately knew who was at the other end of the phone.

"Hello, Max."

"Ah, my butterfly has not forgotten me."

"It's hard to forget a murdering psychopath who killed my friend."

Maxim chortled. "Would it upset you to know that pleases me?"

I bristled. "Your emotions are not my concern, Max. The only feeling I care about is the absolute sense of joyous contentment that your death will bring me. Now, I really must go, I have a prince waiting for me."

"Now, now, little butterfly. It's unladylike to try and make a man jealous. I may fly into a fit of rage and kill someone to prove my feelings to you."

I hesitated just for a second, then cursed myself silently for doing so. My hesitation revealed his words had gotten to me, and that gave Maxim the upper hand. "Fuck off, Maxim," I said through gritted teeth. "Unless you can face me like a man, don't pull dickish moves. Find your balls, and then come find me."

I slammed down the receiver and then ripped the phone from the wall, taking half the wall with it and leaving a gaping hole. Slipping my uniform belt around my waist, I ran my fingers over my sai and left my room behind.

I needed to tell Nickolai that someone had given Maxim my direct extension inside the compound, but I knew he was currently prepping to meet with the President of the Vampires of America. I couldn't disturb him just yet, so I went straight to his captain of the guard.

Yanking open Jack's bedroom door, I instantly wished I had knocked first. Jack and a half-naked Atticus were in a heated embrace, pulling apart suddenly when I came in, and I tried to look anywhere but at them.

"Oh, by Eve, my eyes!" I teased. "I am scarred for life."

"Then you should learn some manners and knock

145

before walking into someone's bedroom," Jack growled as Atticus slipped on his uniform.

Leaning against the wall, I groaned. "This is totally what it feels like when you walk in on your parents about to have sex, isn't it?"

Atticus laughed and Jack shook his head. "What has you storming into my room without so much as a warning, kiddo?"

"Maxim called me on the extension in my bedroom."

Jack's expression changed immediately, and he came over and rested his hands on my shoulders. "Are you okay?"

"I'm grand, Uncle Jack. I told him where to go. Well, I actually told him to go find his balls first and then come find me. And to fuck off."

While I expected to be chastised for baiting the rogue vampire, Jack patted my cheek and smiled. "That's our girl. Why come to me and not Nickolai?"

"Because we need the Americans to side with us, and Nickolai doesn't need to be distracted."

Atticus and Jack shared a look.

"What?" I said, iron in my tone.

"Nothing, kiddo, nothing at all. Let's go charm the Americans."

"If you're hoping for me to be charming, then Atticus needs to take off his shirt again."

I walked from the room to the sound of their laughter and quickly descended the stairs. The doors to the main ballroom were open, and I stepped inside, inhaling a calming breath as I made my way past the gathered vampires. I went to stand with the other guards, slowing so that Jack and Atticus fell into step with me.

My eyes wandered around the room. None of the royal family were here yet. The gathered members of the council stood in their family groupings, and I felt a pang in my chest as I envisioned my parents and I standing beside them.

And then I felt a hand on my shoulder and glanced up at Jack, the freckles on his face crinkling as he smiled. It was then I realized that I was standing exactly where I was supposed to be, where my parents would have been standing—with the Royal Guard.

I slipped in between Atticus and Edison, and the youngest of the St. Clair brothers leaned toward me.

"Did you know President Armstrong has a dome built around his own version of the White House so his vampires can walk around in the sun?"

"You're kidding me."

Edison shook his head. "Nope. Zayn sent Finn a picture of him standing in the midday sun. It's surreal."

"How the other half live, right?"

The doors to the room opened, and the murmur of voices died down as Queen Katerina walked in with a handsome, suit-clad vampire who smiled wider than anyone I'd ever seen before. Anatoly followed his wife, escorting a vampire so stunning she gave Grace Kelly a run for her money.

But before I was able to slip my mask into place, the monster in me growled and snarled as Nickolai led a younger version of her mother into the room by the arm. Her hair was a golden blonde, curled at the ends, a string of pearls adorning her neck. Her dress was a light shade of pink, and she walked in heels that made her almost as tall as Nickolai. Her lips were painted in a shiny pink gloss, and from the way Anatoly glanced back at his son, I knew this was the girl he wanted as Nickolai's queen.

My cheeks heated as Jack glanced back at me. His eyes begged me not to do anything that might strike a match and lead to an international incident. I swallowed my own feelings and kept my head up as Katerina began to walk down the line of the guard with the president.

Atticus and Jack, who already knew the president, greeted him formally and then informally as the president clapped both vampires on the back. The American's eyes wandered down the line as he and Katarina continued, eventually falling to mine.

The president beamed at me; his teeth intensely white. His blue eyes sparked with intelligence as he ran his eyes over me. A strong jawline with high cheekbones, the President of the Vampires of America looked charmingly radiant as he glanced from me to the queen.

"And who might we have here, Your Majesty?" the president drawled.

For a moment, Katerina looked unsure of how I'd react, so I inclined my head.

"Ryan Callan, Mr. President. It is a pleasure to meet you." I held out my hand, which the president took without a second thought. His handshake was firm, sure.

"Ah so this is the infamous Ryan Callan. Youngest guard in history. Second-ever female to hold a guard position. Killer of rogues, and rumored to be as deadly as she is beautiful. Tell me, Katerina," he said, turning to the queen, "what would it cost me to tear Miss Callan away to the other side of the world?"

"I do not sell my vampires, Mr. President, and Guard Callan's place in my court is not up for negotiation."

The president looked at me. "And what say you, darling? I think one of my sons would make you a fine husband."

I flashed my most intimidating smile. "What I might say would not be as polite as what my liege said. I am not known for my diplomacy, sir." I glanced around the president to where his two sons stood waiting, then returned my gaze back at the president. "I respectfully decline your offer, sir. Your sons don't look like my type. I'm not a fan of politicians."

The president boomed with laughter, and Katerina smiled softly at me as they continued down the line. Nickolai tried to catch my eye as he passed, but I ignored him. I knew this would happen, knew that, as every piece of the wall I'd erected around my heart was chipped away, I would end up hurt again.

Once the formalities were concluded, the court broke formation and began to mingle with the Americans. Kristoph was engaged in conversation with the youngest of the Armstrong brothers, and Farrah was smiling at the first daughter, who seemed to be looking at Farrah with surprising interest.

"My sister has no designs on your prince, Guard Callan. Though she does seem quite taken with the Nasir girl. Far nicer than her sullen brother, I might add."

I turned to find the oldest of the Armstrong brothers, his smile as charming as his father's as he extended his hand.

"Lucas Armstrong. Pleasure to meet you."

"Ryan." I shook his hand and noted Lucas's handshake was as firm and confident as his father's.

"I must admit to being rather insulted by your politician comment. I assure you, we would make quite the match. You are by far the most striking woman in this room."

Snorting, I patted Lucas on the arm. "Spoken like a true politician. Listen, Lucas, I'd say I'm flattered, but I'd be lying. I have enough on my plate with a psychotic stalker murdering human in an effort to woo me and a crown prince who thinks it's an inevitability that I will fall for him. Find someone who's a safer bet and might not get you killed. Nice to meet you, though."

Lucas's mouth hung open as I walked away, and Edison stepped into my path.

"Seriously, Callan... that was brutal but totally worth watching."

"St. Clair, you've been stuck to me like an octopus for days. Give a girl a minute, okay?"

Brushing past Edison, I walked smack into Nickolai, who reached out to steady me. I jerked away from his grasp and his gaze narrowed, realization dawning on him as he looked from me to the first daughter. Then he looked from me to Edison, and his smile dropped.

"Getting cozy with Edison?"

"By Eve, Nickolai. Can the possessiveness, will ya? I'm sick of male vampires...maybe I should be trying to woo the first daughter. First Maxim, then the president, then his son. Edison is following me like a bad smell, and now you—you, who flaunted that gorgeousness in front of me—now you accuse me of something with Edison. Gimme a goddamn break."

Nickolai's brow furrowed. "What happened with Maxim?"

I made to answer him when the queen and king, along with the president and first lady, came up to us. I bowed respectfully to Katerina and Anatoly, even as the king scowled at me. Nickolai placed a possessive hand on the nape of my neck, staking his claim in front of all around us, and I couldn't so much as move a muscle, only remain stoic and still as the president clapped Nickolai on the shoulder.

"No wonder the girl turned down my offer and my sons. I see a good match here. Be sure to invite us to the wedding, you hear?"

I felt the color drain from my face as Katerina laughed softly. "Come now, Winston, do not scare Ryan away with talk of weddings."

"She does quite like to run away," Anatoly muttered just loud enough for all to hear.

Katerina shot him a sharp look.

If the president thought much of his comment, he didn't say so. "I would quite like to see a display of fighting skills, Prince Nickolai," he said, changing the subject. "Our army is one of the finest-trained groups of soldiers in the world, but we have adapted to modern weapons. I would love to see how you fight here. It has been decades since I've witnessed a good old-fashioned swordfight."

"That should not be a problem," Nickolai replied, beckoning Jack forward. "I will have Jack arrange for the trainees to run some sparring matches."

"I'd quite like to see Guard Callan in action considering she is, after Jack and Atticus of course, your highest ranking soldier. It would be quite interesting to see her fight with such unique weapons."

Nickolai tensed at my side, but I wasn't sure why. "Happy to give you a display of what we bring to the table, sir," I said to the president. "In fact, my liege and I had planned to spar after this gathering. Our future king is not afraid to bleed for his vampires."

Looking up at Nickolai, I flashed him a grin. "What say you, Nicky? Fancy bleeding a little?"

Nickolai gaze was so intense, so full of pride and lust that I had to stop myself from taking a step back.

"Abso-fucking-lutely."

Chapter 14

I'D BARELY CHANGED OUT OF MY UNIFORM AND INTO A PAIR of leggings and a sports bra when a knock sounded on my door. Ignoring the insistent rap of knuckles, I slung my weapons belt over my shoulder as the irritating knocking came continuously now.

"By Eve," I swore as I marched across the room, slipping into my Chucks as I growled to the person wrecking my head behind the door. "I swear to Eve if you don't stop knocking, I'm going to—"

Halting my words as I swung open the door, my mouth formed an O as I came face to face with Anatoly, my king and liege.

"Please continue, Ryan. I would like to know what treasonous things you would inflict on me."

I bowed my head and fisted my hand over my heart. "Forgive me, my liege. I did not expect for it to be you knocking at my door."

"No need to be polite, Ryan. I simply came to give you a warning."

I lifted my gaze to Anatoly's, noting the bitterness and resentment in his eyes as his lips curved into a scowl.

I wondered what I could possibly have done to draw such a reaction from my king; he seemed angry at my very existence.

"And what may that warning be, my liege?"

Reaching out with a soft, uncalloused hand, Anatoly gripped my chin hard and jerked my gaze to the side as he leaned in.

"Do not embarrass my boy. You will swallow that pride you inherited from your mother and let him best you. You will not insult him or his rule in front of the Americans, or I will make sure your status in the Royal Guard does not last long. Perhaps I'll convince his mother it is time for our son to take a queen."

"If you think Nickolai would want to win in such a way, then I'm afraid you don't know your son very well, my liege."

Anatoly pressed his thumb into the curve of my jaw, and I wouldn't have been surprised if I was already bruised before I even began to spar. Every instinct in me yelled for me to fight back, to remove Anatoly's hands from me and make sure he never dared put a hand on me again.

"Father," a voice behind the king interjected, "Nico and the Americans are awaiting the star attraction. It would be a bad idea to damage the person who seems to have charmed the American president. Let Ryan be."

At the sound of Kristoph's words, Anatoly shoved my chin sideways and turned away. I smothered a growl as the king strode past his son and down the stars without another word. I closed my eyes to center myself, and when I opened my eyes again, Prince Kristoph smiled at me with warmth and affection... and a little remorse.

"I am sorry, Ryan. Are you hurt?"

"You have no need to apologize, Kris. Let's go before

the Americans get impatient."

I descended the stairs with Kristoph beside me, gingerly rubbing my chin as I lingered outside the training room for a few minutes. Kris stayed with me as I found my calm. Then, with a nod of my head and a smile, I flung open the doors and we entered a madhouse.

The entire training area was packed to the gills with vampires. The court families sat on benches all around the room. The queen and king had taken their places in highbacked chairs placed in the balcony above, the president and first lady on either side of the sovereigns. The president's children leaned over the balcony railing, and Lucas let loose a wolf whistle as I strode up to the mat.

Rolling my eyes, I walked toward where Jack stood talking to Nickolai and Atticus. Kristoph wished me good luck and then went to join his parents. Atticus read something in my expression and came over to me, tilting my head to the side to look at the bruise on my face.

Lifting a brow, I grinned at Atticus. "Leave it to me to get a bruise *before* I get hit, right?"

"What happened?" His tone was short, an order.

I stood on his foot hard and he yelped. "Not now. Later."

Nickolai made his way across the mat, grinning as he ran his eyes over me and handed Jack his sword. Then the smug bastard removed his shirt, revealing a stomach and chest tight with muscles. I believe you could call it an eight pack.

There was a chorus of whistles as Nickolai bowed and grinned good-naturedly at the catcalls. I rolled my eyes as Jack handed him back his sword and Nickolai came to face me. His eyes went almost instantly to the bruise on my face but, with a quick shake of my head, Nickolai went back to putting on a show.

Circling me like a predator, Nickolai's gaze never once left mine. "First blood?" he asked.

I snorted. "I won't even break a sweat before I bleed you. One minute and it's over."

"And I remember that you don't like one-minute men."

I laughed loudly, very unladylike, as I followed Nickolai's footsteps. "You may be pretty and all, but trying to distract me with all your abs won't work."

"You think I'm pretty?" Nickolai jested, batting his eyelashes as a titter of laughter rippled through the audience.

Shrugging my shoulders, I slipped my weapons belt off my shoulder, took my sai in my hands, and tossed the belt off to the side. "You can be pretty if you want, Nicky. Whatever gets you through the day. I guess you're Adam Rickitt kinda pretty."

I let the sound of Nickolai's husky laughter wash over me as I kicked off my Chucks. When Nickolai turned to give instructions to Jack, I blocked out everything else and, knowing that Nickolai was within kicking distance, I coiled my leg back and ever so lightly kicked the back of his knee.

His knee instantly buckled, and he turned to me with a growl, his eyes darkening.

"Never turn your back on your enemy, Nicky."

Nickolai smirked and spun his sword toward me, a whistle of sound in the air. I let the blade come close, almost felt the kiss of it, and then I leaned back and let the sword sail over my midriff.

Snapping back into an upright position, I pushed my sai up, slipping them together as Nickolai brought his sword down. The sound of clashing metal rang in my ears as the muscles in my arms burned from holding back Nickolai's sheer strength. He kept on pressing downward, so I slid one of my sai free and slashed across his arm.

The scent of copper hit my nostrils and I growled, flashing my fangs as Nickolai relented and took a step away from me. Glancing down at the slight nick on his arm, his cerulean eyes blazed as his gaze snapped back to mine.

With a sly smile, I tried to look all innocent. "I did tell you you'd bleed first."

"Keep on smiling like the cat who got the cream. It makes me want to kiss you so badly."

He spoke so loudly that there was no doubt every single vampire in the room heard him. I blushed a furious shade of red, my face heating as I snarled and stalked forward.

Nickolai tossed his sword at Jack, who caught it with ease, and I halted my advancement.

"Grab a weapon, Nicky," I said loudly. "I'm not going to have my win spoiled by a whiney prince saying I beat and unarmed vampire."

"I plan on having a weapon real soon, darling."

Nickolai made to grab for me and I ducked, using the momentum to get behind him and kick him square in the ass. As Nickolai stumbled forward, I snuck a glance at the balcony. The fury written across Anatoly's face as the American president chuckled, gave me pause for thought.

I knew Nickolai. I *knew* him. He wouldn't want me to go easy on him, would he?

My steps faltered as I sensed the prince approaching, and even though I could have easily sidestepped him or blocked his advancement, I let Nickolai hit me with his shoulder and I went down to the mat with a thump that rattled my bones.

I rolled to the side as Nickolai made to come down hard with his foot, stumbling to my feet as clumsily as I could so I could pretend not to see the small dagger in Nickolai's hand. He sliced out with the small blade, and I hissed as the sharp end dragged across the skin on my stomach, the scent of my blood now mixing with Nickolai's.

Not once, not once in our entire lives, had Nickolai managed to cut me. He blinked in surprise, his eyes on the very spot where he'd pierced my skin.

I was breathing hard as Nickolai glared at the wound and snarled at me. "Why the hell are you holding back?"

I couldn't stop my gaze from darting to Anatoly's, and Nickolai's own eyes followed mine. Immediately, Nickolai formed a *T* with his hands and dragged me off to the side.

"What happened? Why did you hold back? What did my father say... or do?"

I lifted my gaze. "I was very strongly advised against embarrassing you."

"So, you'll embarrass yourself? Ryan, the Americans cannot stop talking about you. They want to see *you* fight, not me. They are not interested in what us males can do. They want to see the fierce warrior-woman who clawed her way to the top; the rogue reaper who almost killed Maxim singlehandedly and killed a dozen rogues all by herself. Do not let any petty words my father spoke take this away from you."

Nickolai beckoned Atticus over and pointed to my sai. "Give those to Atticus. Everyone knows you can fight with those. Let's show them what else you can do."

Jack came forward and handed me a sword—Katerina's sword, the one she'd had made after I'd advised her that her old one was too heavy. It was a gorgeous piece of steel. The blade itself was inscribed in Russian, and the hilt was free of gems, leaving a simple grip that fit my hands perfectly.

I shook my head as Nickolai took his own sword back. "I can't take this, Nickolai. It's a sword fit for a queen."

"I know."

And then the crown prince strode away, leaving me standing with an open mouth, about to curse him for telling the world our business. He walked to the middle of the mat, then turned and used one of my own moves, *Matrix*-beckoning me with the curl of his fingers. The entire training room was quiet as I re-joined him on the mat.

With one hand behind my back, I pointed my sword at Nickolai. He crossed the tip of his blade against mine and mimicked my stance. Slowly, we circled one another. And then we moved.

Our swords clashed in a din of metal, and I gave myself to the process, losing myself in the movement so thoroughly I didn't know where I began and the sword ended. I cut Nickolai; he managed a slash to my upper arm. We kept on going until we were both breathless and panting.

I realized dawn would approach soon and knew we needed a big finish pronto. As I felt the blazing heat of Anatoly's gaze on me, I sacrificed my leggings (and a bit of flesh) to kick Nickolai in the chest with both feet. When he charged at me, I dropped into a crouch and sliced out with my leg, catching Nickolai at the ankle. He hit the ground just as I rebounded, and I was on top of him in a flash.

With one foot on his wrist, I pointed the tip of my

158

blade to his throat, ignoring the grin on his face. "I win," I said, breathing heavily.

The Americans were on their feet clapping in an instant; the queen smiled softly as she stood and did the same. The entire room followed suit as I removed my foot from Nickolai's wrist and extended my hand to help him up.

His hand was warm in my grasp as Nickolai got to his feet still wearing that grin, and, as the Americans came onto the mat and offered their congratulations, I was engulfed in a wave of questions and queries. I tried to smile and be gracious, but soon enough, I felt a wave of unease settle over me.

Through the crowd, a hand fell on my arm, and I turned to see Katerina smiling at me. Instantly, I held her sword out to her with both hands and bowed my head. "Your sword, my liege. It was an honor to wield it."

"It was a pleasure to see her used properly for once," Katerina said with a softness in her tone that pulled at my heart.

I tried to hand it back to the queen, but Katerina shook her head.

"She deserves to be wielded by more capable hands. It is a gift to you."

I made to speak, ready to argue, but the queen was called away and I was left standing there, holding the sword out to no one. My ears rang and I felt like I couldn't breathe. Blade still in hand, I slipped through the crowds of people as I heard Katerina announce that late refreshments were being served in the ballroom.

I kept my head down, shoving my feet into my Chucks and snatching up my gear, then walking to Atticus and all but grabbing my sai off him. When he tried to question me, I shook my head, quickly sliding through the throng of people leaving the gym and ducking into the storage room that led up to the roof.

Pushing open the door, I gulped in air as I sank to the ground and gazed out into the night. Hugging my knees to my chest, I let out a harsh bark of laughter as a trickle of rain splashed on my skin. I wasn't sure why I was feeling so lost, but I knew that's how I felt.

The night sky twinkled with a dusting of stars that flickered and danced in the moonlight, eerily beautiful yet devastatingly lonely as well. I found a strange comfort in it. But I guessed it made sense that those who walked in darkness were always most comfortable in darkness. I was still sitting there as the rain began to fall in earnest, chilling my skin, and I prayed with all my might to Eve that it would wash away some of what was wrong with me.

I should've been happy. I should've been basking in glory and reveling in the fact that I, Ryan Callan, was sought after and admired by our American cousins. I should've been overjoyed to have such an amazing gift bestowed upon me by the queen. I should've been thrilled that a very-determined prince was vying for my hand. But I wasn't. I felt empty.

Because everything you love or that brings you joy is always taken from you. You are frightened to feel happiness for fear it will destroy you to lose it. You are utterly terrified of letting go of the walls you have built because you may not be able to erect them again should you lose those you let in.

Dragged from my thoughts as a coat was draped over my shoulders, I glanced up to see Atticus about to take a seat next to me. I tried to hide the disappointment it wasn't Nickolai who'd come to find me, giving Atticus a small curve of my lips.

"No need to hide your emotions from me, Ryan. I

160

might not be an Adam Rickitt pretty boy, but Pretty Boy sent me to check on you—make sure you can breathe again."

I snorted a laugh and shook my head, then pulled my weapons under the coat so they wouldn't get too wet, which had Atticus shaking his head. We sat in silence until I could stand it no more.

"What if I'm too broken?" I blurted suddenly. "What if I can't fit in like they all want me to?"

"Ryan." My name was nothing more than a breath as Atticus nudged me with his knee. "You are too stubborn to let anyone break you. You fight against everything, so fight against this. And who wants to fit in? Why do you care what they want you to do? By Eve, Ryan, our very species could be wiped out in a matter of years. Why waste the time we have worrying about what others think?"

There was anger in his tone, and it was my turn to nudge his knee. "What happened?"

Atticus dropped his face to his knees. "I tried to be brave like Farrah," he mumbled. "I told my family about me and Jack."

"Who do I need to stab? If they hurt you..."

My voice trailed off as Atticus peered over at me. "You would, wouldn't you," he said in surprise. "You would march down there and—in front of everyone— you'd rip my parents a new one for accusing Jack of leading me astray. For accusing him of making me... of my being gay as a fad. You know, my mother cried. My father... He left the room after yelling that I was a disappointment and had shamed the family."

I was livid for Atticus. I wanted to do exactly what he thought I would, although in the mood I was in, there'd be a lot more bloodshed than yelling.

"And what did Edison say?"

Atticus shook his head. "He shouted at my parents. Scolded them for being so backward. Told them to either accept me and Jack or lose both sons. He's currently moving into the spare room next to Jack's quarters."

Edison's reaction both surprised and delighted me. Knowing that he'd backed his brother made me more inclined to like him... but not much.

"Then screw your parents, Atticus. Who cares what they think? You love Jack, and he loves you. What else bloody matters?"

Atticus reached up and tugged on my braid. "Maybe you should take your own advice, Ryan. Maybe you should listen to yourself."

And I really wished I could... by Eve did I wish I could.

Chapter 15

EARLY THE NEXT EVENING, I WAS SUMMONED TO AN AUDI-
ence with Winston Armstrong in the Gallery of the Fall-
en. I hadn't stepped foot in that room since the Queen
had ordered me there to attend a meeting that altered
the course of my life forever.

Anxiety and trepidation rested uneasily in my stomach as I opened the door and stepped inside. To my surprise, it was not the president who waited for me, but his
son, Lucas.

His back was to me, his hands clasped behind his
back. As he turned his head to examine a portrait, the
strong jawline of his profile marked him as handsome
even without full view of his features. Dressed in jeans
and a buttoned shirt, he could've passed for any gorgeous college kid. But that was the problem with vampires; they were all handsome in their own way. Some
just didn't have the personality to back it up.

"I thought it best," Lucas said, "for you to think my
father wanted a chance to speak with you for fear you
would refuse to meet with me."

Peering over his shoulder at me, I noted the coy

smile on his lips. It looked out of place; I could tell this boy had never been coy in his life.

I cocked my head, narrowing my gaze at him. "I'm more likely to turn and haul ass out of here now that I know you've lied to me. I can't stand liars."

My tone was harsh, but it needed to be. While I was all for trying to make an alliance with the biggest clan of vampires in the world, I wasn't about to walk into an alliance built on a bed of lies.

Lucas pivoted fully to face me. "Then I will try to be more honest from now on," he said, a now-genuine smile curving his lips. "You are not what I expected, Ryan."

Shrugging my shoulders, I replied, "I never am."

Lucas chuckled at that, then motioned for me to come stand beside him. I did as he asked and waited as he continued to run his eyes over the portraits on the wall. I managed to advert my gaze for all of five minutes before I could not stop myself from looking at the image of my parents.

Lucas's gaze followed mine, and he sighed. "Your parents?"

"Yes, they died when I was seven. They were murdered."

"Seven? I had heard of such losses, but hearing it from your lips somehow makes it more than just a story. I am sorry for your loss."

"Thanks."

Unable to look at the picture anymore, I strode away to perch on the ledge of the bay window as Lucas continued to study my parents' portrait. Finally, he joined me where I sat.

"Why did you ask to meet me, Lucas?" I asked, cutting straight to the point as I folded my arms across my chest.

"My father is considering Queen Katerina's request for soldiers. He wanted to find out why he should say yes from the only person who, he claimed, was honest in this court."

I didn't react to the barbed comment; after all, Lucas and his father were not entirely wrong. There were liars in our court, Maxim had told me so—and even if he was a psychotic SOB, I found myself believing him.

Lucas picked at imaginary fluff on the sleeve of his shirt. "Tell me why we should help you, Ryan. Be honest and up-front, and I will relay to my father what you think we should do."

The fate of the vampire race was not something that should depend on my answer. It was Nickolai who could answer this with poise and grace and not make a complete mess of things. But Lucas was here asking me for my opinion, and I feared that, should I not give it, the Americans would leave us to wage this war alone.

"You guys don't *need* to help us. You can go back to your city under a dome and forget we ever sought your assistance," I began as I tilted my head to look at Lucas. "But what's to stop the rogues from getting bored once they kill us all and head on over to the good ol' U S of A and shatter that dome you live under? What's to stop the rogues in America from gathering up a force and rebelling against you?"

Lucas frowned at my questions, his brows furrowing and his lips forming a scowl.

"If we survive this," I continued, "if we manage to kill Maxim and avert the crisis with the rogues and then we die of starvation, how long before your country, who has a larger ensemble of vampires, is in the same situation? A win for us is a win for all vampires, is it not?"

Lucas was wistful for a moment and then stood.

"Our legion of Children of Eve is four times as large as yours. We will prevail."

"But at what cost? Does America want to be the only country with vampires in it?" I asked. "Would you let us all die because you know that you won't? That's not the brave or strong country I've read about. If you leave us to fight the impending war by ourselves, you'll be returning to your country as cowards, not as 'America the brave.'"

Lucas barked out a laugh, slapping his thigh with his hand. "Damn woman, you don't mince words, do you?"

"I didn't lie when I told your father I wasn't known for being diplomatic."

The door to the gallery opened, and Nickolai strode in, his gaze landing on Lucas sitting too close to me, and a snarl twitched his lips. Lucas smirked, got to his feet, and then grabbed my hand and lifted it to his lips.

"You were not kidding when you said your love life was complicated."

Snatching back my hand, I rolled my eyes. "My life in general is complicated, Lucas. *I'm* bloody complicated."

Lucas laughed, the sound irritating Nickolai even more as he took a step in our direction. The president's son bowed at the waist, and when he lifted his eyes, he said, "You will make a great queen, Ryan Callan. I look forward to that day."

"I don't want to be queen, Lucas. I'm not meant to be that."

"The ones who make the greatest leaders never *want* to be leaders; they just are. It is as Eve designed it to be." Lucas winked as he smiled, stepping away, and then he acknowledged Nickolai with the bow of his head.

When Lucas left us alone in the gallery, Nickolai took the spot he vacated, his shoulder brushing mine.

"What did Armstrong want?"

Batting my eyes, I fanned myself with my hand. "Oh, he professed his undying love for me and asked me to go back to America and live in his dome city with him. He offered me a General's post in the Army and promised to stay home and look after the vampire babies we would have. I mean, I'm seriously considering it."

Nickolai growled, and I could feel the aggression rolling off him in waves, causing me to sigh as I got to my feet. When I stood, I saw Nickolai's fingers twitching as if he wanted to reach for me.

"Lucas wanted me to convince him why they should help us. He wanted me to be honest, so I was. I told them refusing to help would label them as cowards."

Nickolai snorted but didn't rebuke my accusation. Lifting his gaze, I noticed how tired his eyes were, the normal shimmer in his cerulean eyes now somewhat diminished. He seemed exhausted, and I wanted to ease his weariness somehow.

Swallowing hard, I stood in front of him and, even as his body tensed, I wrapped my arms around him, leaning my ear against his chest. Part of me delighted in the sudden quickness of his heartbeat. His arms engulfed me as if he were afraid that I'd bolt at the closeness, and I wasn't ashamed to admit that part of me was considering it.

"What's this for?" he asked softly, as if speaking the words might break the spell between us.

"I just thought you looked like you needed a hug. I read somewhere in the Royal Guard handbook that if my liege needs a hug, I must provide it."

Nickolai chuckled and pulled me closer, and for a blissful few minutes, we remained in each other's arms in silence. Then Nickolai's knuckles ran along my cheek, and I looked up, my teeth biting into my lower lip.

Nickolai licked his lips, and then he lowered his head toward mine. My heart pounded in my ears, and I couldn't even breathe. I was caught between wanting him to kiss me, to feel the press of his lips against mine, and wanting to run far, far away from the implications that kiss could mean.

Lips a bare whisper away from mine, I was utterly petrified and exhilarated at the same time.

"Nickolai!"

I jumped at the sound of Anatoly's voice, a furious blush reddening my cheeks as I wriggled out of Nickolai's embrace and turned away from them both to hide my embarrassment.

"What is it?" Nickolai snapped, anger a red-hot brand in his tone.

"Don't speak to me like that, boy. You are not king yet."

"And don't you dare speak to me as such. I am not a child anymore, Father. I am soon to be king, and you need to get used to that. Now, what do you want?"

Anatoly snarled, and I turned to see Jack reach for his weapon. I shook my head as Anatoly glared at his son. "The Americans have called a meeting. They have things they wish to discuss. Bring the bitch; they requested she be there."

Turning on his heels as Nickolai started forward, I grabbed Nickolai's arm as the king disappeared from view, and Jack closed the door behind him as he left us to deal with Nickolai's anger toward his father.

Without thinking, I pressed my fingers to the faded bruise on my chin, a feeding from a Child of Eve having allowed me to heal the worst of the day's injuries. Nickolai's eyes followed my fingers, his knuckles grazing the skin as I shivered.

"I'm sorry for whatever happened with my father."

I wasn't fool enough to try and lie since Atticus could've told Nickolai or Jack more about my encounter with Anatoly. Or maybe Kris had told his big brother exactly what had happened.

Clearing my throat, I said, "Your father thought it best to warn me to not embarrass you when we sparred. He promised to make things hard for you if I did, and then punctuated the point on my face."

Nickolai growled. "That's why you went easy on me?"

"That's why I went easy on you."

Nickolai was quiet for a few minutes, rage in his scent. I ran my hands up and down his arms, trying to calm him down. After a tense five minutes, he stopped clenching his fists.

"I don't know what his problem is, but I'm done. I'm so fucking done."

"Nickolai, he is still your father."

"I cannot respect any man who can lay his hands on a woman to intimidate them. He's been bitter since I was a boy; he may as well be dead to me."

My blood ran cold, and if Nickolai noticed, he gave no inclination of it. I stepped away from him, wrapping my hands around my waist. "Speaking as someone whose parents are *actually* dead to me, don't wish that upon yourself. You only get one set of parents, Nickolai. Even if your dad is an asshat, he's still your dad."

I strode past him, even as he breathed my name, and was out the door before he could catch me. Jack was standing sentry outside the door, and he pointed to the meeting room without uttering a word. Quickening my pace, I was inside and taking stock before Nickolai came in and took a seat beside his mother.

Thankfully, Anatoly was not present. However, I was surprised to see Kristoph lounging in his father's seat, and he winked at me when I caught his eye. Standing to the right of Nickolai's seat, my arms behind my back in the at-ease stance, I take a moment to look around and see who else is at this shindig.

The president reclined in his chair at the foot of the table, opposite Katerina. Next to him, Lucas had a more rigid posture, and I was beginning to wonder if Winston Armstrong was truly leading his vampires, or if it was his son.

The first daughter sat beside her father, a sulky expression on her face. The first lady was nowhere to be seen, and neither was the youngest son. Jack and Atticus stood behind our queen, and we all waited for someone to speak. I was not entirely surprised that it was Lucas who spoke first.

"I believe we can help each other, Your Majesty."

Katerina smiled her sweetest smile. "I am delighted to hear that, Lucas. Would it not be best to discuss terms and see if both sides are amendable before any decisions are made?"

Lucas leaned forward, resting his chin in his clasped hands. "We have no terms, truly. I was advised earlier today that, should we decline to offer our help, we would be considered cowards, and that is not how we want to be remembered."

Eyes lifting to meet mine in amusement, Lucas dropped his gaze back to the queen. "We will send one thousand soldiers to help rid you of the rogue infestation. We will send two hundred Children of Eve to nourish you while you fight this battle. I will stay behind and command our army with Crown Prince Nickolai."

"Surely you must want *something*," Nickolai said.

"Why offer so much and get nothing in return?"

I was wondering the same myself.

President Armstrong leaned in and whispered into his son's ear, then went back to lounging in his chair. Lucas gave us all a dazzling smile, and I wondered how I could have missed the calculation in his eyes before.

"My father wishes our alliance to bear fruit. He requests a sign of good faith that, once the war is over, our continued relationship will blossom. We think a marriage of our two countries needs something symbolic that unites both our countries and our families."

My breath is stolen from me; the sullen look on the first daughter's face is suddenly understandable; and Katerina sucked in a breath. I saw Nickolai's spine tense as Lucas grinned. I felt like I was underwater—I was certain my worst fears were about to be ripped from my mind and splayed out in front of me.

Nickolai would be asked to marry the president's daughter, and he'd agree to it for the good of his people. And I would be forced to bear witness to it all as my heart shattered into a zillion pieces.

"My son has earned the right to choose his own bride. I will not force this on him."

Katerina didn't need to force it; Nickolai would simply do it because it was his duty.

"Nickolai is free to choose whomever he wants for his queen," Lucas said smoothly. "I feel the crown prince and I are of the same mind as to who would make a worthy successor to you, Queen Katerina. We would like to offer my sister's hand to your youngest son. We feel their marriage will solidify the bond between our two families."

There was a hushed silence in the room. Whatever any of us had expected to fall from Lucas's lips, it wasn't that.

Kristoph blinked, but that was the only outward sign of emotion that betrayed the coolness of the youngest prince.

Oh, by Eve, what the hell would Natalya do now that she was out of princes?

I let loose a snort, and amused eyes turned to me as I struggled to keep my composure.

Katerina ignored my lapse in professionalism and glanced at her son with a sad smile. It was clear she wanted Kris to do this, and Kris slumped his shoulders as if he were already resigned to his fate.

"We will discuss the matter privately and let you know our thoughts," the queen replied. "Both of my sons have free will to choose. I will not force the matter." Rising, Katerina made to leave.

Lucas stood when she did but did not otherwise move. "We have a few more things we would like to say," he announced.

Katerina hesitated for a moment, then lowered herself back into her seat. Lucas followed suit, smiling as he reclaimed our attention.

"It will take six months for us to recall those numbers back to DC and then bring them to Ireland. In those six months, we want all members of the Royal Guard to be trained in firearms as the majority of our soldiers are skilled with guns rather than swordplay. I would bet any vampire here that Guard Callan would be terrifying with a gun in her hand."

"Guard Callan doesn't need a gun to be terrifying; she's terrifying just as she is," I retorted. No one chastised me for speaking out of turn, simply laughed along with my snark.

"Indeed," Lucas said with a smirk. "However, would

172

it not take your enemy by surprise, shooting them point-blank between the eyes?"

"Indeed," Nickolai replied coolly through gritted teeth.

I had the feeling Lucas was building to something bigger than an arranged marriage and asking us to start wielding guns. There was something else brewing that was going to sucker-punch us right in the nuts.

"We will send our Children of Eve over in the new year. That should help you exponentially. We must be forthcoming, though, and admit that we've been contacted by your foe. He has offered us the crown. He's offered to hand over Europe to us so we can join all our nations together."

Maxim. Bloody Maxim...

"Maxim doesn't do anything without getting something for himself," I said. "He will offer you the moon and the stars as he stabs you in the back. He would never be satisfied to simply hand you the crown."

"He would if we handed *you* to him," Lucas replied calmly. "He would if we gave you to him along with the head of his rival. He was quite clear that he did not wish to rule; he simply wants what is his."

"How did he contact you? Do you know where he is?" I asked, a growl escaping my chest. "I swear by Eve, Lucas, if you know where Maxim is and do not tell me, I'm gonna make you bloody, alliance be damned."

Chapter 16

"Veiled threats will not get you anywhere, Ryan."

Lucas's tone irked my already-frayed temper. With a snarl I started forward, a hand on my arm stopping me from advancing. Instead, I bared my teeth at him. "If you align yourself with that monster, then you are no better than he is. He killed an innocent young woman because I was her friend. He carved her up and let his vampires mutilate her body just to prove a point to me."

I let my eyes shift to the first daughter, and I gave her my most primitive smile. "There were so many different fang marks on her body it was hard to count how many vampires had taken a bite. I'm sure there are a few rogues who wouldn't mind the taste of American vampire. I wonder how many bites it would take before you screamed."

"Lucas!"

The little girl whined, and I couldn't bite back the smirk on my face at just how easy it was to frighten her. She'd never survive in our court.

"Stand down, Ryan," Lucas ordered.

I moved not an inch.

"Stand down, Ryan," Nickolai said softly, though his tone held a hint of authority.

"Yes, my liege." I strode back to where I had been before, letting the ice-queen façade slip into place.

Lucas watched me with careful eyes before turning back to Nickolai. "I have no desire to align myself with the rogue or give him his homeland in order to gain a seat of power on this side of the pond. Like my human brethren, we do not negotiate with terrorists."

"And we do not suffer fools who think the best way to garner trust is to flaunt the enemy in our faces. If you know where Maxim is hiding, tell us," Nickolai replied coolly.

Lucas shifted in his seat. "Last we knew, he was working out of a back room in his gentleman's club."

I snorted. "Your info is outdated, Lucas. Been there, killed some rogues, suffered the wounds from jumping out the window to save my ass. Maxim isn't stupid enough to keep using the place as his base of operations."

"Then tell me all about Maxim Smyrnoi, Ryan."

Tilting my head to the side, I narrowed my gaze at him. "Maxim is smart, deadly, calculating, and determined. He wears his grievances against his former court like armour. He is handsome and charming and uses that to influence his followers. Much like a cult leader, once he's ensnared someone to his cause, they will follow him even into death. His one downfall is that his anger at our court is easily triggered, and he feels like the universes owes him."

"You think he is handsome and charming?" Lucas asked me with amusement.

"I also think tigers are handsome and charming," I replied. "Doesn't mean I'm about to go pet one."

This caused Jack and Atticus to laugh, even managed to drag a smile from Katerina. Nickolai, however, remained still in his chair. The tension in the air intensified, and Lucas snarled in response as aggression suffocated the air. Nickolai was reacting to my assessment of Maxim, a vampire who Nickolai felt was a rival for my affections. He wasn't; he never would be.

Stepping forward as Nickolai gripped the arms of his chair so tightly the wood splintered, I crouched down so my lips were almost at his ear. "You need to calm down. I'm not interested in Maxim like that. Killing my friends doesn't make me want to be with someone. Maybe I'm crazy, but I'm more interested in the vampire who rented out an entire cinema for me to watch Christmas movies in November. But the possessive idiot routine doesn't do much for me, so every point you scored is quickly disappearing."

Straightening, I returned to my spot, and the tension slowly ebbed until it was gone. The American delegation eyed us with suspicion, but Lucas grinned at Nickolai.

"Did you really rent out a cinema for her?"

"Absolutely."

"And they say romance is dead."

"Puh-lease," I scoffed. "He made me watch *Die Hard*." The smile my comment earned from Nickolai made my knees weak.

"I think now would be an appropriate time to adjourn while we ponder your terms," Katerina said as she rose and motioned with her hand for the Americans to leave. The president rose and escorted his daughter out. Lucas smoothed his shirt and grinned as he made to leave.

"Lucas?" I called, waiting until he turned to look at me. "How long have you been leading the American vampires instead of your father?"

Lucas gave me his politician smile. "Brains and

beauty," he said silkily, "along with epic fighting skills. As I said, Ryan, it's always the ones who don't wish to lead who eventually make the best leaders."

Offering his hand to Nickolai, Lucas shook it firmly. "That girl is a keeper," he said.

"I know."

Rolling my eyes at the smugness in Nickolai's tone, I blew out a breath and went to pour myself a glass of water. I drained it as the door closed behind Lucas, and Nickolai waited a heartbeat as the sound of Lucas's footsteps disappeared.

"The Americans are to tour the city tonight. I want them surveyed in case they come into contact with Maxim. I fear the president's rule is ripe for a coup, and we do not want to be embroiled in that. Atticus, take the Royal Guard and the trainees, follow their every move. No doubt they are watching ours."

Atticus bowed and left. When I made to follow him, Nickolai held my elbow.

"Where are you going?"

"Well duh, I'm going with Atticus. If the Americans *do* run into Maxim, then I want to make sure Maxim runs into my sai."

"I need you here."

"Bullshit."

"I'm sorry?"

"Bull-shit... Do you need me to spell it for you?" I snarl.

Jack dragged me away from Nickolai. "By Eve, Ryan. Can you not hold your tongue for a minute? Let Nickolai speak."

It took a lot for Jack to be furious at me, so I pinched the bridge of my nose and turned back to Nickolai. Katerina was standing nearby but staring at her youngest son, as if she hadn't noticed the interaction between me and Nickolai. Kristoph hadn't moved from his seat; his head was down, and his hands were clenched on the table.

"Hey, Kris, you okay?"

"I thought I was safe."

"Safe?" I asked, my heart breaking at the sadness in his voice.

"Being the second son has always granted me some liberties. Unless Nico dies, I am nearly irrelevant. I chose not to learn to wield a sword. I chose to dabble in the financial side of the court. I thought I would avoid having a marriage forced on me, yet here I am, readying myself to say yes for the good of the species. By Eve, was this always to be my fate?"

Katerina walked gracefully over to her son and placed a hand on his shoulder. I glanced at Nickolai as if begging him to say something to help his brother even as Katerina squeezed Kris's shoulder.

"I would never have agreed to let you marry Natalya, Kristoph. If you were waiting for Nico to take the throne and grant you this, he agrees that you are not a right match."

"I love her, Mother."

This conversation was delving into areas I did not want to be privy to. I snuck a peek at Jack, and he looked as uncomfortable as I did. Backing away slowly, I tried to remain silent as Kris lifted his gaze to Nickolai's.

"Would you deny me this also, Brother?"

"I agree with Mother. Natalya is not meant to stand at your side. You are sixteen years old. Even if you do not marry the American—which I am also against, by the way—you have plenty of time to find love with someone who loves you and not your crown."

Kristoph jerked out of his mother's touch and his chair scraped backward as he stood up. "Don't patronize me, Nico. You of all people should understand about having the right to choose. You've followed Ryan around like a dog on a leash your whole life, and you claim I cannot know myself at sixteen? I won't marry the girl. I won't marry anyone. But I will remember what transpired today."

Kristoph stormed from the room, and Nickolai began to go after him until Katerina called his name, asking her eldest son to leave Kristoph be. Katerina swayed on her feet, and I was the first to move, catching the queen by her waist before she collapsed. Jack helped me ease her into one of the chairs.

Nickolai crouched in front of his mother, taking the glass of water I handed him and lifting it to Katerina's lips until she drank. Her brow glistened with sweat as she glanced up at Nickolai with a small smile.

"I find that I am tired of being queen. I don't suppose you want to become king sooner rather than later?"

There was a teasing tone to her voice, yet Nickolai flinched.

She patted his cheek, lifting her gaze to mine. "You must think I am a terrible mother."

"Until I am a mother, I cast no aspersions on how you raise your children, my liege."

Katerina glanced from me to Nickolai as she smiled. "I would very much like to be a grandmother one day."

The color drained from my face as Jack chuckled.

"My liege, just as you advised the president not to speak of weddings for fear of scaring Ryan, I'd advise against speaking of babies for fear she might bolt."

Katerina laughed tenderly. "Imogen was the same when we were girls. When I dreamed of my wedding and having children, Imogen scoffed at the thoughts. Until she met Tristan, that is."

Before I could stop myself, I was out of the room and ignoring the sound of my name as I bolted up the stairs and crashed straight into Edison. I shoved him aside with a growl, and he hit hard against the railing.

"Hey, Callan, what gives?"

Ignoring him, I took the stairs two at a time until I was safely in the comfort of my room. I sucked in a breath, not realizing just how much panic I felt in my chest as I bent over and fixed my eyes firmly to the floor.

"Would it be so bad? To consider a future like that with Nickolai?"

A pair of shoes stood ever so close to mine, and I wondered if I reached out and touched them, would it bring my friend back to me? I wanted so much for her to be alive and listening to me as I explained all my fears to her. But Krista was dead, and insanity could be passed on to your kids.

"I'd be a terrible mother."

"I bet every person thinks that. I wanted to be a mom. I wanted a dozen mini me's or mini Conrad's running around the place. I wanted a picket fence and a dog and a soccer-mom car."

"I'm sorry, Krista. I took that away from you."

As I straightened and leaned my head against the door, Krista smiled. "So, you've moved on from blaming Nickolai to blaming yourself. It's progress I guess, just not the kind of progress I wanted."

"I've always blamed myself. It was just easier to be angry at Nickolai when I was always angry at myself."

A tap sounded at my door. "Ryan, I'm coming in."

"I'd rather you didn't."

Nickolai chuckled at my response, and I glanced at

Krista, who was grinning at me with ghostly creepiness.

"I'll leave you two lovebirds to chat. There has got to be a sexy, half-naked vampire *somewhere* in this place."

I laughed and stepped away from the door as she vanished from view. Twisting the handle, I opened it, stepping back to let Nickolai inside. I was finding that the more time I spent in his company, the more space he took up in a room. Part of that was just Nicky; part of it was the alpha presence he carried with him.

Nickolai made himself at home as he placed himself on my bed, folding his arms behind his head as I closed the door, walked toward my bed, and hesitated at the end.

"Could you not find anywhere else to sit?"

Nickolai flashed me an expression of fake horror. "You don't expect me to sit on the floor, do you?" he asked, his lips curving into a smile.

I clutched my hand to my chest. "Perish the thought of His Royal Highness sitting on the floor like a commoner!" I said, eyes wide. "Perhaps you could use one of your Royal Guard to follow you around with a pillow for your royal ass."

He smiled mischievously. "Maybe I'll make you do it."

"Only if you want me to smother you while you sleep," I replied, wanting to sucker-punch that smile off his face.

Nickolai let loose a chortle of laughter as I busied myself tidying things that didn't need to be tidied. Nickolai let me fuss around the room, and when I was done, I perched myself upon the cupboard, far away from Nickolai and my bed.

"Did you mean what you said?" he asked.

"I tend to say a lot of things. You need to be more

specific."

"When you told me you were interested in me. It's the first time you've admitted it out loud."

I swallowed hard, tasting my own lies before they left my mouth. "I told you what you needed to hear to calm down. I've also told you that my body might want you, but you and me can't be together, Nicky."

"Why does it sound like you're trying to convince yourself?"

I sighed, preparing for a deep dive into the truth he more than deserved to hear. "There is this constant pressure," I admitted, "that everyone is watching and waiting for us to get together. But what if we do, and once we've given into whatever this is, we end up hating each other? I've lost too many people, Nickolai. One more might kill me."

"You could never lose me, Ryan."

I sighed, shaking my head. "You don't get it. You are not invincible. My parents were two of the most capable warriors ever to grace this world, and they both died surrounded by their fellow soldiers. You *could* die. Tell me my fears are irrational, tell me that I'm silly for worrying; but you worried when I went after Maxim by myself."

"*I* didn't go out looking to die, Ryan. You were ready to let me lose you all over again without a single thought of how I would feel if Maxim killed you because you hated me."

"I never hated you, Nickolai. It was simply easier to blame you than it was to carry the blame myself."

Nickolai slipped off the bed and came to stand in front of me, resting his hands on my thighs. My entire body came alive at his touch, and I fought against my reactions as the prince gave me a fangy grin.

"You never did answer my question truthfully."

"I told you," I replied, cursing the husky tone in my voice, "I told you what you wanted to hear. Out of you and Maxim, you are the saner choice. I mean, if it's a choice between you and Tom Hardy..."

My throat dried up as Nickolai leaned in and, with his nose on my neck, inhaled my scent and sent a shiver dancing alone my spine. The barest hint of fang grazed my skin, and a treacherous purr sounded in my throat. My pulse raced as Nickolai pressed a kiss to the curve of my neck and I forgot how to think or speak.

Nickolai grazed his fangs over my pulse, and my body arched into his, my hands twitching with this sudden need to touch him. I fought against it, reining myself in even as Nickolai whispered against my flesh.

"Let go, Ry. Let yourself go."

His hands slid up to my waist, the hem of my tee rising as his fingers moved beneath the fabric, his skin touching my abdomen. All at once I felt overwhelmed, like my body was making a decision that my mind hadn't quite caught up to. I grabbed Nickolai's wrists to stop his hands from travelling any farther. I couldn't bring myself to pull away from where his lips now pressed lightly against my collarbone.

"Nickolai, please..." I couldn't get all my words out, I couldn't think. I couldn't breathe.

"Please what?"

My heart felt as if it would burst out of my chest as Nickolai sealed his lips over my pulse, his mouth hot against my skin.

"Please stop." The words came out in a whine, and Nickolai instantly stepped away from me. My body arched to go after him so strongly I nearly fell off the cupboard.

Horrified by the treachery of my own body and the

perplexed look in his eyes, I slipped off the cupboard and went to the sink, splashing cold water on my face to regain some composure as Nickolai stood simply watching me.

After what felt like forever, Nickolai broke the silence. "What just happened here, Ry?"

"I'm not really sure," I admitted. I had no rational reason for stopping Nickolai except that I had started to lose control and that's when I began to panic. I decided to be honest and see if that would send him running.

"I felt myself lose control. I wasn't in control, and I panicked. I don't panic, but I did. I'm sorry."

"If you want to be in control, I'm totally down with that," Nickolai said with a grin as if my admission was nothing. Nickolai wasn't the sort of vampire to relinquish control, though, no matter what he said.

I pointed to the door. "Can you just leave so I don't die of embarrassment? And can we never speak of this again?"

Nickolai laughed, and I let myself smile. "You do realize you never said you didn't like my lips on you, right? You never said you didn't want me to touch you."

My mouth hung open as Nickolai retreated, a lopsided grin on his face. As he reached the door, I told him to forget that any of this had happened. Nickolai paused with his hand on the door handle.

"Darling, I hate to tell you, but I'm already in your veins. You wanted me today. I just have to convince you that losing control can sometimes be fucking amazing."

Chapter 17

"This shit is bananas!"

My exclamation was met with a chortle of laughter as I dropped my duffel bag to the ground and took in the magnificence of Nickolai's new apartment on campus. The penthouse apartment was twice the size of his previous accommodations, with spacious dining and seating areas. The kitchen was off the dining area, and a chef's mouth would have watered at the glorious countertops and workspaces—all of which were wasted on me considering I could only nuke stuff in a microwave.

When you arrived into the apartment, having a door this time rather than a lift opening straight to the room, you had to go up three steps to be able to get the full impact of the room. Tinted privacy windows curved in a circle that led out into a balcony so you could eat dinner and gaze down onto the campus below.

The bathroom was heaven in a wash of blue tiles and a jacuzzi-style bath with a seating area big enough to fit my entire training class. I couldn't wait to sink into some bubbles and ignore the world.

Across the hall from Nickolai's apartment were a

bunch of smaller apartments that would house Jack and Atticus and some of the trainees. With everything going on, the queen decided we should return to college with added protection.

Nickolai came up behind me. "The floor below us has a fully equipped gym. I know what makes my girl happy." He grinned and dropped a kiss on my cheek that had said cheek flaring in embarrassment as I growled and swatted him away.

Since our little... I dunno what to call it... Nickolai had been driving me mad, dropping not-so-subtle comments and going out of his way to touch me. Vampires were starting to notice, and he was beginning to get on my last nerve.

Storming away from him, I opened the bedroom door and screamed inwardly. Inside the room was one king-size bed. This place was bloody ginormous, and he couldn't arrange for a single bed for me?

I made a point of slamming the door and very loudly opening and closing every single door in the place. Wincing with each door slam, Jack asked me if I was all right. The moment my eyes landed on Nickolai's smug-ass grin, my temper reached the boiling point.

Now, if I was honest with myself, I wasn't really angry, just embarrassed that everyone seemed to know my business and eyes constantly watched me. But I'm rarely honest with myself.

Grabbing my duffel, I headed for the door, ignoring Jack calling my name behind me.

Nickolai slid in front of the door and blocked my exit.

I bared my fangs at the crown prince. "Get out of my way, Nickolai."

"Tell me what has you seething and running out the

door first, Ryan."

"No."

"Then you don't get to leave."

"Like hell I don't."

I stomped down on Nickolai's foot, and he yelped. I used the distraction to not-so-gently push him aside, and then I was out the door and striding into the first apartment I came across. Well, these were more like soldiers' barracks with two single beds, a kitchenette, and a bathroom; nothing like the luxury across the way.

Edison St. Clair was midway through changing into a tracksuit and tee when I burst into the room. He stopped mid-change as I tossed my duffel on the bed, and when he made to speak, I growled. Now dressed, Edison held up his hands as I began to take clothes out of my duffel and scatter them over the bed.

"No offense, Callan, but wouldn't you rather be sleeping over there where you can keep an eye on our liege?"

"Mind your business, St. Clair. Mind your business."

A growl rumbled in my chest as a knock sounded on the door and Jack stood in the doorway.

"Hey Edison, give me and Ryan a minute."

"No problem. We are going to try out the new gym, Callan. Come join us if you want."

I ignored Edison, who exchanged a look with Jack before he left. I sank down on the bed and Jack sat opposite me. There was so little space between the beds that our knees almost touched. I folded my arms across my chest, no doubt a vicious scowl on my face.

"What's got you all up in a heap, kiddo?"

"Nothing."

Jack smiled. "Sure, and that's why you're over here trying to bunk with someone you hate."

I blew out a breath and unfolded my arms. letting them fall into my lap. "Nickolai needs to stop with the PDA. We are not dating. He is driving me mad, and I want to stab him."

Jack laughed, the freckles on his cheeks creasing as my scowl deepened.

"I'm glad my murderous intentions are funny to you."

Sobering at my tone, Jack reached over and rested his hands on my knees. "I'm sorry, kiddo. I didn't mean to laugh. Nickolai is doing what every male vampire does when he is interested in a female. He's trying to make you crazy enough that you think only about him. Did something happen to encourage him even more? I mean, you guys had been sleeping in the same bed at home."

Getting up from the bed, I turned away from Jack as tears welled in my eyes. I didn't want to cry. I wasn't sure why I was getting so emotional. It'd been two days since what had happened in my room, and I'd made sure not to be alone with Nickolai since then. But Jack was right, I couldn't stop thinking about what had happened. Even in my dreams, I imaged what it would have been like to keep going, to let Nickolai stake his claim, to let myself feel.

I never expected to feel like this; I never wanted to feel like this. I never imagined I'd be this close to someone, but I had no one to turn to for advice. My chest ached to be able to sit across from my mom and ask her about everything going on in my head, maybe even Krista, but I was surrounded by men and had no one to confide in.

"Ryan, are you crying?"

"No," I bit out with an unconvincing sniffle.

"Talk to me, kiddo." Jack's tone was encouraging and gentle, but I still wasn't going to talk to him about how

I was feeling.

"I can't," I hissed through clenched teeth.

"Of course you can."

I spun to face Jack, and his face fell at the tears leaking down my cheeks. "I really can't, Jack. You can't understand. I mean it and I'm not being dramatic, but I'm surrounded by male vampires and have no one of my own gender to talk to. I want to talk to my mom. I want a hug from my mom and for her to tell me it will all be okay. Do you understand what I'm saying? You can't understand because you aren't female and you aren't my mom!"

Realization dawned on my uncle, and a blush tinged his cheeks. I rubbed the spot over where my heart was hoping it might dull the ache, but it did nothing to soothe me. With my other hand, I wiped away my tears and cleared my throat.

"I'm sorry I shouted at you, Jack."

"It's okay, kiddo. I just never expected to have this conversation with you. Ever."

Rolling my eyes as Jack paled a little, I said, "Don't worry, Jack. I know where baby vampires come from. I'm not asking you to have the sex talk with me."

"Thank Eve not."

That had me laughing as Jack got to his feet and held out his arms. "I'm a poor substitute for your mom, but I'm an excellent hugger."

I let Jack embrace me in a hug, huffing out a tired breath as Jack pressed his lips to the top of my head. "I'll tell Nickolai to back off. In the meantime, Rose has been asking after you. Maybe you could go check on her so she doesn't chew my ear off."

I hadn't been to see Rose in the weeks since I'd left her to get myself injured, and I knew I should go thank her for her kindness. Maybe then she would tell me her story.

I nodded my thanks and, leaving my clothes on the bed, yanked my dad's leather jacket on as I made sure my weapons belt was hidden under the length of my T-shirt. As I made for the door, Jack called after me.

"Take Edison with you. We don't leave the apartment alone."

Letting my shoulders droop, I groaned, shaking my head as Jack went back inside the apartment. Nickolai was sitting on the steps just inside, and for a minute our eyes clashed and I forgot to breathe. Snapping myself out of the fog, I saw Jack sit down beside him. I heard Nickolai ask why I'd been crying and ducked my head as Jack explained and a look of pity pained Nickolai's eyes.

Swallowing down my emotions, I slipped into the staircase and headed down to the gym. The last thing I wanted was to take Edison with me to see Rose, but I wasn't about to disobey Jack's order, either. Well... I'd considered it but decided no.

Pushing open the door, I slipped into the hallway and listened to the sounds inside the gym. They were the sounds of teammates who were completely secure in their group, laughing and joking as they sparred. I imagined that when I walked in, they'd be working in pairs, spotting each other on the weights and all the stuff I'd had to do alone.

I yanked open the double door and, I kid you not, the entire gym halted. Every pair of eyes turned to me as my own eyes scanned the gym for my intended victim. With a bored expression on my face, I let my hand fall to one of my sai and motioned with my head.

"St. Clair, with me."

Edison grinned before I turned and walked out the

door, following after me quickly as he slipped on a black hooded sweatshirt.

I waited for a second and then asked, "Have you a weapon?"

"Of course."

"Then let's go."

We walked in silence for a good while, Edison so far being the perfect companion as we crossed campus and headed into Cork City. As I let the chill of the night awaken my senses, my mind wandered over the last two days, when the Americans had left, unhappy that the queen would not agree to the proposed marriage. She'd said if our cousins could not come to our aid without such stipulations, then the Royal Court of Romanov would prevail without their help.

They left swiftly after that, with Lucas extending an offer to me that, should things get progressively worse, he was always at the other end of the phone and I always had a place in America.

I'll let you imagine what my reply was, but it did involve swear words in at least four languages.

As we ventured deeper into the city, I directed us toward Rose's shop. When we were two streets from Rose's, Edison put a hand on my elbow and went to a coffee cart. Coming back to me, he handed me a coffee and took a sip of his own.

I muttered my thanks, walking again as soon as I'd gulped down a large drink of coffee.

"Why did you bring me along if you aren't even gonna speak to me?"

"Jack told me to bring you. He didn't say anything about making conversation."

I expected Edison to balk at my directness and was pleasantly surprised when he laughed. "Damn, Callan. I knew you were brutal, but spare a guy's feelings, would you? Right now, I am the envy of all my classmates, and I'd like to brag that you chose me."

I gave Edison a noncommittal shrug of my shoulders. "Tell them what you want. Doesn't matter to me."

"So, no chance of us being friends?"

I skidded to a halt and spun to face Edison. "I don't have friends, Edison. Being my friend gets you dead. Whatever crush you had on me or have on me; you need to let it go."

Edison's cheeks reddened as he took a step back from me. "I did have a crush on you when we were younger. I can't change that. And I can't change the fact that I was an asshole to you or that we were intimidated by the unbreakable Ryan Callan. I'm just trying to make amends here, Callan. No ulterior motives—I mean it."

I stalked away from Edison as I mulled over his words, even as he fell into step beside me. As we turned into the alleyway where Rose's shop was, something in my gut prickled, and an awareness sent my senses into overdrive. I held up a fist to Edison and felt him ready for a fight beside me.

The door to Rose's shop was slightly ajar, light spilling into the darkened street. Rose knew better than to leave her door open this late into the evening. Unsheathing my sai, I slowly inched toward the door. Holding up three fingers, I lowered them one by one, and as soon as all three were lowered, I pushed open the door and slipped inside.

I could smell the scent of Rose's perfume, a sweet smell reminiscent of her name. I felt the heat form the heater she kept in the shop for cold winter evenings like tonight. Inhaling another breath, I smelled the herbal tea that was chilling on the cash desk just inside the door, and then relief washed over me as I heard Rose speak sharply to someone.

"I told you not to come by at night. If the vampires knew I was aiding you, then I'd lose all the privileges of being a Child of Eve."

"I'm sorry, Rose, but Darragh was too ill to bring during the day. I came myself because he needs the medicine for his lungs."

The scent from the second voice was strange as if not quite human, but still. I pressed a finger to my lips as I straightened, pushing open the door and stepping into view as Rose glanced in my direction, not at all surprised by my sudden appearance.

Rose's companion, however, stank of so much fear that I licked my lips at the taste of it. Her hazel eyes darted from side to side as she contemplated trying to make a break for it.

"I wouldn't even try if I were you. The only way out of here is through me and my companion, who is guarding the door, or up through a small skylight in the attic." Sheathing my sai, I walked over and stood beside Rose, who greeted me with a little smile.

"Ryan."

"Rose, what have I told you about leaving that door open this late? You never know what can get in."

Rose chuckled as I continued to observe the creature in front of me. She was younger than me by two years, if her appearance matched her actual age. Her hair was a dark shade of brown, and a recent scar puckered on the curve of her eye. It was quite noticeable, despite the thick-rimmed glasses perched on her nose.

"Look, I don't want any trouble, especially from Ryan Callan. I'm just going to take my medicine and poof, I'm gone, never to be seen again."

I pushed away from Rose's side and circled around the young girl who was utterly terrified of me. It was nice to know my reputation preceded me. The scent of her fear was like a draw to me, and I leaned in and inhaled deeply as the girl jerked back.

"Ryan, stop teasing poor Emer and say hello properly."

With a fangy grin, I extended my hand. "Ryan Callan."

"I know who you are," Emer said with a little venom in it that instantly made me like her a little.

"You hear that, St. Clair? She knows who I am!"

Edison stepped into the room and instantly made it smaller, but now Emer would have no means to escape.

"You shouldn't have said that," he said to Emer. "She'll be more insufferable now."

I allowed a slow smile tug at my lips as Emer glanced at Rose as if Rose would help her. I wasn't sure what Rose could do or why she was dealing with this woman, but I needed to find out more.

Reaching out, I took the box of medicine from the counter as Emer started forward. I held up a finger as I examined the box. This was medicine used to treat a lung infection. Someone important to this Emer was ill.

I handed the box to the girl, and she clutched it to her as if she were handling the crown jewels. And maybe to her, she was.

Looking to Rose, I grinned. "You are full of surprises, old woman."

"Less of the *old*, dear. You are not too old for a clip round the ear."

Walking away from the two, I hoisted myself onto the counter and swung my legs back and forth. "So, who is going to tell me exactly what's going on here? Rose?

Emer?"

"I owe you no explanations, Ryan."

"No, Rose, you don't. I'm just curious how a Child of Eve and a species thought to have died out could happen across one another in a city like Cork. There hasn't been one of her kind around in centuries if I'm correct, and somehow here she is, terribly human, but not."

I wet my lips as I leaned forward and pinned Emer with my stare. "Where did you come from, Emer? Who is your father?"

"I don't know."

Tasting the truth in her words, I changed tactics. "Then answer me this, little *dhampir*. How many of you have been hiding in plain sight in my city?"

Chapter 18

Dhampirs used to be as common as vampires, when our numbers were greater and before vampires became elitist snobs who believed that true-blood vampires should only mate with other true-blood vampires. When our numbers began to dwindle and female vampires were seriously outnumbered by males, those who wished to start a family did so by having a child with a human mother, resulting in a *dhampir*.

This offspring was born half-vampire, half-human and could walk in the sun. They couldn't heal like us, but they did crave blood, had more strength than an average human, and usually suffered from illnesses—like this person called Darragh—due to their genetic makeup. A great number of mothers also died while carrying *dhampir* offspring,

During the early 1940's, the number of *dhampir* children was three times greater than true-born children. One court vampire, paranoid that vampires would be wiped out and replaced by these half-breeds, went on a murdering spree and claimed to have rid the world of *dhampirs* altogether.

It was still possible for a male vampire to sire a child with a willing human female, it was just never spoken of.

If Emer was residing in Cork, and by her accent she had grown up here, then there had to be others around here. Her father might even be a current member of the court; although, her father could also have died in the same battle as my own parents.

Dhampirs, though not as strong as a vampire, had far more strength than a standard human. This Emer looked like she couldn't fight her way out of a paper bag, but appearances could be deceiving. I knew that better than most.

Emer took a step, and Edison moved when she moved. I needed to know if Emer had more *dhampirs* lurking in the shadows, but I knew the girl would give me no information. I'd have to be sneaky... and I liked being sneaky.

"Let her go," I said.

Edison stared at me. "Are you for real?"

"I outrank you, Guard St. Clair. Are you questioning my orders?"

"No, ma'am."

"Good," I said coolly, waving my hand for Edison to step aside.

Emer's gaze slid from mine to Rose's and then to Edison, who had stood to the side. Talking a hesitant step toward the door, I could see the moment she intended to bolt.

"Emer," I said in a singsong tone, then dropped my tone to make her a promise. "I'll see you again."

Then the girl darted out the door, and I could hear her heavy steps running up the alley. I was off the counter a second later, pointing at Edison. "Stay here and make sure Rose doesn't do anything stupid like try and

197

warn the half-breed."

"You shouldn't go out there alone." Edison's tone was cold, very much the soldier. I approved.

Patting his cheek, I grinned. "Don't worry, I'll make sure to tell our liege that I ordered you to stay. It's all on me. I'm not afraid of his royal highness."

And then I bolted out the door and followed the scent of the little *dhampir*. If I'd been her, I would have tried to lead me on a wild goose chase, but the poor girl was taking me right to her home, the scent of her fear so strong that any predator could easily track her. She carried on running through the city, past the bus station and out toward the now-vacant train station, Kent Station having been decommissioned.

Emer went down the steps and walked along the platform, glancing from left to right before jumping down to the tracks, balancing herself carefully on the rails as she disappeared into the tunnel. I stood on the bridge, watching as she disappeared out of view, and then I dropped down to brace myself on the tracks.

I expected her to keep going on through the tunnel, however she stopped at a maintenance door and knocked three times. The door opened with a creak, and a young boy around Emer's age, his scent entirely human, stepped out and embraced her.

"What's wrong, Emer?"

"The vampires found me. And not just any vampire—Ryan feckin' Callan!"

I grinned to myself in the shadows, enjoying my celebrity status just a little more than I should.

"You came face - face-with the rogue reaper? Is she as hot as they say?"

Biting back a smirk as Emer punched his shoulder, I thought now would be the perfect time to make an entrance.

"I don't consider myself hot, but they do call me the ice queen."

Emer let out a shriek and made to duck inside the maintenance door.

I *tsked*. "And here I thought we were friends, Emer. If you lock that door, I'm gonna be forced to break it down."

My ears twitched at the sound of a cry inside the door, and I raised a brow. "Yours?"

"Oh god no!" she exclaimed. Realizing her mistake, she shut down quickly, but the damage was done. Now I knew there were more inside.

Looking to the human, I smiled. "Hey kid, what's your name?"

The boy refused to answer me, simply whistled through his teeth as he pulled a stake from his pocket.

Amused, I cocked my head to the side. "Dude, I'd snap your neck before you even lifted that piece of tree. Put it away before you hurt yourself."

The slight tremble in his hands made my lips twitch. I had no intention of killing him, but he didn't know that. He made to stand in front of Emer, and I secretly commended him on his bravery.

Footsteps sounded in the distance, and soon a dozen or so more came through the door and formed a protective circle around the teens. Humans and *dhampirs*, all hiding out in caverns under this train station—the farthest point away from the court. It was smart, and as *dhampirs* needed blood, though not as much as a vampire, having humans on tap was very smart.

The court could learn from them.

Shoving my hands into the pockets of my jeans, I bounced on my feet as a man came through the door carrying an oxygen machine, the tubes of which ran from the machine to his nose. The man looked tired, as if it hurt for him to be standing. He smelled like a *dhampir*, and as he opened his lips to smile, I saw the tiniest hint of his fangs, smaller than a vampire's.

I ran my eyes over the man who I now believed to be the leader of this band of unlikely warriors. Everything about him was unremarkable; he wouldn't stand out in a crowd. Brown hair and eyes, a face that would get lost in a city like this, he was small in stature, almost the same height as me. Apart from the aura of leadership that hung off his shoulders, this man was nothing.

But he was everything to his people.

"Darragh, I presume?" I inched a step closer, extending my hand which he declined to take. I wasn't offended.

"What can we do for you, Ms. Callan?" His tone was clipped, but he could not mask the hint of admiration in his tone.

Chuckling, I held my hands up. "Please tell your friend with the crossbow to lower the damn thing. His hands are shaking so much, he'd stake me in the shoulder rather than the heart. I've enough scars there, thank you very much."

A baby let out a cry again, and my eyes darted to the door. Every single man, woman, and teen moved to block the door.

Again, I held up my hands. "I'm not here to hurt anyone. I was just curious."

"Vampires always have an agenda," a voice called out, and I glanced toward the man with the crossbow.

Letting loose a snort, I nodded my head. "I can't argue with you on that. I spent my entire childhood navigating court politics."

Darragh cleared his throat. "I will ask you again, Ms. Callan. What can we do for you?"

Grinning, I shrugged my shoulder. "I mean, the fact that you guys have heard of me is enough to give a girl a complex. I'm flattered, really."

The group shared a look of disbelief as if they weren't sure what to do with me, and I wondered what I was going to do next.

Suddenly, out of the corner of my eye, I spied a chubby-faced toddler peeking round the door, her auburn hair bouncing as she waddled out into the tunnel and then ran toward me. The adults around her were too focused on me to see her daring escape until she was out of their reach and within mine.

"Chloe!"

An agonizing cry came from one of the human women who lurched forward, the father of the child, a *dhampir*, snarling as the child bounced up and down in front of me, her little arms reaching out to be picked up.

I scooped the little girl into my arms, and she bared her little fangs at me and snapped her teeth. I mimicked her actions and she giggled at me, totally unafraid of mean ol' Ryan Callan.

"Vampire!" the little girl exclaimed, reaching for my mouth.

I flashed her my fangs, ignoring the collective gasp as she went for the sharp points, and I gently held her wrist. "Uh oh, sharp," I said with a smile, my peripheral vision watching as her father made to come forward and Darragh stopped him.

"Sharp?" Chloe asked, her eyes filled with wonder.

Bracing her on my hip, I nicked my thumb with my fangs and showed her the welling blood. "Yup, sharp."

I tried to set the little girl down, but she clambered up my body again and rested her head on my shoulder, playing with the strands of my hair. Aware that I had lit-

201

tle chance to reach for a weapon should they try to attack me, I inched closer to the crowd, then threw caution to the wind and strode right through the group, stopping before the father, who was glaring at me like I was Lucifer himself reborn on earth.

I ruffled the little girl's hair and pried her from my side. Lifting her up, I tapped her nose. "You are a brave little one, maybe the bravest of us all. Stay brave even when the world forces you not to be."

Handing the child back to the father, the little girl waved at me as her mother fled back into their home. I was surrounded by terrified people who all despised my kind. They were justified in their hatred; true-born vampires had hunted their kind for centuries.

I decided to see how this would play out, hoping Darragh would see there was no sense in trying to kill me. I was too high profile to simply disappear, and even if they could blame my disappearance on the rogues, it probably wouldn't end well for them.

"Stand down," Darragh said. "Go back inside. Ms. Callan and I need to speak alone."

I admired how they all hesitated but ultimately obeyed his command, and soon, Darragh and I were the only ones standing on the abandoned track. He coughed, a harsh, ragged sound that rattled his lungs. I let him gather himself after the coughing spasm and then leaned against the brick.

"If you wanted to prove a point," he said quietly, "you could have killed Chloe."

"And show that we vampires are monsters?" I quipped. "I mean, we are, and I am, but I don't hurt innocents who cannot fight for themselves."

Darragh blinked, his eyes wandering over me in newfound respect. "You are not what I expected."

Rolling my eyes, I replied, "I've been hearing that a lot lately. I tend to exceed people's expectations."

The *dhampir* laughed, and that brought on another burst of coughing. Emer snuck out of the doorway with a bottle of water and the pack of tablets she'd gotten from Rose. She helped Darragh as he swallowed the tablets and then drank half the bottle of water. When finished, he cupped her cheek in thanks, and she beamed before heading back inside.

"How long do we have before the court come for us?" he asked, turning back to me.

"Why, did you invite them?"

His gaze narrowed. "This is not a game; this is our lives. I will not let my children become collateral damage or orphans. If we need to move, then tell me now so I can get the children to safety at least."

I had told the truth when I'd said I was curious; I really had no intention of telling the court about this little community. If I'd learned anything at court, I'd learned it was wise to keep a secret or two in one's back pocket.

"I give you my word that I have no intention of telling the crown about any of you," I said. "When I say I would rather walk into the sun before inflicting the pain of losing a parent on a child, hear the truth in my words." After a slight pause, I added, "Tell me, do you plan on rising up against the vampires?"

Darragh snorted. "Do I look like I'm in any condition to stage a rebellion, Ms. Callan?"

"Then your people and I have no quarrels. And please, call me Ryan, since we're buddies and all now."

Darragh stood motionless as I strode forward, pausing at his shoulder. "If you ever need help, ask Rose to pass on a message to me. I will come."

He squinted. "Why would you do that? You don't

203

even know us."

"I'm a softy really, but don't tell anyone. It will ruin my badass reputation."

Darragh huffed out a laugh as I turned to leave the tunnel, pausing as Darragh uttered my name.

When I turned back, he looked me dead in the eyes. "I am sorry for your loss."

"Yeah, me too."

I could feel Darragh's eyes on me as I crouched and leapt up, grabbing the underside of the bridge as I rocked back and forth and used my momentum to swing myself up to the top of the bridge.

Once my feet were braced on the top of the wall, I jumped down lightly and said, "I need to tell how badly you follow orders."

Edison shrugged his shoulders. "I guess I've spent too much time learning from your example."

Well, he had me dead to rights there.

"You are not going to say a thing to anyone about what we saw tonight."

"Why not?"

I got in Edison's face—well, I tried to anyway, but he was almost as tall as his brother—and dug my finger into his chest. "These people have done nothing wrong. We're the ones who made them feel like they must hide from us. You want me to trust you, Edison? Here is where we start."

"That's all fine and dandy, but you need to come up with a reason as to why, when Jack called Rose to make sure you were okay, you weren't there but I was.

Shit.

"When Rose told him, he shouted at me to go find you," Edison continued. "Seems like they all think you might end up finding trouble."

Groaning, I lifted my gaze to heaven and ushered Edison forward. "I take it Jack is on his way over now to pick us up?"

"Yup."

"Last one back takes the blame?"

Edison grinned. "Sure, but I'm faster tha—"

I took off at a sprint, ignoring Edison's growl. He *was* faster, but I knew these streets better than he did. I had stalked every darkened alley in this town in hopes of finding Maxim, and Edison wasn't used to the twists and turns like I was. Picking up my pace regardless, I was sitting on the step outside Rose's shop when Edison stomped into the alley.

"Ah, little tortoise, you finally made it."

"Best two out of three?"

"Not a chance." I replied with a grin.

Edison let out a whoop of laughter, holding out his fist. Rolling my eyes at his grinning face, I bumped his knuckles just as Jack flung open the door to Rose's shop, causing me to jump up to stop myself from being hit in the back with the door.

"And where the hell were you?"

"Shopping?" I replied with a raised brow.

"Do you expect me to believe that?"

"Maybe?"

Jack snarled at me as I tried to look all innocent, and then his eyes wandered to Edison, who, Eve bless him, didn't so much as squirm under his commander's steely gaze.

"St. Clair, where was Guard Callan?"

"I believe she said she was shopping, sir."

Jack came down the steps and stood inches from Edison's face. "I didn't ask you what she said, soldier. I asked you a direct question. Where was Guard Callan?"

205

Edison remained tight-lipped and refused to answer. I felt bad for him, but I think Jack would respect his loyalty to me and his courage at not ratting me out.

"Jesus, Jack," I said, trying to ease the heat for Edison. "I went to get some shopping... *feminine* shopping. I can bloody show you if you want." I prayed to Eve Jack wouldn't insist as I rummaged round my empty pockets.

"Okay, okay, stop. I believe you. You should still have let Edison go with you."

"Noted, sir."

Jack shook his head as he pointed to the waiting car. "Get in before I explain why your story smells fishy."

"That's just Edison; I made him run."

Jack growled as the two of us hightailed it to the car, Edison slipping into the back as I claimed the passenger seat. I waved through the window at Rose as Jack walked to the car.

Twisting to face Edison before Jack reached the car, I held out my fist. "Thanks for having my back."

Edison gently bumped my fist. "Anytime, Callan."

Jack got in and glanced at the two of us smiling. "Since when are you two all chummy?"

"Didn't you hear, Jack? We're bros now."

Jack scowled as Edison chuckled, and I leaned my head against the headrest and closed my eyes.

Chapter 19

THE NEXT DAY, NICKOLAI WENT BACK TO CLASS. I HAD OF-
fered to go with him, but he declined my offer very politely and asked Atticus to go with him instead. My eyes
had narrowed, meaning to ask him what I had done to
get dismissed like that, but Jack shook his head.

When Atticus and Nickolai left, I whirled on Jack.
"What gives? Are you punishing me for disappearing last
night?"

"No, kiddo. Nickolai doesn't even know you went
MIA last night. I asked him to give you some space. Well,
I told him off and ordered him to give you space."

I ground my teeth together. So that was why I'd been
left to sleep in the bunk room with Edison. I had managed to fall into a deep sleep in the car, not waking as I
was brought inside and tucked snugly into bed. I woke
in the middle of the day, disorientated and wondering
where I was. It took a few minutes and a few loud snores
from Edison before I realized. I'd been surprised and a
little perplexed as to why Nickolai would let me sleep in
the room with Edison, but now I understood. Jack had
basically put a gun to Nickolai's head and told him to

back off.

But that was what I wanted, right?

"Did you manage to chat to Rose last night?"

I shook my head, walking over to the window to watch Nickolai and Atticus leave the building and make their way across the campus. As if he sensed my eyes on him, Nickolai glanced over his shoulder and gave a little wave, although I was certain he couldn't actually see me.

Turning away from their retreating forms, I caught Jack watching me. "What?" I asked as my adopted uncle pulled out a chair and motioned for me to sit. I did so cautiously, my senses prickling with awareness. I had fed earlier in the evening and the blood pumping in my veins had me a little on edge even after the post feed high.

"Christmas is coming up soon and I know how hard that is for you."

Despite my love of cheesy Christmas romance movies, I hated the actual holiday because it was also my father's birthday. Tristan Callan born in his little village almost a century ago not quite on Christmas Day, arriving kicking and screaming with mere minutes left on Christmas Eve.

I usually got through the holidays with an unhealthy amount of alcohol but that was most of the days that the loss of my parents felt even more unbearable. Since being ordered to watch Nickolai, I didn't think anyone would let me crawl into bed and ignore the holiday period.

"I'll be fine, uncle Jack." Jack didn't look convinced and I guess neither was I.

"Nickolai was thinking of asking you to go away with him for Christmas. Asked me my thoughts."

My stomach plummeted. "And what did you say?"

"I told him that if he continued to put pressure on

whatever relationship you both are heading toward, then he might just push you too far. I told him to let you set the pace."

"Thanks, I guess," I said with a small smile.

"Did I do wrong? Do you want him to take you away?"

"By Eve, no!" I exclaimed, shifting uncomfortably in my seat. "I just... By Eve, this is awkward. I mean, we can't just let things happen, can we? Not without talk of weddings and babies and queendoms. Do they not realize I'm an emotionally stunted, feral seventeen-year-old who's just been forced into the world after years of isolation? I half-expect Katerina to burst into the room, if we do eventually kiss, with a measuring tape for my wedding dress."

Jack laughed softy. "It's a lot of pressure, eh?"

"I guess."

Jack reached out and took my hand in his. "But you do realize he'll be king, yeah? That is who he is meant to be. But he would give it all up if you asked him to, kiddo. He would happily run off into the sunset with you and live a normal existence, but Nickolai was destined to be king—it's who he *is*. Would you ask him to give that up?"

I snatched back my hand, suddenly angry as the pressure built in my head. "Of *course* I wouldn't. I never have. But does anyone wonder what I want? If *I'm* willing to give up who *I'm* destined to be just to be with *him*? For the same reason I would never ask him not to be king, I resent his asking me to be something I'm not."

I got to my feet, not liking where this conversation was going. I couldn't understand how Jack would side with Nickolai and not with me. I felt betrayed. "I guess I can't offer you fancy titles or grant you permission to be open with your boyfriend, but I thought I meant more to you, Jack. I opened up to you; do you know how hard that is for me? I expected more from you."

Jack shot to his feet, palms up in a show of peace. "Hey, kiddo, you are reading too much into this. I'm trying to look after you both. You're my family, and he will be my king. This uncertainty is killing you both, and you both need to be honest with each other about where you stand."

A bark of laughter, bitter and venomous fell from my lips. "If you think to put the blame on me, Jack, then we ain't family; I'm just the orphaned daughter of your best friend, whom you feel obligated to look after."

Jack stumbled back like I'd shot him, but I wasn't done taking aim. "I told Nickolai from the start where I stood. He's the one who blurred the lines. He's the one who begged me to let him in. I should've listened to my gut. Every vampire for themselves, eh, Jack? You're more like the council families than I ever thought."

Turning, I marched down the steps and slammed the door so hard on my way out that the frame rattled. I crossed the landing and walked into the room I shared with Edison. Grabbing my phone and a pair of headphones, I threw on a hoody and, popping the earbuds in, chose an angry playlist to match my mood.

I wasn't mad enough to be stupid, so after stomping down the five flights of stairs, I jogged around the main square of the campus, letting the heavy sounds of Fiver Finger Death Punch soothe my soul. I looped around the quad more than was possible for a human, not even breaking a sweat. I could feel Jack watching me, and I leaned over pretending to be winded.

As the songs faded from one to another, NF's "Leave Me Alone" blared in my ears, and I couldn't help but laugh out loud. Lowering myself into the grass, I lay my head down and stared up into the night sky. Starless tonight, a mass of gray clouds hid the moon for the most part, its pale yellow glow peeking through whenever the clouds gave her space to do so.

I lay there for an age, until the crunch of footsteps on gravel shifted to the swish of footsteps in grass, signaling someone was coming toward me. I sat upright, the muscles in my stomach bunching as I plucked out my ear buds, and saw the human teenager who'd embraced the little *dhampir* nearing.

He stopped shy of me, his face pale as if he were terrified of me... which he should be.

"Hello, little human."

"I'm taller than you," he retorted.

"The taller they are the harder they fall," I said with a smile. "Now, what brings you looking for the big bad wolf?"

The boy inhaled a breath and before he began, I motioned for him to keep his voice down as I spied Jack out on the balcony.

"Darragh sent me to say thanks for not ratting us out."

"I don't think those were Darragh's words," I retorted with amusement in my voice.

"Well, his version had big words I couldn't pronounce, so I improvised. He wanted to return the favor and said he hopes we can remain friends. He said to tell you that Maxim Smyrnoi landed into Cork Airport on a private plane just before sunrise yesterday. A car collected him on the tarmac, and he spent an hour at his club before he vanished."

My heart hammered in my chest as my eyes scanned the quad for a threat. Jack was still watching me from the balcony; somehow, I'd missed Atticus and Nickolai's return, and they had joined Jack. When I was certain that Maxim was not going to leap from the shadows, I inclined my head to the teen.

"Tell Darragh I'm grateful for the information and appreciate any more information he may happen across. Tell him I ordered supplies to be delivered to Rose as a thank you for his trust, and she will contact him when they arrive."

The teen nodded and turned to walk away.

"What's your name, little human?"

The boy snorted. "Liam."

"I'll see you again, Liam."

And then the teen took off through the throng of people who'd just emerged from an exam in a nearby building. I brushed the grass from my butt and headed back toward the base of operations, ignoring the stares from above.

To delay the inevitable questions, I strode upstairs, stopped off in my room to throw my phone down, and changed out of my sweaty clothes, pulling on lounge pants with hearts on them and a vest top. I was hungry enough after my little run that I decided to risk going into the apartment to feed myself considering how shite I was at cooking.

I walked in to see Jack and Nickolai having a heated discussion. They stopped when I came in, and I bypassed them and went into the kitchen.

"Don't mind me. Continue talking. Doesn't bother me. I'm only here for the food."

I listened to Nickolai tell Jack to leave as I pulled a bar of chocolate from the fridge. By the time I'd devoured the entire bar and washed it down with blood, Nickolai was leaning in the doorframe.

"Who's your little human friend?"

"My little human friend is none of your concern."

"Does this have anything to do with why Jack has his boxers in a twist?"

I flicked my tongue along the rim of the bottle. "Nope, totally unrelated."

"By Eve, Ryan, can you stop being so evasive?"

I brushed past him, let my feet keep moving until I stood at the top of the stairs. "The little human is not your concern. Jack is pissed because I called him out for looking after your interests instead of mine. Have you been pouting, my liege? Have you felt put out because I wouldn't?"

"What the hell are you talking about?"

"Well, your captain of the guard basically accused me of being a tease and leading you on. Is that what you think? That I'm playing some game?"

"By Eve, Ryan, I'm sure he didn't mean it like that. I asked him for some advice, and he read too much into it."

"Is it just about sex?"

"*What?*"

My heart pounded inside my chest as I crossed my arms and pulled my tank over my head. I fumbled with the tie on my lounge pants and would have pushed them down if Nickolai's hands hadn't stopped me.

"What are you doing?"

"I would think that's pretty obvious, Nicky. Do it. Fuck me. Get it out of your system, and once it's over and done with, we can get on with our lives and forget it ever happened."

Nickolai stepped back like I had burned him. Bending down, he took my vest in his hands and held it out for me. I was suddenly embarrassed and yanked on my top.

"Now you can tell Jack where we stand, and he can leave me alone."

Spinning on my heels, I went to head down the

stairs when I heard Nickolai murmur.

"I've done this all wrong, haven't I?"

I didn't reply, but I did turn back to face him. Nickolai had retreated to the sofa, his head in his hands, and I had to stop myself from going to comfort him.

"I'm just sick of talk about weddings and babies and crowns and psychotic vampires who want to make me their butterfly. I'm tired of everyone having an opinion on us—it's like this pressure in my head that won't turn off. It's like everyone is pressing fast-forward and rushing me. I don't like all the scrutiny. I don't like my uncle basically telling me to stop being a tease."

Nickolai was silent for a minute, then he lifted his head just a fraction and I was forced to lose myself in his eyes. "It's not all about sex, Ryan. I want you. I want all of you. I'm fighting against my nature, here, that's demanding I claim you. You are it for me; you always have been. I waited ten years to get you back. I can wait a little longer."

"I'm not asking you to fight against your nature, Nickolai, and I appreciate the honesty. So, I'm gonna be honest with you. I do have feelings for you. Just for you. I'm willing to try and see where this might go, but I can't do that with your mom talking about babies and Jack accusing me of trying to get you to give up the crown."

Nickolai's head snapped up. "That was taken completely out of context. I made a flippant comment that I'd give up the crown for you. I'll talk to Jack."

"Then you didn't mean it?"

"Of course I meant it. I'd give it *all* up for you."

I sighed. "I'd never ask you to."

"I know you wouldn't. And I would never ask you to be something you're not. Where in the rulebook does it say a queen cannot be a warrior?"

214

I held up my hand. "You were doing so well up until you mentioned me being queen."

Nickolai chucked, sitting up straight. "Would you let me hold you? Just while it's us?"

I considered saying no, but I was sitting in his lap with my head in the curve of his neck before I could reconsider. Nickolai let out a breath, the tension leaving his body. His fingers played with the strands of my braid, and I closed my eyes as I imagined that there was no one but Nickolai and me in the world.

I didn't want to break the spell, but I knew I would have to tell him about Maxim sooner rather than later. Lifting my head, I patted his cheek and he tried to bite my finger.

"Listen, I hate to break this up, but I have information on Maxim, and you know I hate to repeat myself. So, you might as well call the guard in here so I don't have to."

"Any chance this has something to do with teenage boys following you about?"

"No comment."

Nickolai reached for his phone and sent out a message. I made to get up when his arms tightened around me. "I don't want to let you go."

Snorting, I pressed a quick kiss to his cheek, ignoring the blush on my face as I get to my feet. "Alright, Romeo. Time to get back to business. Now, before the horde arrives, I'd like some more chocolate please?"

I ignored the way Nickolai's hands traced where my lips had touched as the door to the apartment opened and all the guard, current and trainees, flooded in. I allowed Atticus to ruffle my hair as he sat down next to me, however I couldn't look at Jack just yet. He sat opposite to where I sat and kept trying to catch my eye, but I pretended not to notice.

As the trainees unfolded chairs to sit, Edison walked around to sit behind his brother, stopping first to bump fists with me. Nickolai strode out of the kitchen with my chocolate and a coffee, and I made grabby hands for them.

"What was that?" he asked, his voice teasing with no hint of jealousy.

I took a long sip of coffee, conscious that everyone was watching us. I guessed we'd never escape the circus. "Oh, didn't you hear? We're cool now."

Nickolai looked at Edison, who flashed a toothy grin. "We're bros."

I was aware that quite a few vampires had open mouths, including Edison's brother. I offered him a square of my chocolate to give his mouth something else to do. Nickolai took the seat next to me, and I tensed, expecting him to stake his claim in front of the other male vampires.

I was more surprised when he didn't.

Holding up his hand, he silenced the chatter. "Ryan has some important information about Maxim."

Growls and snarls greeted me as I cleared my throat, wrapping my fingers around my mug. "Maxim returned Cork yesterday morning just before sunrise. He flew in on a private plane and then paid a visit to his strip club. He stayed for about an hour before disappearing from the club."

"How reliable is your source?" Jack questioned.

"Very." My clipped tone had the rest of the vampires glancing at each other. "I suspect Maxim will come looking for us sooner rather than later."

"We will be ready when he comes," Nickolai said with a growl, and his soldiers echoed his growl.

"Why are we waiting?" I asked. "Why can't we go get him? I'm tired of Maxim being two steps ahead of us all the goddam time. I say we walk right up and ring his doorbell."

I expected to be shot down, expected them all to say defense was the best offence. I *fully* expected Jack or Nickolai or even Atticus to ask me to stop riling up the vampires.

I wasn't expecting for them to agree with me.

"What's you plan?" Nickolai asked.

I grinned as I sipped my coffee. "I'm gonna lure Maxim out into the open and kill the bastard. But first, I need to call in a favor." I glanced over at Edison. When his brow quirked in response, I said, "Hey, bro, fancy going to a strip club?"

Chapter 20

"You want me to *what?*"

I tried very hard not to roll my eyes and let out a frustrated sigh as Farrah Nazir paled considerably. The vampire was seated across the table from me and Nickolai, with Edison, Atticus, and Jack standing off to the side. They had followed my lead and invited Farrah here, but none had known exactly what I planned until I began explaining the plan to Farrah.

That was ten minutes ago, and she still couldn't believe what I was asking of her.

"You only need to open the window. Then Edison and I will slip in, and you get your ass out of there. Not a soul except those in this room know you're involved in this, and I will bleed anyone who dares spill the secret."

Farrah shook her head, her dark curls bouncing vigorously. "I'm not like you, Ryan. I can't be as calm and collected as you are walking into danger."

Leaning forward in my seat, I rested my chin in my hands. "And you think I'm not scared when I go into a fight? Of course I am. But the fear doesn't cripple me. I just let it fuel my desire to survive. I'm not asking you to kill anyone, Farrah; you just need to go into the club, feed from the human you already go to the club to see, and then open a window. The rest is up to me."

"And me," Edison chimed in, the biggest grin on his face that reminded me of how much he looked like Atticus.

"I can't do it, Ryan. I just can't."

"Have you been training like I asked you to?" I questioned, trying to soften my voice and be reassuring, even though it wasn't in my nature.

"I have."

"Then this is your first test. I will keep you safe, Farrah. I give you my vow."

Farrah swallowed hard, and I stared at her with a comforting smile as her upbringing battled against her desire for change. Finally, she nodded her head stiffly, and I winked at her, anticipation flooding my veins as Jack led Farrah out of the room to make arrangements.

I watched Jack go, my stubbornness not allowing me to make the first move to clear the air. I mean, it wasn't my place to make him feel better, right? He was the one who'd chosen Nickolai's feelings over my own.

Nickolai leaned back in his chair and let out a small snarl. "What the fuck is it with you and goddamn windows?"

I shrugged as I bit back a grin. "Listen, I'm starting a tradition. I want enemies to know I'm willing to break stuff in order to survive. What's a few windows between immortal enemies?"

Atticus chuckled and, pulling out a chair, slumped down in it. "You should let me go with you, Ryan."

Shaking my head, I jerked my head to Edison. "You gotta cut the apron strings at some point, Atty. Besides, I'd never forgive myself if something happened to you.

I'm more likely to use Edison as a shield anyway, if it means I get to escape."

Edison chuckled, excusing himself to go have a nap before we left. He ruffled my hair just as Atticus did, and I growled. He left the room with a grin on his face as I glanced up at his older brother.

"You don't have to be nice to Edison for me. I know he can be a massive asshat and has been to you."

"We came to an understanding, Edison and I. His actions spoke louder than any insult he threw at me."

Atticus turned to look out the window and then faced me again. "Can I ask a favor of you?"

"Sure. I mean, you can ask, but I'm not agreeing to anything," I replied with a shrug of my shoulders.

Running a hand through his hair, Atticus cleared his throat, and my heartbeat kicked up as I realized what he was going to ask. "Talk to Jack," he said. "He is beating himself up so bad about your last conversation."

"Jack is a grown vampire who doesn't need his boyfriend to fight his battles. If he wants to talk to me, then he needs to grow a pair and come to me. He was in the wrong here, not me."

Atticus sighed. "Did Jack go about it the wrong way? Yes. But you are so wound up over certain subjects, Ryan, that you strike back with words that are sharper than any weapon you wield. Jack loves you like his own. It's killing him that you think he would choose Nickolai over you."

I let out a short bark of laughter. "I *expect* him to choose Nickolai over me. It is his *job* to choose Nickolai over me. However, it's not his job or his right to tell me how to live my life. When it comes to my life or Nickolai's, it's our liege's life that matters. When it comes to any personal relationship between me and Nickolai, Jack has no say—just as I have no say in yours."

Atticus smiled, getting to his feet. "I get it. And Jack will, too. But before you go out there, don't let this drive a wedge between you two. Neither of you would forgive yourselves if something happened to the other and the last conversation you shared was an argument."

With that, Atticus left me alone with Nickolai, and I let my head fall onto the table and banged it once and then a second time for good measure, hoping to bang the frustration out of my head. When I lifted my gaze, I spied Nickolai watching me with an amused expression on his face.

"What?"

"Absolutely nothing," he replied, yet the grin didn't fade from his lips.

Folding my arms across my chest, I glared at the crown prince and said, "We need to talk while we're alone."

"I could think of better things to do while we're alone."

The look in his eyes nearly melted my skin, and I felt heat creep into my face as I rolled my eyes and tried not to think about how Nickolai's hands had felt on my skin, or how much I wanted his lips on me. I ducked my gaze so he couldn't read any of what I was feeling.

"Ryan..."

Shaking away my thoughts, I jerked my head up. "You can't be anywhere near this tomorrow night."

"Like hell I can't."

Banging a fist on the table, I snarled. "By Eve, Nickolai, listen to me for one goddamn minute and be reasonable. It's my job as your personal guard to ensure your safety. I won't be by your side, and I can't let my attention waver to wonder if you're safe. One slip in concentration could land me with a sword through my heart."

"You can't expect me to sit back in safety while you go off to chase down a madman."

His words were clipped and his tone dangerous, but it wasn't like I was doing this because he couldn't hold his own. I was doing it because I cared about him. I had to convince him this was the best course of action, and I knew only one way that I could.

"If you want me to believe that you becoming king and us starting something won't affect who I am as a soldier, then yes. I do. You and Atticus will stay on campus, and you will go to your last exam. If Maxim's rogues are watching you, then they aren't watching me. Please, Nicky, trust me to come back to you."

Nickolai considered me for a moment, and I could almost hear the internal battle raging inside his mind. His expression changed into a cool mask, the one he wore when he was trying to block out his emotions. Finally, he looked at me again and smiled a sly smile.

"I will agree to your terms and do as you ask, with one stipulation. I will use that time to speak with my mother and tell her to halt all talk of weddings and children. Then, once you come back to me, we will be a partnership. The entire court will know that I intend to make you mine, and you will not let fear drive you."

Panic flared in my chest at the thought of the entire court watching and waiting for me to fall on my ass. The court spent so much time watching us that if Nickolai declared his intentions as was tradition, we would never have a moment's peace. I would not live my life in a fishbowl.

"I counter your stipulation with an amendment."

Nickolai inclined his head as if he and I were negotiating world peace and not our relationship—or lack thereof—at the moment.

"You do as I ask and stay away from the club tomorrow night, and when I come back, you give us six months to figure out if what we have is real or not. No interference from the court, no declarations, nothing. Then, if we decide we want to be together, I will... I will..."

I couldn't get the words out; they were stuck in my throat. To say them felt as if I were sacrificing a part of my soul. I would only be eighteen, with a couple of centuries ahead of me before I was reunited with my parents in Eden. I was terrified that once I agreed to anything, as soon as Nickolai had that crown on his head, things would change and I would lose myself for him.

"I agree to your terms, Guard Callan. No more running, Ryan. No more walls."

I snarled at him with a look of murder in my eyes, but the prince just looked smug as hell. What, by Eve, had I just done?

Before I could contemplate my impending downfall, the door to the apartment opened and Jack strode in. He wore an expression that could only be described as determined as he strode up the steps and stopped in front of the table.

"My liege, I would ask for a moment to speak with my niece in private."

"Then perhaps you should ask your niece if she will speak with you instead of me, Captain O'Reilly."

Jack bristled at Nickolai's tone as the future king of vampires rose and pressed a kiss to the top of my head. Then he crossed the room and slipped inside the bedroom, closing the door with an audible click.

Leaning my chair back, I crossed my leg and let my knee hold me up as I balanced two legs of the chair off the ground. I tilted my head to the side as Jack took a seat opposite me, and we sat there in silence for what felt like forever.

When Jack didn't open his mouth, I blew out a breath and let the chair fall back into place. I got to my feet, shaking my head as I went to leave.

"Ryan, wait."

Turing to face Jack, I couldn't help but feel a little tug in my heart as I saw him scrub a hand down his face, scratching the faint stubble on his chin. He looked older than he should, a tiredness in his eyes. I owed Jack a lot, so I returned to my seat and gave him a chance to have his say.

"I went about this all wrong. I was trying to protect you both, and I ended up hurting you. I didn't mean for you to mistake my words as concern for anything other than what I said."

"Look, as I told Atticus, I expect you to choose Nickolai over me. It's our job. But you expected me to be like all the other female airheads in court and didn't even consider that what happens between Nickolai and me is not your business. It only becomes your business if whatever may or may not happen puts his life in danger."

Jack nodded his head. "I let my lines get blurred, kiddo. I wanted to protect you both, but I never meant for you to think Nickolai's happiness mattered more than yours. I'm so grateful to have you back after all these years that I was afraid of losing you again."

"You never lost me, Jack. I spent a lot of time with you."

With a small smile, Jack let his shoulders slump. "The moment your parents died, you shut a part of you off. I remember speaking to Atticus once after I had taken you to a fairground. You laughed and joked like it was automatic, like you knew what I needed to hear in order to sleep during the day, but your spark was still gone. It went out as we washed your parents' blood off the floor, and nothing I did ever brought it back. But now—now it's back, and I was so fucking terrified that Krista's death, Maxim's infatuation, or even Nickolai himself would snuff out that spark, and the little girl who felt too much would come back and I would lose you, kiddo. I can't lose you again."

I remembered that night out, when an old-fashioned fairground had come to Cork and Jack had taken me out. He'd fed me cotton candy and ice cream, and we'd ridden together on the Ferris wheel—I remembered watching the city below, the lights like a cascade of fireflies in the night. High above the city, I had felt as though I could fly. For the first time in a long time, I'd forgotten all the pain and sorrow and was just Ryan.

"I remember that night, Jack. We have different recollections of it, but it's one of my happier memories. I pushed people away for selfish reasons. I was afraid of losing more people that I cared about." I tapped a fist to my heart. "I couldn't bear anymore of the intense sadness."

Jack watched me, surprise flashing in his eyes before I inhaled a breath and then spoke again. "I know that you spoke with the best intentions, Uncle Jack, but mine and Nicky's relationship is off limits. I told him and I'll tell you—the pressure in my head over it is making me want to go back to that person who was alone. You can't expect me to just open the door one day and forget everything I've been through."

Jack reached across the table, and I let him take my hands in his. "Then I'm sorry for adding to your stress, kiddo. I would never want to upset you."

"And I'm sorry for suggestion that you were as bad as the court vampires."

225

"In that moment I was, so you have no need to apologize."

An awkward silence stretched out between us, and I gently pulled my hands back and rolled my shoulders. I'd spent far too much time spilling my guts over the last twenty-four hours, and I was suddenly exhausted. I just wanted to go to bed and wake up tomorrow, happy at the prospect of watching Maxim die a long and painful death.

"What's got you smiling like an idiot?"

I hadn't even heard Nickolai come out of the bedroom, but I shrugged and said, "Murder."

Jack barked out a laugh, and Nickolai smirked. Getting to his feet, Jack came around to me and dragged me up into a hug before he shook hands with Nickolai and left. I stood facing Nickolai, the first hints of dawn's arrival prickling along my skin, and yawned.

"Can I walk you back to your room?" Nickolai asked politely.

I blinked in surprise. I thought back to what he had said about going against his very nature by not claiming me as his own. Vampires were possessive, it was part of our animal nature, and I suddenly realized how much of himself Nickolai was holding back in order to not spook me. He fully expected me to bolt like a gun-shy horse during a thunderstorm. I glanced toward the door and shrugged. "Sure. I was planning on staying over here today considering I want as much rest as I possibly can before tonight and Edison snores like a helicopter. But if you'd prefer I go, then that's okay, too."

"How princely would it be of me to send you back to your room, then, and rob you of a good day's sleep?"

"Not very. But no funny business, mind."

Holding up three flingers, Nickolai grinned as I

226

made to walk past him. "Scout's honor."

A snort slipped from me as I pushed open the bedroom door and climbed into bed. I curled onto my side, squeezing my eyes closed, willing myself to sleep as I felt Nickolai slide into the bed beside me. I waited for him to curve his body around mine. But he didn't.

I could tell from his breathing that Nickolai wasn't asleep. I could almost feel the waves of tension in his body, and he wasn't even touching me. I had all but thrown myself at him earlier, and he'd calmly handed me back my top. Not many vampires would have done that, but Nickolai wasn't like most vampires.

A memory washed over me, and I lost myself in it for a minute.

My clothes were soaked through, my skin drenched as rain continued to fall from the sky, as if my tears and the rain were in sync with one another, as if Eve herself was crying with me, as if the first of our kind felt my pain and answered it with a sorrow of her own.

But Eve now held my parents in her embrace, and I wanted so badly to join her.

I screamed out into the night, not stopping until a hand rested on my shoulder and the rain stopped falling on my skin. My head snapped up, and eyes of cerulean blue studied me with concern. Nickolai stood over me with an umbrella in one hand and his coat in the other. He draped the coat over my shoulders, then sank down into the grass beside me, not uttering a word.

He had been with me when I was eavesdropping and heard of his father's intentions to send me away. That being in the court was not healthy for me. I heard Jack argue in my favor, telling Anatoly that sending me away from those left who cared for her would not help my grief. Even the queen herself had questioned if sending me away was for the best.

"Don't worry, Ry. I will never let them send you away. I will never stop being your friend."

I *pushed down the anger in me and leaned my head against Nickolai, knowing that maybe I needed to free myself from any chance to have my heart broken.*

My eyes flew open as I remembered how the very next day, I'd begun the process of letting Nickolai go. I'd shut him out, and still he'd kept his promise.

The chemistry between us had always been too much to ignore.

Swallowing hard, I felt another of my walls come crashing down as I turned in the bed, shifting my body so that I snuggled into Nickolai's side, hooking one of my legs over his. A shiver ran through Nickolai's body, his arm wrapping around me, his fingers the barest touch on my hip.

Chapter 21

I woke to the feel of a very warm male body next to me, having slept like a baby. The sound of a shrill shrieking was coming from the other room, and I groaned, rolling away from Nickolai and swinging my legs out of bed. An arm ensnared my waist and dragged me backward.

"Maybe if we just stay here, she will get distracted by something shiny and go away," Nickolai murmured against my neck.

I laughed. "You are definitely spending far too much time with me, Nicky. That's a line right out of my book of snark."

"I'm not complaining one bit."

He nipped my shoulder gently, sending a shudder through me. I was tempted to see where this might go, but another shriek assaulted my ears and Nickolai let go of me. Pulling on a tee, he strode from the room.

"Natalya... Always a pleasure."

Rolling my eyes, I counted to ten and then got out of bed, following Nickolai out as I pretended to yawn and run my fingers through my hair. Nattie glared at me with so much hate and poison, a lesser vampire would have been intimidated. She took a step forward, but Jack's hand on her arm halted her.

I was impressed by how together she appeared. Her makeup was pristine, her lips painted a crimson shade that should have been too much, but she made it work. Her hair had not a strand out of place. Natalya Smyrnoi wore her clothes and beauty as if they were her best weapons, and perhaps they were. I mean, those shoes had points so sharp she could dust any vampire with them.

I ignored her laser beams of hate and, grabbing my weapons belt, I sat at the table and began to prepare my weapons for the inevitable fight I would have tonight. Nickolai went to his own trunk and snagged a cleaning kit. I flashed him a grin as I took out the *nugui-gami* and began tending to my sai.

"What can I do for you, Natalya?" Nickolai asked, sounding as bored as possible.

"I would speak with you when your guard dog is not present."

"Anything you say to me can be said in front of my personal guard, Natalya. And Jack will remain as well. The night isn't that long, so get on with it."

Nattie's eyes snapped in my direction, and I let my inner monster surface, flashing my fangs and letting the animal into my eyes as I said, "Woof."

A muscle in her cheek ticked, and I went back to cleaning my sai. The air thickened with tension, and while I growled at the aggression, Nickolai remained impassive and calm.

"Speak, Natalya. I grow tired of this drama."

Natalya slammed her thousand-euro purse down on the table. "How dare you tell Kristoph that you forbid him from marrying me? How dare you use your influence like that! Is it that you want me for yourself, Nickolai? Can you not bear to see me happy with someone else, even if it's your brother?"

Her voice had started as a low snarl, but it quickly crescendoed to a scream that rang in my ears. I brought my head up and cleared my throat.

"My liege."

"I beg your pardon?" Natalya replied with an indignant tone.

I examined my sai, then pointed it in Nattie's direction. "When you speak to your prince and future king, you will address him as 'my liege.' You will address the future king with the respect he deserves, or I will make you."

"Then should you not follow your own warning, Ryan? Do you not disrespect him every time you call him *Nicky*? Should you not address him as 'my liege'?"

I ran my thumb up the middle blade of my sai, not so much as flinching as the sharpness drew blood. "I call him by that name very often. He hates it when I do. Now I say it just to piss him off."

Nickolai nodded his head in agreement. "I do hate it when you call me that."

"S'okay, Nicky. I promise to only call you 'my liege' when the occasion calls for it."

"Thanks, babe."

I almost burst a gut when Nattie stomped her foot on the ground. "Don't you dare mock me. You cannot do this to me. You cannot prevent me and Kristoph from being together. I won't stand for it."

Nickolai folded his hands across his chest. "You forget who I am, Natalya. A union must be approved by a reigning monarch. My mother will not approve of her baby boy marrying a viper like you, and neither will I."

"How dare you! By Eve, I will see you suffer for this. I will not stand for this. You will rue the day that you dare—"

I didn't let Nattie finish her sentence before launching myself over the table with a snarl. I had Nattie on her knees, my sai at her throat before she could say another word, the tip of the blade hungry for blood. I zoned out everyone else, focusing solely on Nattie.

The scent of her fear was intoxicating, and I enjoyed watching the sweat on her brow trickle down her face, leaving a streak in her no-longer-flawless makeup.

"Do you dare threaten our liege?" I asked quietly. "Are you so stupid as to threaten your future king while I am in the room? I should feed your blood to my blade right now."

There was a moment of hushed silence, and I focused on the racing of Nattie's heart. Leaning closer, I inhaled the scent of her fear. "Go on, Nattie, piss yourself with fear. Show us how weak you are."

"That's enough, Ryan. Let Natalya to her feet."

With a feral snarl, I jerked my blade back, and Nattie fell forward, her hands hitting the ground before she all-but-crawled away from me. While she clambered to her feet, I went to stand by Nickolai, who cupped the back of my neck with his palm.

"I really do hate it when you call me 'liege.'"

I shrugged my shoulders. "The occasion called for it."

Nickolai chuckled as Nattie scowled. She ran her hands over her clothes, smoothing and adjusting them, and then snatched her purse from the table, making to leave. Jack blocked her way automatically, and she turned back to us.

"Remember," Nicholai said calmly, "I can make your

life difficult, Natalya. I will never agree to you marrying Kristoph, and if you fight me on this, I'll be more than happy to send Zayn some company in America."

Nattie placed her fist over her heart. "My liege."

Her tone was sarcastic enough to draw a snarl from my lips, and I took a step toward her, weapons still in hand.

"My liege," she repeated, this time respectfully enough to halt my advance.

Before she could make things any worse for herself, Jack escorted her from the apartment.

I stayed perfectly still as Nickolai's grip on my neck intensified for just a minute before he released me with a growl. Jack returned a second later, and his gaze wandered from me to Nickolai, who had now found something interesting to look at outside the window.

Setting my sai on the table, I took myself off to shower and change. I washed the scent of Nickolai off my skin, or at least I hoped I did, and quickly dressed in a black long-sleeved T-shirt, a black hooded sweatshirt, and leggings. I was sitting on the edge of the bed, lacing up my boots when a knock sounded on the door.

"Coming!" I yelled, twisting my hair into a braid as I exited the bedroom. The room had filled up nicely, with the entire guard dressed in similar gear as me. I crossed the room and began looping my belt around my waist. When my belt and my sai were a comforting weight around my waist, I turned my attention to Jack and listened as he gave orders. And then, he inclined his head to me.

The weight of the entire guard's gaze shifted to me, and for once, when I looked at my peers, not a single expression was one of pity, contempt, or loathing; it was respect.

233

Swallowing the lump in my throat, I folded my arms across my chest. "Farrah Nazir should be making her way to the club by now. Once she gives us a way in, Edison and I will do a full sweep of the club and then signal if Maxim is present. All of you need to stay a comfortable distance away so as not to spook the rogues."

I nodded to Atticus. "Atticus and Nickolai will leave shortly and act as a distraction, meaning those rogues who scour the campus for Nickolai will follow him and report back to Maxim. I want five guards on the prince and Atticus the *moment* they step into the night. The rest of you divide up and make your way to the rooftops around the club."

Jack stepped forward. "Dismissed."

The guards fisted hands over their hearts and slipped off into the night, some waiting outside to follow Nickolai to class. Edison waited patiently for me, keeping his face impassive as Jack leaned his forehead against Atticus's before they shared a kiss and Jack pushed away from his love without saying a word.

My uncle paused at my shoulder, turning his head to me. "Give him hell, kiddo." And then he was gone.

My heart clenched, and I realized how right Atticus had been about clearing the air before everything went down. Atticus motioned for Edison to follow him, and they went down the stairs and out the door, leaving me and Nickolai alone.

Nickolai's stance was tense, and I knew how much it was costing him to leave me to hunt down the big bad wolf without him. He didn't close the distance between us as we faced each other.

"You will be careful."

"I promise."

"And try not to leap through any windows unless absolutely necessary."

I grinned. "Yes, my liege."

Nickolai laughed sharply. The air around us crackled, and my heart raced as I considered that he might kiss me. If he kissed me now, I would think of nothing else, and I couldn't afford any distractions. I needed to be the calm ice queen, a cold-blooded killer.

"I'm not going to kiss you. Even if all I want to do is brand you with my lips. I want you to still wonder what it will be like, to wonder what it will feel like to feel the nip of my teeth on your bottom lip. I want you to go out there tonight and be your badass self, and then, when this is over, I will finally get to taste you like I've wanted to do for fucking *years*."

"Nicky... I—"

Nickolai held up his hand. "Don't Ryan, please. I need you to walk out that door before I do something stupid like take advantage of the fact that we both want this and convince you not to go."

The heat in his gaze was enough to convince me, and I spun on my heels and nearly bolted from the apartment. I flung open the door and darted around the corner, slamming into Edison, who let out a surprised grunt and reached out to steady me as I stumbled.

"You good, Callan?"

"Five by five, St. Clair. Let's go kill something."

Instead of heading down to the foyer, we climbed the stairs upward until I pushed open the door to the roof, a blast of frigid air whipping against my skin as I took off in a sprint without waiting to see if Edison was behind me.

Coming to the edge of the roof, I leapt up to the ledge and pushed myself off. I flew through the air and landed on the next roof as if the gap between buildings was nothing. Pumping my arms, I continued my surge forward, leaping from roof to roof, racing across walls and any other surface that connected one building to another.

Edison kept pace with me, following in my footsteps, and as we neared the seedier part of town, I slowed my pace. I came to a halt on the rooftop opposite the club, pausing to inhale a couple of breaths. A smile curved my lips as I watched Farrah sweep the curtains to the side and open the window to the private room. I let out a low whistle, and she ducked inside again.

I rolled my shoulders and glanced at Edison. His face was serious as I regarded him.

"You ready, St. Clair?"

"Let's do this."

I backed away to the farthest point of the roof and then ran forward, my legs still moving as I soared thought the air, my fingers reaching for and grasping the window ledge as I hit the side of the building with a grunt. My legs dangled as I waited for a couple of heartbeats and then swung myself up and through the window.

I braced myself to be attacked as my booted feet hit the wooden floor, quickly taking in my surroundings, from the fur-covered walls to the giant pink bed in the center of the room. It screamed tacky. I was expecting to be set upon by rogues or be standing in an empty room. But Farrah Nazir stood by the door, her fangs bared, a dagger in her palm even as fear scented the air. She glanced at me as Edison came through the window and closed it quietly.

"I told you to go once you opened the window."

"And I wanted to make sure you weren't ambushed."

Despite her scent of fear, there was steel in her tone and I couldn't have been prouder. I gave her a clipped incline of my head and cleared the short distance to cautiously open the door and peek outside.

The halls were empty, the music from the club pounding softly. There were no familiar scents in the air, and I closed the door softly and turned to Farrah.

"You done good, Farrah. Now get your ass out of here before things go any further. You've got five minutes to clear the building before we leave this room."

Farrah nodded rapidly and her hand went to the door handle. "Ryan, something's not right in the club. It's far too quiet. It's never this quiet. Even the rogues are on edge."

Then the girl slipped from the room, leaving me with Edison. I glanced at my fellow guard and opened my mouth.

"Before you say it, we do not split up, Callan. I'm not the distraction so you can go off and get yourself killed trying to get that psycho."

I knew it was pointless to argue with him, so I eased open the door again, just as a bloodcurdling scream ripped through the air. We both took off at the same time, Edison slightly behind me, racing down the corridor to where another scream broke over the sound of the music.

I yanked open the door that led from the private area to the main club. It was still as cheap and tacky as it had always been, the flashing lights hurting my eyes as I focused on where the screams were coming from, hoping that Farrah had made it out and I wouldn't be responsible for another senseless death.

"Callan, look."

Edison pointed to the dancefloor, and my stomach plummeted to my feet. Across the center of the room, five humans were lined up seated in chairs, each one

237

bleeding from bites and cuts, and each one wearing a set of butterfly wings. Maxim had known we were coming; someone had tipped him off.

Projected on a screen behind the humans was video of Nickolai and Atticus wandering through the campus and ducking into one of the buildings, the English building, where Nickolai was due to take an exam. The timestamp was an hour ago, which meant that in one more hour, whoever was watching Nickolai might strike.

I glanced up at Edison, who shook his head at my unspoken words. "I'm not leaving you."

"You have to. Nickolai and Atticus are in danger. You need to get outside and warn Jack. Please, Edison. I can't lose him any more than you can lose Atticus, and Maxim wants me alive. Plus, I outrank you so don't make me order you to do it."

Edison's expression darkened. "Stay alive, Callan," he snarled, then turned and did as I'd asked of him, leaving me all alone to face Maxim... if he were here, that was.

I peered down at the dancefloor, then jumped down the steps toward the human captives. It was only then that I noticed the contraptions with blinking lights on the chairs they were strapped to.

"Maxim wanted to be here in person, but he has a bigger catch in mind."

I whirled to face the direction from which the voice had come. A male vampire I didn't know moved toward me, his eyes gleaming red, his fangs stained with blood that dripped onto the already-bloody floor. His skin was a rich mahogany color, his head was bald, and his body was thin and light. He was dressed in a long, dark trench coat that screamed cliché, but that was his own business.

"So," I said lightly, "he sent you to me as a present to kill? Maxim must not value you as much as his other

238

rogues. Sucks to be you."

The rogue grinned as he nudged open the trench coat, lifting his hand to show me the trigger device. This idiot was about to blow us all to Eden for a coward who didn't want to get his own hands dirty.

"Maxim has asked me to show Eve my loyalty by sacrificing myself to him as her vessel. I will be welcomed into Eve's bosom with open arms."

"Only if there's enough of your body left to hold, buddy. Listen, Maxim isn't the savior you all think he is. He's a bitter old vampire who wants what he can't have. He doesn't follow Eve but his own need to... I dunno... rebel against what he was born into."

The humans behind me whimpered, and I knew in that moment that I'd never convince the rogue of Maxim's true intentions. I toyed with the idea of trying to free the humans, but I knew I'd never save them in time.

The rogue dropped to his knees, and I crouched, launching myself upward with all my might. I landed in the bar area and raced toward the door, hoping to get out before he blew me to Eden with him.

"Hail to the king!" the rogued yelled, and I knew it wasn't Nickolai he spoke of.

The world around me exploded and the building folded in on itself, a large piece of wall hitting me on the head as I hit the ground. My vision darkened, my head spinning as I tried to get up, but my foot was pinned under another piece of rubble.

As the building shook, I offered up a prayer to Eve, another explosion rattled the very foundation, and the roof fell down to crush me.

Chapter 22

"Ryan, come on baby girl, it's time to wake up."

"I'm too sleepy, Papa. Let me sleep, okay?"

"There's no time to sleep, baby girl. The future waits for no one, even if she is a future warrior princess who will be the stuff of legends."

A giggle escaped my lips. "Silly Papa," I muttered drowsily. "I am not a princess."

"You will always be my princess, Ryan Skye Callan. Now wake up and fight, baby girl, it is not time for Eve to claim you just yet."

I didn't understand what my dad was telling me and snuggled into the warmth surrounding him.

"Wake up, Ryan!" he said sharply with a growl. "By Eve, wake up."

"Callan! Callan! Wake the hell up!"

I groaned at the sound of my name and tried to sit up, momentarily forgetting what had happened. My body screamed in protest; my legs were trapped under a mountain of rubble. I reached down and tried to yank my legs free, but I couldn't. My vision swam as my stomach lurched, and I gagged. Something sticky dripped down my face, and I brushed my fingers against my forehead, looking in disbelief at the blood staining my fingertips.

"Callan! By Eve, you almost gave me a heart attack."

Edison's face came into my field of vision, and I swallowed, coughing as I tasted dust and ash in my mouth. The mouth of a bottle came to my lips as Edison tipped some water into my parched mouth, and I drank greedily. When I started coughing again, he took the bottle away and pressed a piece of cloth to my forehead.

"My legs. Edison, my legs are trapped."

I couldn't mask the panic in my tone as I feared I wouldn't have enough time get free and drink blood to heal whatever damage was done to my legs.

"Ryan! By Eve, are you okay?"

Jack's voice rang though the night, and I heard his heavy boots on the concrete.

"Jack, Maxim's going after Nickolai. Leave me here and go to him."

Jack shook his head, his ginger hair falling into his face. "I sent reinforcements to the college, Ryan. Let's get you free, and then we can all go kick that bastard's ass."

I closed my eyes as Jack and Edison worked to free my legs, listening to their grunts and groans as they moved stone and rubble off me. But I only knew I was free when Jack scooped me up into his arms.

I couldn't feel my legs. I let loose a sharp cry, and Jack paused because he thought he'd hurt me.

"Jack, I can't... I can't... I can't feel my legs."

I must have lost consciousness again because the next time I opened my eyes, my fangs were embedded in someone's arm, and I almost roared with the hunger. With every pull, my legs started to tingle, then burn as the bones slotted back together, and then I yanked my mouth away to let loose a scream that was caught in my chest as I felt the pain of them breaking and realigning.

Shrinking back, I gulped in a lungful of air and then blinked to clear the haze from my vision. Rose was standing next to me looking extremely pale, and I saw Jack run his tongue over her wrist, which had just fed me. I'd fed so much from her Jack had to hold her upright. There was another groan nearby, and my eyes darted to Edison holding up Kallum, who was out for the count, his skin as pale as death.

I had almost killed him... I had almost turned rogue.

I staggered to my feet, bracing myself on the countertop as the room spun and my legs screamed in protest. The Children of Eve's blood coursed through me, and I felt invincible even as I felt disgusted by myself.

"Ryan, you need to take it easy," Jack said. "Let your body recover."

"Where is Nickolai?"

Not a soul answered me, so I growled and took a menacing step forward. "Where. Is. *Nickolai?*" I bellowed.

"By Eve, Callan, you are a scary SOB when you want to be," Edison said, eyes wide. "The rest of the guard went to campus, but they couldn't find Nickolai or my brother. They vanished from the exam room."

"What the fuck do you mean 'they vanished'?"

"I mean," Edison growled, his own worry bleeding into his features, "that they went into the building and never came out. There was no trace of them. They are gone."

If my heart could've imploded, it would have in that moment. Ice ran through my veins as all my fears bubbled to the surface, and I let go of a hysterical laugh. This was why I didn't let people in; this was why I needed to keep my distance. I was cursed to lose the ones I

242

cared for most. Still laughing hysterically, I wrapped my arms around myself, beginning to panic when I realized I couldn't stop the laughter even to breathe.

My head cracked to the side at the force of the slap that struck my face, the shock and sharp pain causing me to gasp loudly. I whipped back around with a snarl as Rose glowered at me.

"Get yourself together, Ryan Callan. I did not come out of retirement to feed you and keep you alive just so you could lose your sanity. You have people out their depending on you to bring them home safely. Sort your shit out and pull yourself together."

Damn, she was right.

I rubbed my cheek and raised an eyebrow at the woman with so many secrets. "That was one hell of a slap, Rose."

"Spending my youth with Imogen Callan has taught me a thing or two."

I blinked in surprise. I knew that Rose knew my mother but not that she'd spent more time in my mother's company that I ever had. I stared at her hungrily, desperately seeking any link to the parents I had lost so violently.

"I will give you the answers you seek, Ryan, when this is all over. I fed you today as I did the day you were born. Go and show those rogues exactly who you are."

Jack put a hand on my shoulder. "We need to go and hunt for Nickolai and Atticus, Ryan. We need to find them."

I heard the choked emotion in his voice and reached up, placing my hands on either side of his face with a smile. "I'll bring him back to you, Jack. I give you my vow."

Before he knew what was happening, I smashed his

head through the counter and watched his body crumple to the ground, his head lolling to the side. He was knocked out cold.

I braced myself for Edison to attack, but my new partner in crime simply nodded his head.

"Probably best he has a little nap for now. Let's go, Callan."

"You stay here."

"Bullshit. You go, I go. Atticus is my brother, Callan. You ride in like a knight and save the prince—I got Atticus."

My hands on my hips, I growled, but Edison wasn't intimidated.

"Last time I left you behind, a building fell on your head. Not this time. I got your back, Callan, until Eve comes calling."

I snorted. "That might be sooner rather than later, St. Clair, if you hang around with me too long."

"Then it's Eve's design."

"Then let's go tempt fate, St. Clair."

Despite my reservations, I gave Rose a hug, asking her to tell Jack that I was sorry. Then, with Edison at my back, I stepped out of the shop to find a sleek black town car waiting for me.

The driver's door opened, and a rogue stepped out, walked around the car, and opened the back door. "Maxim is expecting you, Ms. Callan."

Maxim knew exactly what buttons to press. He knew I'd go to him. I walked to the door and made to climb in, when the rogue blocked Edison from following me.

"You must come alone," he said.

I rolled my eyes and sighed. "Listen, St. Clair and I already had this conversation, and he was having none of it. So, if Maxim wants to see me so bad, then it's a

244

two-for-one special today. The fool will just chase the car anyway, so he might as well come with us."

The rogue nodded his head, and Edison slipped in beside me. When the door was closed, in the brief seconds we had before the driver got in, I gritted out a plan to Edison under my breath.

"If the chance comes, you get our liege and Atticus out, you hear me? That's an order, St. Clair."

Edison didn't get the chance to answer me as the rogue slipped into the driver's side and reversed the car out of the alley, driving us off into the night. I stared out the window, taking in my surroundings as the car edged out of the city and toward the airport. I expected him to drive right up to a hanger like all villains seemed to in movies, yet as we came to the roundabout, the rogue veered left and continued driving another ten minutes before he turned the steering wheel left again and we drove into what looked like a large field. All the blood in me froze.

A small building sat in the middle of this field, the ground around it covered in wild, knee-high grasses from neglect. Trees surrounded the area, blocking the edges from view, but even in the dead of night I lost count of how many red eyes stared back at us as we drew to a halt.

The driver opened the door and both Edison and I got out, standing side-by-side, our shoulders touching.

"By Eve, Callan," he said quietly. "There are bloody hundreds out there."

The rogue held out a hand and gestured toward the door to the building, as though he were a chauffeur showing me to my hotel and not leading me to my possible death. I hesitated, glancing to Edison, hoping that I could persuade him to flee, but the firm set of his jaw and the determination in his eyes told me there would be no convincing him.

The red eyes seemed to step toward us in one sweeping motion, and I had little choice but to follow the rogue into the building.

"I hope this one is a little sturdier than the other one Maxim owned. I'd rather not have another building fall on my head tonight, thank you very much."

Nobody seemed to appreciate my attempt to relieve the sinister tension in the air, or else they didn't find me funny, because no one laughed. All I managed was a smirk from Edison. Closing the door behind us, the rogue asked for our weapons, and my middle-finger response simply made him sigh.

He pushed open another door and stepped into a great hall. There was a little stage at the end of the hall, upon which Nickolai was tied to a chair, his head hanging down, the scent of his blood drawing a snarl from me. Atticus was coiled around the prince's feet, ready to strike, even as blood gushed from a wound on his forehead.

Edison started forward, but my hand on his arm stopped him. "Wait," I implored.

The sound of my voice caught Atticus's attention, and his gaze clashed with mine. Then his eyes widened as he spied Edison.

Between us and them were a dozen rogues standing to attention. The rogue who'd driven us here dragged a chair across the room, the sound of it like nails on a chalkboard. He smiled and patted the chair for me to sit down on like advising a child.

Without comment, I strode over to the chair, hoisted in above my head, and smashed it to the ground. Between one breath and the next, I grabbed a broken shard of the chair and slammed it through the heart of the patronizing son of a bitch.

Yanking the makeshift stake free, the rogue's body crumbled to the ground and elicited a cohesive growl from all the rogues in front of me. I gave Edison one of my most intimidating smiles before turning it on the rogues standing between me and my people.

Edison pulled a pair of blades from his back and I braced myself for attack, but the rogues simply stood to attention, blocking our path.

A female rogue stepped forward, her hair the same shade of red as her eyes. Her teeth were stained with blood, a familiar trait of most rogues, as she stood front and center.

"Relinquish your weapons, and we will not be forced to disarm you both."

I chuckled. "Try it and see how dead it gets you."

Rolling up her sleeves, the rogue charged for me and I sidestepped, digging my sai into her back as she stormed past me as Edison used his twin blades to separate her head from her shoulders. Her head hit the ground with a reassuring thud seconds before her body followed. The rogues were getting antsy now, no doubt baying for our blood. Their feet shuffled restlessly, and I wondered how many more we'd have to kill before they lost patience all together.

I whistled the tune to "Don't Fear the Reaper," and Edison chuckled beside me. The rogues snarled.

"Oh, come on guys, have a sense of humor."

That earned me more snarls, and I stalked back and forth in front of the horde, waiting for them to move. Not a single rogue attempted to step up to me, and I was getting a little bored. But while the rogues were watching me, none were paying attention to Atticus or Nickolai, and Atticus used the precious, unobserved moments to try to free Nickolai from his restraints.

"Aw, come on, Max. I'm bored now. Send more rogues for me to kill. Didn't anyone ever tell you it's rude to keep a girl waiting?"

Another rogue rushed from the back of the crowd, a wicked-looking trident in his grasp. He leapt up, drawing back his arm and aiming for me, but the problem with all this show of testosterone was that I knew Maxim wanted the pleasure of killing me himself as much as I wanted to do the same to him. I was positive the rogue aiming for my heart couldn't kill me on his boss's orders.

I, however, had no qualms in killing him.

Dropping to my knees, I felt the trident whoosh over my head and I whipped out my second sai, stabbing upward. I struck the rogue right in the chest and then sliced down, managing to get out from under him before his guts spilled on top of me.

I picked up the trident and, with all the strength I could muster, sent it sailing through the air until it hit home, square in the wall behind where Nickolai was tied to the chair. I'd given them half a chance of escape now.

Wiping a streak of blood from my face, I raised my voice. "Come on, Max. I'm here just like you wanted. Don't get performance anxiety now. Come out and face me, or are you too much a coward? I'm tired of playing with the monkeys, Max. I came to kill the organ grinder."

A deep rumble of laughter sounded, and the rogues parted as their illustrious leader strode through them like Moses parting the Red Sea. He was as handsome as I remembered, the sensuous curve of his lips almost inviting as Maxim smiled at me like I were the sun and moon and not his would-be executioner.

Dressed in a pinstripe suit that somehow didn't look like his usual attire, the crimson shirt he wore made his

248

eyes seem even more red. I couldn't help but wonder what color his eyes had been before he'd killed a human and become a rogue.

Maybe I'd ask him before I yanked his eyes from his head.

"Ah, my little babochka, you have finally come home to me."

The rasp of his voice caused the hairs on the back of my neck to stand to attention. Maxim kept on walking until he was at the head of his gathered horde, and they stepped back in line as once cohesive unit. It would have been impressive if they weren't mindless killers following a zealot who only looked out for himself.

A groan from the back of the room snapped my attention to the vampire whose cerulean eyes widened in surprise at the sight of me, and my breath seized in my lungs. It was then I realized that despite my best intentions, Nickolai had burrowed his way into my heart. Even though I'd admitted I wanted him, I hadn't admitted to myself that what I felt for him was more than just physical.

But I couldn't dwell on that now, so I dragged my eyes away from Nickolai and back to the monster standing in front of me. As I stared into the sanguine eyes of the rogue who had killed Krista, my fingers itched to use the sai in my hand to stab the smirk right off his face.

"Hello, Ryan."

"Hello, Max. Tonight's a good night to die, don't you think?"

249

Chapter 23

As if we were the only two in the room, Max circled me, and I could feel his eyes wandering over me, the very action causing my skin to crawl and my stomach to sour until bile crept up my throat. His finger trailed up my arm, and I sucked in a breath.

"I do so love it when you flirt with me, Ryan." His voice rasped as he walked around to face me once more.

"If you think this is flirting, Max, it's no wonder you can't keep a girl."

The rogue continued to smirk, but my remark did cause his jaw to tick, so I knew it had irked him. My main goal was to anger him to the point where he lost his cool and made a mistake. Considering I was an expert at pissing people off, I felt the odds were in my favor.

"Speaking of romance, Max... I mean, dropping a building on a girl isn't the best way to ask her out on a date. Neither is kidnapping and beating up her friends. Although I do appreciate the fact that you gifted me three of your rogues to kill."

Maxim rubbed his chin with his fingers, and I almost cringed at how silly he looked. He snapped his fingers, and one of the rogues brought forward a chair. Max glanced at me before he took his seat, taking the time to unbutton his suit jacket before sitting down. Considering what happened the last time I had a chair within reach, the rogue didn't bother bringing me a chair. What I wouldn't give for a fresh stake to drive right through his black heart.

"You've got me here now, Max. What do you want?"

"I want what I have always wanted, Ryan; you as my queen."

If I rolled my eyes any harder, the damn things would've fallen out of my head. "What the hell is it with male vampires wanting to put a damn crown on my head?"

"Most women would be flattered that a king wishes to make them a queen."

With a snort, I shook my head. "You are not a king, Max. And in case you hadn't noticed, I'm not most girls."

Maxim leaned back in his chair, a smirk toying with his lips. "I had noticed, Ryan, that you are unlike any woman I have ever known. That is why we are here. And what makes a king a king? Do I not have loyal subjects who look to me for guidance?

"Guidance?" I scoffed. "They are sheep who are lost, and you're the dog herding them to death and destruction."

"Enough!" His bellow echoed throughout the hall, and even his own rogues flinched. Fury was written all over his face, his eyes darkened to an even more vicious shade of red, and his cheeks reddened as he gritted his teeth together.

Oh, looks like I hit a nerve. Such a shame...

As quickly as his temper flared, it dissipated; the calm and collected exterior of the former royal court

251

member turned rogue slipped back into place, and he regarded me with intrigue.

"You know just what to say to yank my chain, don't you, Ryan Callan."

I assumed that wasn't a question, but it wasn't in me to hold back my thoughts or my words.

"It's not metaphorical chains that I want to yank, Maxim. I would like very much to wrap a chain around your neck and drive Nickolai's very expensive car at high speed down the road, dragging you along for the ride."

His smile deepened as if he were proud that I'd clapped back at him. "I do like a girl with a vicious streak. That's why Mia, despite her beauty, was never meant to be mine. She was too delicate a flower to embark on this journey with me. But you—you would take to this world without any adjustment."

I paced back and forth. "You see, Max, this is where you and I differ. I will never become a rogue. I will never kill a harmless human just because I can. I would never kill an innocent girl just to prove a point. You killed my friend just because she was my friend; one day, I will have justice for her."

Nickolai murmured my name, and I fought against the urge to go to him. Instead, I turned back to Maxim. "Come on, Max. Let the prince and Atticus go. Edison here will take the car outside and drive them all away. I will stay here, and I won't fight you."

"You won't fight me, Ryan, because you care for the three vampires in this room, and you would rather hurt yourself than see them hurt."

I kept my features neutral as I tilted my head to the side and shrugged. "Then what the hell do you hope to achieve by this, Max? Cut the pomp and posture and get to point already."

252

Maxim leaned back in his chair, resting his right leg over his left and clasping his hands together. A slow, deliberate smile played over his lips. "I am here to offer you the same deal I offered you before. Come with me now, and I will leave Ireland tonight; and the crown and its reign will be safe."

Sheathing my sai, I folded my arms across my chest. "What's the catch?"

"There is none. You hand over your sai to me, and I let your little paramour leave to be crowned another day. My army will stand down, and once we are out of Ireland, the rogues will follow us to wherever we touch down."

My heart sank even though I was resigned to the fact that this might happen, that I might be forced to go with Maxim and kill him another day. Nickolai, Atticus, and Edison would be safe, though, and that was all that mattered.

"Send the rogues outside as a sign of good faith, Max, but I will never hand my mother's sai over to you willingly. I give my word, however, that I will not try and escape. My word is my bond."

Maxim snapped his fingers, and all but three rogues swept from the room. I watched as Atticus freed Nickolai's legs and then tried to stand. One of the rogues jumped up to the stage and brought his foot down on Atticus's knee. The bone crunched with a sickening sound and Atticus howled. I had to hold Edison back from charging to help his brother.

"Rein in your vamps, Max. If they cause any more injury, I'll make sure the last thing they see is my face."

Barking an order in Russian, the rogue dragged Atticus forward and tossed him at Edison's feet. Edison dropped to his knees to check on his brother, and I stepped forward. Maxim stood, buttoning his suit jacket

253

and motioning with his hand. I hesitated, my eyes darting first to Atticus and then to Nickolai.

"Let me say goodbye. Let me give him closure, or else he'll not stop coming after me."

Reaching out his hand, Maxim cupped my cheek, and I fought against the urge to shudder, his hand on my skin making me want to scrub my face clean.

"I do not think, even if you offer him this farewell, that our fair prince would stop his hunt for you. I know I am not capable of doing such a thing myself. But say your goodbyes, my little butterfly, if it will soothe your soul."

Nothing would soothe my soul; it felt as if every single fiber of my being was being torn apart, piece by piece.

Turning my back to Maxim went against my nature. I quickly crouched down and lifted Atticus's gaze to mine. "Thank you for keeping him safe. Now Edison will keep you both safe. Thank you for being my friend, Atticus St. Clair, and even though I never said it, thank you for saving my life. Tell Jack that I love him and that I gave myself willingly."

"Ryan... don't..." Atticus moaned, trying to reach for me, but he just wasn't up to it.

I gave him a hurried hug, careful not to linger in case Maxim ran out of goodwill.

Standing, I faced Edison, the boy I once thought of as an enemy but who'd quickly proven himself far from it. "St. Clair, you make sure that they get back to court safely, you hear me? That's an order, my friend."

His eyes widened at my final words, but I couldn't stay for the sentimentality that might break me. Instead, I lifted my chin and went to do the hardest thing I'd ever had to do—say goodbye to Nickolai.

His eyes held mine as I removed the gag from his

mouth, and he breathed my name.

"Hey, Nicky." My words were spoken softly, private, even though every ear could hear us.

"Dates with you are always exciting."

I shook my head as I laughed. "What I wouldn't give to be back in that cinema watching *Die Hard* with you."

"Don't do it, Ry. Don't give yourself up for me. Fight your way out and go. *Please*."

"I don't have a choice, Nicky. You haven't given me any other choice. You chose me as your guard so I would give my life for yours. I am fulfilling my duty, and I am at peace with that."

"Well I'm bloody not."

I smiled as I brushed a stray strand of hair from his eyes. "You need to let me go, Nicky. You need to get me out of your system."

"Darling, you're already in my veins."

My heart broke at the words he had spoken to me before, and I wondered if this was truly what it felt like to die inside. I had wasted so much time trying to avoid this pain when no matter how hard I tried, whether Nickolai left me behind today or I stood by and watched him take a queen as he should, this pain was unavoidable.

I had so much more I'd wanted to experience, and I'd wanted to experience it with Nickolai. I wanted an epic romance story worthy of a Hallmark movie. But it wasn't meant to be. My life was a never-ending wave of tragedy that swept me along for the ride.

I ran my fingers over his lips, tracing the fullness of them. "You know, if I could have given my heart to any-one, had it not already been so broken, I think I could have given it to you. I'm sorry I wasted so much time in my own head, Nicky. I'm so very sorry."

I had made promises to Nickolai about what would

happen when this was over, and now... now I would never know what could have been. There would never be any kind of future for him and I.

It was selfish, I felt it deep in my bones, but I could not walk away without knowing what it felt like to be kissed by Nickolai Romanov.

I closed my eyes and leaned in, pressing my lips to his, tasting the salt of tears I didn't even feel falling from my eyes. This kiss was far from the one I wanted, our passion stilled by this torturous separation, but when I pressed my lips to his it was familiar, and a memory raced through my mind as I jerked back in surprise.

I stumbled through the dark of the party, the music vibrating the floor and the warmth in my veins from the copious amount of alcohol that I had drunk, making the room spin. I stepped on my red cape and stumbled, cursing myself for dressing as Red Riding even more than I cursed myself for showing up to this party.

This year, for Samhain, the queen had decided to hold a fancy-dress party, and everyone was forced to attend. I was already drunk when I arrived, emptying my flask of vodka so quickly that I was wasted—so wasted Jack demanded I leave.

I supposed it wasn't appropriate for one's fifteen-year-old niece to tell the queen to piss off quite loudly.

I stumbled again, but this time a strong arm caught me before I face-planted on the ground. I glanced up to see a vampire wearing a Zorro mask looking at me with concern, but I was so drunk I couldn't make out who was holding me upright.

"Let's get you to bed."

That sounded like a brilliant idea.

"Oh, let's," I said as I flung my arms around his neck and dragged whoever it was down, my lips on his as I pressed my body close. The receipt of my kiss returned my passion with

his own, and when I tugged at his bottom lip, he jerked back.

"Not like this. Not like this, Ryan."

I ignored his words, whoever the hell it was, as my stomach heaved and I vomited into one of the queen's potted plants.

My fingers touched my lips, my eyes widening. The boy I'd kissed, the one who I always thought had stolen my first and only kiss until now, had been Nickolai all along.

"It was you," I said. "It was you dressed as Zorro. All this time and you said nothing."

"That night was not our first kiss, and this forced goodbye will not be the last time I kiss you, Ryan Callan. I have loved you since before I understood what love was. I have loved you even when you could not love yourself, and I will love you until the end of time and then some. I will cross oceans and countries to find you, Ryan Skye Callan. Until my dying breath, I am yours and you are mine."

My heart was bleeding inside my chest, and I was powerless to stop it. I opened my mouth to tell him that I loved him, too, but that would be cruel, wouldn't it? To tell him what he'd wanted to hear every moment we were together our whole lives, and then to rip it out from underneath him? He would follow up on his promise; he'd cross oceans to find me. The pain in my chest burned as I got to my feet and staggered away.

"Edison, get them the hell out of here, right now."

Edison came forward and pulled off the remaining ropes that bound Nickolai. He hooked one arm under Nickolai's and helped him off the stage. Nickolai teetered forward, trying to reach for me, but I shrank back from his grasp even as my nature screamed at me to go to him.

Nickolai shoved Edison away, calling my name over

and over again, begging me to fight, to never stop fighting like I fought with him every single day. Thankfully, Nickolai was weak enough that Edison could overpower him and kept him moving. When Edison paused for a second to lift Atticus up with his free hand, Nickolai used every bit of strength he had left to try to get back to me.

Idiot.

I kept watch over them until I could no longer see them. With every step Nickolai took away from me, I pushed down memories of the people I had let back into my life and who'd brought me back to life. As Edison, Atticus, and Nickolai turned out of sight, I shoved the last bit of the girl I was down with the rest of my memories and locked them away for some future time when I might need them, to comfort me on the path I was now walking.

With the best parts of myself now safely in stow, I turned slowly toward my captor, feeling the old walls surrounding my heart refortify. The ice queen had returned.

It was like the song said—I guessed my fairy-tale had a few plot holes.

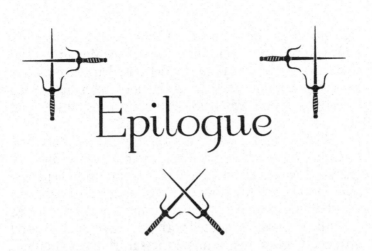

Epilogue

Maxim wrapped his hands around my throat, leaning in to inhale my scent, and I cringed; I couldn't help myself. His hands roamed from my throat down my arms, and then he made an attempt to reach for my sai.

"Do it and I will bleed you, Max."

"I am not your enemy, Ryan," Maxim sighed as he stepped away from me, his tone suggesting he believed his own words. "We can be friends, you and I."

"In case you don't know, Max, you're the villain in this story."

He cupped my cheek once more, and this time, I jerked away with a hiss.

"We are all villains in someone else's story, Ryan."

I went to retort when the door burst open and Edison charged in; the damn fool had not left when I'd ordered him to. The three nearest rogues descended on him in a blur of movement, and even through Edison gave as good as he got, they were too strong for him.

Two of the rogues held Edison by his arms as the third brought one of Edison's own blades to his neck.

Without thinking, I reacted automatically, lunging

for Maxim and knocking him to the floor. I managed to sink one of my sai into his shoulder as Maxim bucked underneath me, but then his fist collided with my jaw, sending me flying. I slid along the floor, readying to leap back into action, when the room suddenly filled with rogues.

With a snarl, I leapt into the fray and did my best to inflict as much damage as possible before my face smacked against the floor and my vision swam. I spat my own blood onto the floor as I was dragged upright, my butt landing in a chair as I snarled and tried to break free.

Maxim's face was filled with a murderous rage as he crouched before me, yanking the sai from his shoulder. Grabbing my face, he jerked my chin so I'd look at him, then placed the tip of my own blade at my throat.

"How *dare* you disrespect me so? I offered you peace, and you spit in my face. I thought you a butterfly, but I should have known that a butterfly could never love a spider."

I wasn't sure where Max was going with his little rant, but I was just a spectator now, watching this unfold. His hands trembled, and I refused to blink as he pierced my throat with my blade. I swallowed down my disgust as he licked up the curve of my neck, shuddering at the taste of my blood, and tried not to vomit.

Getting to his feet, Maxim smoothed out his suit and shouted at the rogues in Russian.

"Clothes don't make you a man, Max. Nor will they make you something you can never be."

"And what is that, Ryan."

"A real vampire. You can't go back—there is no back for the likes of you."

Maxim smiled coldly. "I am a spider, Ryan, and I fell in love with a butterfly—a beautiful butterfly with ice-

260

blonde wings and lavender eyes. But now it is time to evolve, my love; and if a butterfly cannot love a spider, then I will break you and make you into a fly. And then you will fear me."

A chortle of laughter, bitter and sad at the same time erupted from my lips. "I could never love you, Max. You're so delusional you need a padded cell to handle your crazy."

Maxim growled and strode away, and I was dragged upright. One of the rogues kicked Edison square in the stomach, and I snarled and kicked out in retaliation. Maxim stopped, turning back to me with a smile.

"Bring the guard with us in case Ryan decides to misbehave," he said to the rogues. "I think she will be more compliant if I have someone else to take my frustration out on."

My heart pounded in my chest as I screamed at Maxim, cursing him in every language I knew. Fury boiled within my veins as I elbowed one rogue in the nose and then kneed the other so hard in the groin that I was sure he'd feel it for weeks.

Ignoring his bellow of pain, I stalked forward with murder on my mind. Maxim stood waiting for me, and just as I neared him a young boy with an unusual scent stepped up beside him. He was no more than fifteen, with reddish-brown hair and pale skin. He looked like he should've been worrying about school and girls, not hanging out with a murderous sycophant.

"*Stad*."

He ordered me to stop in my father's native tongue, and my entire body froze at the damn command.

"I swear by Eve that I will rip your tongue from your mouth while you're still alive," I snarled at the boy. "I will fuc—"

261

"*Bí ciúin*," he interjected calmly.

When the new addition told me to be quiet, I felt the tingle of magic on my skin as my voice went silent. I had never felt anything like it before, and I fought against it with every fibre of my being.

"She is stronger than she appeared to be. She carries her own magic in her blood."

A growl rumbled in my chest, and with great effort I manged to move one leg forward. And then another.

The boy eyed me with a morbid curiosity before he glanced up at Maxim.

"Do it," Maxim bit out as he walked away.

I snarled at the magical hold on me, and it snarled back.

In English, the boy began to speak to me, and I knew from his words that he was far older than his appearance.

"I can see why Maxim is obsessed with you, Ryan Callan. I look forward to seeing inside your mind. But for now, sleep."

Ryan's Personal Playlist:

- Five Finger Death Punch—Got Your Six
- Disturbed—The Vengeful One
- Volbeat—A Warrior's Call
- YUNGBLUD—Die A Little
- Post Malone—Goodbyes (Feat. Young Thug)
- Raleigh Ritchie—Stronger Than Ever
- YUNGBLUD—Falling Skies (feat. Charlotte Lawrence)
- BANKS—Fuck With Myself
- Foals—The Runner
- LYRA—Mother
- Fozzy—Nowhere To Run
- Simple Creatures—Thanks, I Hate It
- Halsey—Graveyard
- Sam Fender—You're Not The Only One
- Bea Miller—NEVER GONNA LIKE YOU
- Written by Wolves—Secrets
- The Hunna—One
- The Hunna—We Could Be
- Anth—Medicine
- FLETCHER—I Fall Apart—Recorded At Electric

Lady Studios NYC

- YUNGBLUD—original me (feat. dan reynolds of imagine dragons)
- Bring Me The Horizon—Can You Feel My Heart
- Bring Me The Horizon—Sleepwalking
- MEDUZA—Lose Control
- James Arthur—You (feat. Travis Barker)
- Deaf Havana—Saviour—Edit
- Frank Carter & The Rattlesnakes—Why a Butterfly Can't Love a Spider—The Bloody Beetroots Remix
- Phantogram—In A Spiral
- blackbear—hot girl bummer
- CamelPhat—Breathe
- Seibold—Hush
- Machine Gun Kelly—I Think I'm OKAY (with YUNGBLUD & Travis Barker)
- YUNGBLUD—casual sabotage
- Dermot Kennedy—Dancing Under Red Skies
- PVRIS—Old Wounds
- VÉRITÉ—faded
- PVRIS—Nightmare
- PVRIS—Things Are Better
- Bea Miller—THAT BITCH
- Mike Shinoda—fine
- Bring Me The Horizon—Ludens
- Snow Patrol—Made Of Something Different Now
- James Arthur—Maybe
- Marshmello—Tongue Tied (with YUNGBLUD & blackbear)
- Frank Carter & The Rattlesnakes—Nothing Breaks Like a Heart
- Eminem—'Till I Collapse
- Limp Bizkit—My Way
- Limp Bizkit—It'll Be OK

- Limp Bizkit—Lonely World
- NF—Leave Me Alone
- Too Close To Touch—Here's A Thought
- Written by Wolves—Let It Burn
- Bring Me The Horizon—±ᵃþ³§ (feat. Yonaka)
- Bring Me The Horizon—¿ (feat. Halsey)
- Marmozets—Major System Error
- Dermot Kennedy—What Have I Done
- Halsey—You should be sad
- Billie Eilish—everything i wanted
- Oshins—Out of Control SAINT PHNX—Bury a Friend

My Writing Playlist:

- Avenged Sevenfold—Hail to the King
- Twin Atlantic—Novocaine
- Avenged Sevenfold—Crimson Day
- Twenty One Pilots—The Hype—Alt Mix
- GAITS—Other Side
- Lindsey Stirling—Love Goes On And On (feat. Amy Lee)
- Foals—Syrups—Vincent Taurelle Remix
- Ryan Sheridan—Walk Away
- The Hunna—Lover
- Sam Fender—Saturday
- Bring Me The Horizon—Deathbeds
- The Pale White—Swim For Your Life
- Jake Isaac—10 Steps to Heaven

- Maren Morris—The Bones—with Hozier
- Sam Fender—Two People
- YUNGBLUD—hope for the underrated youth
- Marilyn Manson—God's Gonna Cut You Down
- Of Mice & Men—Deceiver/Deceived
- Harry Styles—Sign of the Times
- Written by Wolves—As Long as It Takes
- Cigarettes After Sex—Touch
- HAIM—Now I'm In It
- Too Close To Touch—Chasing Highs
- Limp Bizkit—Build A Bridge
- Dean Lewis—Half A Man
- Apocalyptica—En Route To Mayhem
- Trash Boat—Synthetic Sympathy
- Alter Bridge—Wouldn't You Rather
- Radio Company—Sounds of Someday
- Simple Creatures—The Wolf

Acknowledgments

WRITING A BOOK MIGHT BE A SOLITARY PROCESS, BUT THERE are so many people who contributed to this book.

My parents - Thank you for all that you do for me. I love you guys very much.

LJ and Taylor- I love you both to infinity and beyond

I have to thank the amazing ladies of Clean Teen Publishing, Rebecca, Courtney and Marya, and their continued belief in me and my books. I'm truly blessed to be part of such an amazing company.

Melanie Newton- Thank you for being my person, my sounding board, the person who believes in me no matter what. I am truly blessed to have you in my life and even more so that I get to call you friend.

Marya- the cover for Butterfly Effect is just as gorgeous as Chaos Theory. Thank you so much for another breath-taking cover.

Special thanks to Chelsea Brimmer for taking such good care of Butterfly Effect and making sure this book is ready for readers to sink their teeth into.

Jaime Cross- My trusty beta reader...thank you for

all you do!

Krista Meyers Gill- I'm so grateful that you loved book you as much as I do. And it's not over yet. (Wink, wink)

To my friends, Michelle, Helen, Orla and Susan, thank you for keeping me sane and supporting me.

To Melanie's Musers- The best group of people you could ever meet in your life! You guys don't know just how awesome you are.

Thank you to all the readers, who have embraced Ryan and her story. Thank you for joining Ryan and I on this journey. It's gonna be epic!

About the Author

SUSAN HARRIS IS A WRITER FROM CORK, IRELAND AND when she's not torturing her readers with heart-wrenching plot twists or killer cliffhangers, she's probably getting some new book related ink, binging her latest tv or music obsession, or with her nose in a book.

She loves to hear from her fans, so be sure to visit SUSANHARRISAUTHOR.COM to find out where you can stalk her!